ACCIDENTALLY APHRODITE

USA TODAY BESTSELLING AUTHOR

DAKOTA CASSIDY

Published 2015
ISBN: 978-1-944003-07-4

Published by Book Boutiques. Copyright © 2015, Dakota Cassidy

Manufactured in the USA by Book Boutiques
support@bookboutiques.com

BLURB

"Sweet Baby Jesus in booty shorts! Thank you, Dakota Cassidy. I'd read the damn phone book if you wrote it!" *New York Times* bestselling author, Robyn Peterman.

Dakota Cassidy, *USA Today* bestselling author of *The Accidental Dragon*, brings you a laugh-out-loud romantic comedy *Accidentally Aphrodite*, Book 10 in the Accidentally Paranormal series. Get swept away to Greece in this international romp where you'll meet a few Gods and Goddesses, and fall in love with Quinn Morris as she transforms from a heartbroken mess to the goddess of love.

Mythology buff Quinn Morris has always wanted to visit Greece, where her inner hardcore romantic envisioned proposing to her boyfriend. And she's finally here—with her friend Ingrid. She might not have found love at the Parthenon, thanks to her cheating ex, but she has found big boobies…and swirly purple eyes…and sparkling skin. Oh, and Greek hottie Khristos, who claims to be descended from a goddess and swears Quinn's the new Aphrodite.

With help from Khristos, and support from Ingrid's employers—Nina, Wanda, and Marty—Quinn has to learn all the tricks of the matchmaking trade, STAT, lest she has her new friend Cupid sticking arrows in all the wrong places. All while dealing with her man-hating mother, guarding her own heart from Khristos, and protecting herself from an invisible foe who might want to snatch Quinn's newfound powers from her—dead or alive.

AUTHOR MESSAGE

Darling readers,

I'll confess straight up, I've stuck my nose deep into the mythology surrounding Aphrodite and her legend. Then I tweaked, dabbled, distorted, and overall gave it a good shaking up. So please understand, while I mostly adhere to Aphrodite's basic story, I did put my own spin on her for my own selfish modern-day purposes. I hope you enjoy it as much as I enjoyed splashing around in the pool of Greek mythology!

For anyone new to The Accidentals, I've included a link to *Interview With An Accidental* dakotacassidy.com, a free, quick (mostly painless), interview-style introduction to the women who are the heart and soul of this nine-book series originally published traditionally. If you're a repeat offender (YAY to repeat offending, you rebels!), skip right to chapter one!

DEDICATION

First, enormous, humble thanks to Katie Wood, who's been my cover artist from the very start of this series, and was willing to jump off the cliff with me when I went indie. She's amazing, kind, insanely talented, and she really listens to how I see my characters. I'm awed you were willing to partner back up with me—humbled by the beauty of my book covers brought to life!

And to my editor Kelli Collins, here we go, kiddo! Welcome to the wonderful world of all the crazy antics constantly zipping around in my brain. You are a goddess among mere mortals for sinking your teeth into this project, and I love you madly for your never-ending support and your dedication to coming as close to editor perfection as any one human can get.

To my BFF Renee George, who helps me plot, hears me whine, loves me anyway. I love you. Always-always.

To my sister from another mister, Robyn Peterman, who just wouldn't take no for an answer when I doubted rebooting this series on my own. Love you, Pooks. Cassman 4-ever!

Finally, this edition is for all you amazing fans who've stuck around for nine (nine!) books, and to my amazing Glam Fam at Team Tiara, for all the laughter on my Facebook and Twitter pages, the emails, *The Walking Dead* and GoT conversations, the sharing, the absolute delight I experience when you taunt me with the color yellow—number ten's for you!

Dakota XXOO

CHAPTER 1

"Jesus in a flippin' muumuu, Quinn! What the hell happened?"

Quinn Morris's stunned eyes flew to her college study partner and much younger friend Ingrid Lawson's face, crimson from the heat of the Grecian day.

Hysteria threatened to take over, forcing Quinn to put a hand to her chest to catch her breath before mumbling, "Something?"

Quinn winced when Ingrid lifted a finger and pointed it directly at her. The digit trembled a little as it silently circled Quinn's chest area. Her mouth opened then snapped shut, as though she couldn't quite put into words what she was seeing.

Quinn nodded in agreement because, yeah. Holy, holy shit! Plucking at the front of her billowy white blouse, the one she'd specifically picked for this trip because it looked like it was straight off the back of some eighteenth-century poet, she looked down into it.

Then she gazed upon her nearly shredded bra, and gasped. The sound of her shock echoed off the Parthenon columns and reverberated in her ears.

Then she looked once more and gulped.

Oh dear.

Ingrid fisted her hands and brought them to her forehead, shaking her head as though she were trying to shake off some terrible memory.

Which was odd...

When she looked back up at Quinn, her eyes, hidden beneath the dark gothic makeup she favored, bulged from her head. Her words burst out of her mouth like a ball from a cannon. "OhmyGodohmyGodohmyGod! *Boobs! Big, big boobies!*" she shrieked, her multicolored Mohawk bending in the humid breeze.

Quinn nodded numbly, a hot wind swishing her flirty skirt around her ankles. "So, so big…"

Ingrid clutched the straps on her backpack, her voice shaky. "*How* did this happen?"

"Um, I don't exactly know. But I can tell you one thing for sure. They're no longer the size of crab apples. In fact, they're a lot more like Shawna Sutter's cantaloupes now, don't you think?"

Even in her horror, Ingrid managed to scrunch her face up in distaste. "Don't even mention that woman's name at a time like this. No one, and I mean no one, wants to be like Shawna Sutter or her stupid cantaloupes!"

Quinn shrugged a little, because even in their shared horror, the truth was the truth. "But you have to admit, she has really nice cantaloupes. Igor seems to think so anyway."

Igor—her cheating, lying, bottom-feeding almost-fiancé, and the very reason she was here on her dream trip to Greece with Ingrid instead of him—now belonged to Shawna "Cantaloupes" Sutter. Lock, stock, and brainless banter.

"Igor is a bag of dicks!" Ingrid yelped. "Forget about him and that stupid, vapid, silicone-sporting Shawna and explain why you're literally sparkling like a bunch of rhinestones on some cheap, homemade beauty-contestant dress?"

Quinn's eyes flew to her hands and forearms, but she paused. "Do you think it looks cheap? As sparkling goes, I think it's sort of glowy and ethereal."

Sort of.

Ingrid scoffed her impatience, letting her hands slap her thighs. "Is that really the point here, Quinn?"

She took another deep breath, inhaling the hot air and realizing, no, that wasn't the point at all. She backtracked in her mind, trying to remember how this had all gone down. "Remember that little old lady on the tour bus on the way here?"

Ingrid nodded and wrinkled her nose. "The one who smelled like a goat?"

"Uh-huh. But it's not her fault. She raises them to sell their milk. A girl's gotta make a living. Anyway, did you hear the story she told me about there being a golden apple etched in one of the Parthenon's columns?"

Ingrid's breathing hitched, her lower lip, glossed to the max, curled inward. "Was that before or after the anus-head called you to ask where his nostril clippers were? I can't even believe the size of that dick's clangers."

Enormous. Igor's clangers were enormous. So was his anus-head. "I know, right? Especially seeing as he was doing it from between the very sheets we used our Bed Bath & Beyond fifty-percent off coupon for."

Ingrid's eyes narrowed, the crinkle of her leather, spike-studded vest crackling when she threw her arms up in the air. "Did he actually tell you he was in *bed* with that cantalouped trollop?"

Quinn shook her head, letting her straw bag fall to the ground. Suddenly, everything felt very heavy. "Not exactly. I heard Shawna in the background, attempting to pronounce the color *fuchsia* from the package. I know the word was on the package of sheets because it's hard to find sheets in fuchsia. Or fuck-see-a, as per Shawna's interpretation. Igor, in all his kindly professor-ness, helped her sound it out."

Ingrid's eyes grew glittery with outrage. "Ohhh, I *told* you when you packed all the things you had in his apartment you should have taken the sheets, Quinn. I don't care if the fifty-percent off coupon came from a sale circular addressed to *him*. He deserves sheets made out of burlap—not Egyptian cotton."

Quinn's arms sagged forward a little, but only a little, because it was hard to relax them with her huge new knockers in the way. "You're absolutely right. I was just trying to be fair, but my regret is real."

Ingrid peered at her, rolling her hand for her to continue. "So the old lady on the tour bus. Before or after Igor called?"

Grabbing the length of her long braid, Quinn wound it around a finger and tried to remember. "I think it was after. It had to be after, because then she heard you give me hell for even answering the phone, knowing he was on the other end of the line. So of course, she heard my pathetic story about how I'd saved a lifetime for this trip and thought Igor should be the one to take it with me because...well, you know the rest..."

The rest being Quinn's intention to propose to Igor in the place she considered one of the most romantic on earth.

Ingrid's head fell back on her shoulders, her pale throat exposed to the glaring ball of buttery Grecian sun. "Oh, you did not fall for that story she fed you, did you? She must've heard you going on about how Igor was a total jerk, and how you'd had it with romance and love for good."

"Well, I have," she defended. She had, too. All her life, her mother had told her to knock off the daydreaming about her Prince Charming and find a man who was real—if she had to find one at all.

If real meant finding a man who scratched his love sac and burped while watching the Playboy Channel, she'd rather keep daydreaming about her Mr. Darcy.

Until her ugly breakup with Igor, that is. Since the night she'd found out he'd been sleeping with a leggy redheaded waitress who worked at the Spotted Pig, two doors down from the bookstore where she worked, she'd thrown in the towel.

Ingrid's ringed fingers flashed in the sun in protest. "Stop. Even with everything that's gone down with that cheating slug, you *still* listened to that crazy woman on the bus. Which means you, in all your unicorns and cinnamon sticks, could manage to find romance at the urologist's. You're a diehard, Quinn. Your soul-mate take on life alone could feed a buffet of the love-starved. It'll come back. Right now, you're just butthurt. That aside, she was probably just trying to make you feel better. And you, an expert on all things Greek and mythological, fell for it? I don't get it."

She bit the inside of her cheek. She *had* fallen for it. Which meant her romantic bone still needed work if she was going to be more of a realist about love. "To be fair, it was a really compelling story."

She loved a good story. Almost any story, in fact. As long as it was about love—tragic, happy, or anything in between. Until she'd decided no more romance. She'd promised herself from here on out it was sci-fi and cookbooks only.

"Quinn Morris, you know the ins and outs of Greece and all its rich history almost better than you know your own home country. You did *not* believe her, did you?"

Quinn crossed her arms over her chest in exasperation. Well, she almost crossed them. Her big, big balloons really prevented a lot of extra-curricular activity. "Blame, blame, blame. How could I not investigate what she told us, Ingrid? I mean, you have to admit, even *you* were a little curious about a mysterious golden apple no one's ever heard about. It was pretty spectacular. How could I not at least take a peek? Seriously, I actually thought she'd probably go home and wet clear through her Depends laughing after feeding me such gibberish, but..."

Ingrid's eyes rolled upward. "You did it anyway. Now, if you tell me that you actually confessed your heartbreak to a damn produce item in some marble column like she told you to do because she claims the gods can hear your love woes, I'm going to deflate your new cans one at a time. Ping-ping," she said, making a gun with her forefinger and thumb

Quinn gave her a sheepish look. "But I *did* find the column with the apple. It looked just like it had been stamped there. So I thought, what the heck? Who better than Aphrodite's shoulder to cry on, right? Goddess of Love, blah, blah, blah. And before you say another word—I was just talking out my grief over my breakup, Ingrid. You know, kind of like one big, ugly purge, never really-really expecting anything to come of it, and then…"

"And then?" she asked in that tone she used when she became irritated with Quinn, who was usually much more cautious and less impulsive.

Except today, of course. Today she'd thrown caution to the wind like she was pitching for the Yankees.

The hot breeze whipped at Quinn's flowing skirt, tugging at her sunhat with the silky pink tulle streams of ribbon tied around the brim—another piece of her "must haves" wardrobe for this trip. Because it was romantic and frilly and she loved both of those things.

"*Quinn?*"

She gave Ingrid another embarrassed glance, her mouth dry. "And then I said something about Igor being a wolf in sheep's clothing and how he was going to regret his infidelity so hard. And I swear to you on my beloved copy of Keats, I heard a deep rumble of laughter."

Ingrid's eyes grew suspicious, flying upward and then to the surrounding landscape, brilliant and white under the glare of the sun, clearly looking to see if anyone else was around.

Wait—why isn't anyone else around? How could the Parthenon be so deserted when it was one of the biggest tourist attractions in Greece…?

"Get to the big, big boobies, Quinn," she ordered, pulling her phone from her backpack.

To not go all the way with this was just putting off the inevitable. "So then the wind picked up with a huge gust of hot air, all while I was going on and on about Igor being a cheat, and how ridiculous that must sound to someone like Aphrodite and a bunch of gods who aren't exactly opposed to a good genital jamboree. And…"

"*And?*"

Quinn swallowed hard, her gulp loud and thick. "And then there was this weird, soothing vibration coming from the ground that rumbled my feet. It spread up my legs and worked its way all along my rib cage. It was incredibly peaceful…er, at first. But then the pillar shook with a god-awful heave, splitting the marble and shooting chips of rock at me in every direction—and it fell! I swear! It fell right out of the column. Just splat, hit me on the head and rolled right to my feet."

"The apple?" Ingrid squeaked.

"Yes! It was as if the column had given birth to it. I swear I'm telling the truth, Ingrid, because look!" She dug around in her straw bag and retrieved the apple, holding it up as it gleamed, gold and perfect in the sun.

5

Ingrid's breath shuddered in and out, her voice skipping when she spoke. "*This* made your boobs bigger? An item from the produce section?"

Quinn whirled in a circle, letting her arms flap open wide. "I don't know, Ingrid! I just know the second it fell from the column, my boobs inflated at least two cup sizes. How, I ask you, does Shawna even breathe with these things?"

Ingrid held up a hand and took a long breath, her eyes again scanning the area surrounding the Parthenon. "First, put that thing down."

Quinn obliged, setting the apple at her feet—feet she could no longer see past her poofy chest.

"Don't touch it again. Now, I'm calling Nina. She'll know what to do. So let's just stay calm and breathe."

Fear sped up Quinn's spine as a mental picture of Nina Statleon formed. A brooding, hoodie-wearing, angry, foul-mouthed woman who was nuts with a capital Crazypants. And though absolutely, breathtakingly gorgeous sans makeup and all manner of finery, she was, oddly, very, very pale.

Nina, along with Marty Flaherty and Wanda Jefferson, were Ingrid's bosses at the office she worked in while studying to become a vet tech. The basement office in Manhattan Ingrid never allowed Quinn anywhere near when they had study dates. Which now, come to think of it, was pretty strange.

Nina evoked fear in her belly after their last encounter, when the woman had discovered what Igor had done and how Quinn had considered not taking this trip to Greece. Nina had been full of *all* kinds of opinions about it. They'd been littered with colorful language and sometimes even threatening stances and the words "limp" and "dick".

She was the one who'd suggested Ingrid come with Quinn in Igor's stead, to keep Quinn from throwing herself off the top of Mt. Olympus.

Which was a hasty assessment of her mental state, if you asked her. Okay, so she'd cried. She'd cried a lot that night she and Igor broke up and Nina happened to witness it. Cried so much, Nina had offered to chew her way through Igor's chest and eat his heart for her.

No doubt a kind act of girl-power solidarity. But she hadn't just cried about Igor. She'd cried because no matter what she did, Quinn Morris sucked ass at getting a relationship right.

Regardless, she was a little afraid of Nina

But it didn't make any sense that they'd call her for anything unless they needed a creative swear word or the eating of someone's face.

Quinn latched onto Ingrid's arm. "Nina? Why would you call her? How can she possibly help me with my huge lady lumps?"

Ingrid looked as though she was weighing her options and then she said, "There's some stuff you might need to know about Nina and my other bosses, Marty and Wanda. But not right now. Right now, I just need you to trust me, Quinn."

Trust. Sure. What else did she have but trust—and big boobs.

Holding up her phone, Ingrid grimaced. "Ugh! I can't get a damn signal. Stay right here and don't move. I'm just going to go over there and call her."

"But—"

"Not another word, Quinn. I know Nina scares you, but she's not just my boss, she's a good friend, and she *will* know what to do. She can help, and I promise to tell you why later."

Quinn couldn't imagine Nina as helpful. Maybe she'd be helpful if World War III erupted, but in something as sensitive in nature as this?

Fat chance.

She watched as Ingrid walked away, stomping over the debris of the column, kicking up dust with her heavy black work boots in search of a cell signal.

"Quinn Morris?" a deep, velvety voice asked.

Whirling around so fast she almost lost her hat, Quinn found the face that went with the voice.

Oh, and the body.

Yes—dear future soul mate and Jesus forgive her—*the body*.

She blinked in the glare of the bright sun. "Yes?"

A man with wavy hair like rich dark chocolate and sprinkled with golden highlights approached her. He took the strides separating them with confidence, on thighs that bulged beneath his tailored white trousers. When he stood before her, the apple resting in the gap between their feet, he smiled at her.

Winningly. Beamingly. His smile left deep grooves on either side of his mouth and flashed a set of brilliantly white teeth offset by a deep olive complexion. Yet, Quinn was able to note, even in her fear, his smile didn't quite reach his liquid amber eyes.

No. His eyes were cold and wary. And suspicious. Very suspicious.

"Who are you?" And hey. How did he know her name?

The upward tilt of his lips grew sly, and his burnt-orange knit shirt rippled against his broad chest when he said, "That's my apple. Excuse me, if you would."

In a matter of seconds, Quinn not only realized once more the enormity of what had just occurred with the pillar, but that possibly the apple could be some sort of rare Greek artifact, and this beautiful man was some kind of Indiana Jones in search of his Temple of Doom.

It wasn't every day an apple plopped from marble as if it had fallen off a tree. Which had to mean it must have some kind of value, and *she'd* found it.

The chiseled man eyed the apple. His expression flashed with apprehension so briefly, Quinn might not have caught it if she wasn't looking, but he instantly relaxed his utterly gorgeous face and covered up any trace of his worry with an arrogant gaze down at her.

Huh. Yeah. Something wasn't kosher here. Without thought, she gave him a blank look to distract him before swooping downward, using a deft hand to sweep the fruit off the ground.

"That's my apple," he repeated, low and easy.

"I beg to differ." She held it up, ignoring the fact that he could be dangerous, and waved the gleaming fruit at him. Just who the hell did he think he was? "I think it's *my* apple."

He edged closer, his spicy cologne lodging in her nose, his stance not quite one of menace but most definitely one of impatience. The sheer size of him made her knees waver.

"I assure you, it's my apple," he cooed in a silky-rich timbre.

Quinn's eyebrow cocked upward in haughty fashion. "By what authority?"

"My ancestors'."

"And who are your ancestors?"

"You'd never believe it."

"Try me. An apple—a shiny golden one I've never heard of in all my studies on Greek mythology—just fell out of a pillar in the Parthenon. *A. Pillar.* I'm game for just about anything."

His luscious lips thinned in obvious aggravation. "It's none of your business."

Quinn bristled. Hold on. Maybe this was an enormous archeological find and he was some bad guy who wanted to sell it to the highest bidder. What if this was a part of Greek history and he was going to cheat the people of this fine country out of something rightfully theirs and sell it for some ridiculous amount of money?

Briefly she thought of all the movies she'd seen and the idea that maybe she was going too far with the fantastical.

But how far was fantastical? Didn't an apple just fall out of some inanimate marble? Didn't she have boobs reminiscent of basketballs?

Planting her free hand on her hip, she used her best I'm-in-charge-of-this-rodeo voice and said, "I guess it's my business if you hope to prove this is really your apple. If you don't want to share and give me a good reason for claiming ownership, I'm sure the Greek authorities would be pleased to hear all about this *apple falling from a pillar,* which is insane to begin with. But I bet they'd really like to hear all about how it's *yours.*"

This time he didn't just edge closer, he loomed over her, his height, in her estimation, a good ten inches taller than her five feet four. "Give me the apple, Quinn," he demanded, his smooth jaw clenching.

When he spoke her name, it slid off his tongue like a dollop of warm caramel. And again, the romantic in her wanted to savor this moment and take the time to create a story for the piece of fruit and its connection to this walking, talking sex god. However, the big, albeit hot, goon obviously wasn't going to let her.

No. He glowered at her. Glowered so hard, were she a tea rose in an English garden, she'd have withered under his glare.

Quinn smiled, suddenly filled with adrenalin and totally fearless. Maybe it was the way Igor had so callously treated her, or maybe it was just more than past time, but suddenly she was a take-no-shit kind of girl.

Holding the apple closer, Quinn glared back at him in defiance and brought the gleaming fruit to her mouth, taking a long lick, ignoring the bitter taste of the skin on her tongue.

Hot Stuff planted his hands on his lean hips with a sigh of exasperation and rolled his beautiful eyes. "Now why would you do that, Quinn?"

"Five-second rule. Whoever licks it owns it."

He waved an admonishing finger, shooting her a teasing, almost playful glance. "No. I think you're confused. The five-second rule is only in play when you drop food on the ground. It means it's safe to eat as long as it wasn't on the ground longer than five seconds. And you forgot to kiss it up to God, thus blessing the five-second rule. *That's* the five-second rule."

Confusion furrowed her brow for a moment. Was that the rule? She'd never been very good at those sorts of playground games. While everyone else was jumping double Dutch or playing hopscotch, she'd been too busy making up stories about Jane and Dick running off together into the sunset with Spot as their trusty sidekick.

"I don't care what the rule is. I licked it. That means it's mine."

"This conversation's a little ridiculous, don't you think? Please hand over the apple."

"No. Not until you identify yourself and give me a good reason to hand it over. Otherwise, it goes to the authorities. And where did you come from, anyway? I didn't see you get off the tour bus. In fact, I didn't see you anywhere here in the Parthenon."

His lean cheeks puffed out in a huff of frustration. "On the count of three or I'll take it from you, Quinn."

Was he threatening bodily harm? Right here in the Parthenon? She began to back away. "If you touch me, I'll scream. A lot. Loudly. With vigor!"

His hand snaked out, his fingers wrapping around her wrist, capturing her in a tight grip. The contrast of their skin—hers pale and translucent, his deep and dark—fascinated rather than frightened her.

"First, I don't want to hurt you. Not at all. But I'll be long gone by the time someone arrives to help you either way."

She frowned up at him. "Hey. No fair. You said I had until the count of three."

His grip loosened a little, his handsome face growing deceptively serene. And then he smiled gorgeously, as if in apology for breaking the rules of their game. "My bad. Onetwothree! Hand over the apple, Quinn!" he roared.

With all the strength she had in her, she jerked her wrist, bringing them eye-to-eye. "Not gonna happen."

He sighed, visibly relaxing. Yet, there was a vein in his sun-browned temple that throbbed, giving away his impatience. "Quinn, Quinn, *Quinn*. Will you make me pry it from your pretty hands?"

Instead of heeding his words, which was certainly the smartest alternative to him roughing her up, she reacted by tightening her grip and shaking her head. "Nope."

By God and Greece, or whatever entity, she was going to get this apple to the proper authorities.

But he tightened his grip, steely and unmoving. "You're making an enormous mistake, and you've been warned. Now, for the very last time, please hand over the apple."

Maybe it was his tone, all silky-sexy but so demanding, or maybe it was that she felt as if she were in some strange tug-of-war on behalf of Greece and all its lush history, but *the hell* she was giving him the apple.

The. Hell.

May the power of Indiana Jones compel her.

"And I said *no!*" With that, Quinn yanked with such force, her hand snapped back then forward, nicking the apple on her two front teeth.

Simultaneously, the tall, sexy man bellowed the word "Nooo!" so loudly her ears literally hurt before letting her wrist go and stumbling backward.

As the juice of the apple hit her tongue, Quinn gagged. For a piece of fruit that looked as if it should have its own display case in Tiffany's, it was unbearably bitter, the juice running down the back of her throat like a trail of battery acid.

She ran her teeth over her tongue in a scraping motion. "Gak," she spat, letting the remainder of the apple fall to the ground, where it trembled eerily then came to rest at her right heel.

His sigh of aggravation made the ground beneath her feet rumble and a warm wind stir to a frenzy. It whipped around her head, leaving behind the minty scent of his breath in her nostrils.

Which, if she wasn't in some horrible nightmare, was impossible, wasn't it?

"You've done it now, Quinn." His tone rang with warning as he took another step back and crossed his arms over his chest.

She opened her mouth and made a clucking noise from the back of her throat to rid herself of the taste then wiped her knuckles over her tongue in repulsion, reaching into her bag for her bottle of water. "Tahth's disgussing," she said around her fingers.

His nod was sharp and all-knowing. "I'd bet it is, knowing my mother. But give this a second or two and you'll see what you've done."

Quinn pulled her fingers from her lips. His mother? "Your mother? And what exactly did I do but graze an apple, that tastes like a Jersey landfill, with my teeth?"

He glanced at his shiny gold watch with one raven eyebrow raised. "You'll see in five, four, three, two, one."

What was it with him and the counting?

But then Quinn's body jolted forward, making her drop the water bottle as the earth began to crack beneath her and the skies darkened to a deep purple. She broadened her stance, leaning back against the stranger who'd swiftly moved to stand behind her, tucking her into the shelter of his rock-hard chest.

And for about a half second, his chest was a very nice place to end up sheltered—except for the fact that he was a traitorous, likely black-market dealer of stolen and exotic goods.

But she forgot all about that when images flashed in front of her eyes in a tornado-like funnel of Greek gods and goddesses sitting on thrones, shooting arrows and, oh my...Doing things she assumed only happened in the movies they ran on Cinemax in the wee hours of the morning.

And then there was silence—deafening and frighteningly still.

Dazed, Quinn's hand went to her head to push back the wild tangle of her tattered braid from her eyes just as her chest heaved and her legs buckled, making her fall forward.

Vibrations of warmth skirted her spine, slipping along every available surface of her skin.

Fear turned to panic when she began to experience a simmering heat on her flesh worse than the hottest fever she'd ever had. It came in waves, rushing and relenting, bending and twisting until it finally subsided, leaving behind a residual warmth she had no words for.

As Quinn fought to gather her senses, the man let her go and paced before her in short jaunts, the heels of his loafers scraping against the loose stones.

He stopped to stand in front of her. His glare was angry, his sharply angled face tight. "Did I or did I not say the apple was mine?"

Once more, her mouth fell open. Words eluded her. Fully formed thoughts, too.

"And now look. Do you see what's happened here, Quinn?" He grated out the question between clenched teeth.

"Wha…"

He shook a long finger at her. "Oh, I'll tell you what. You've gone and done it now. Really done the hell out of it. I bet you're wondering what exactly you've done the hell out of, aren't you?"

Out of nowhere, Ingrid flew into her line of vision, skidding to a halt in front of her, eyes bulging when she scanned Quinn's face. Her mouth formed an O then her jaw fell before snapping shut. "What in the ever-lovin' fuck?"

Quinn's gaze flew to the stranger's before latching onto Ingrid's, wide with surprise, in a plea for help.

"Oh. My. Hell!" Ingrid shouted, pulling at her backpack to dig out a compact with the name Bobbie-Sue on it and flipping it open. "Look!"

Quinn blinked at her reflection under the hot sun. Her hands flew to her eyes. Wow. If in the choosing, she would have had any say in her eye color upon her birth, this amazing shade of bright, swirly purple would have been high on her list.

Much higher than her own dull, mousy brown. And they weren't just purple—they were purple with a capital P. As though someone had popped contacts from some Halloween costume store directly into her sockets.

"What did you do since I left you, Quinn?" Ingrid fairly seethed.

"I…" What had she done?

The man sauntered up to Ingrid, his bronzed arms crossed over his chest. "Here's what she's done. She's—"

But Ingrid halted his explanation by backing up, pushing Quinn behind her and reaching into her pocket for her cell. "Who the hell are you?" she spat, yanking her phone out and flipping open the keyboard. She began to type without letting the man out of her sight. Her fingers flew as she eyeballed him with a fierce stare.

"I'm Khristos with a K, for future reference—a descendant of Aphrodite and the man who's apple your friend Quinn here stole." He bowed regally at the waist before rising and glaring his obvious displeasure at Quinn.

Ingrid's stare whipped over her shoulder. "You stole his apple? Wait. It was *his* apple that fell out of the pillar? An apple did all this?" She swished her finger around the vicinity of Quinn's breasts.

Khristos nodded curtly, clearly attempting to keep his anger in check. "It was definitely the apple that did," he swept his hand up and down, "this."

When Quinn finally found her voice, it was raspy and thick. "What is *this?*" She plucked at her shirt in disbelief. "Is the apple really why my… my—"

"Her cans are the size of life rafts? Are you serious?"

Khristos chuckled—fondly, if she was hearing right. "The gods, in all their antiquated, outdated beliefs, think only women with," he cleared his throat, "um, *fuller* figures appeal to men. I've tried and tried to convince them to jump into the year 2015 with me, but old habits die hard. We're still working on diversity and all sorts of sensitivity training when it comes to body shaming. That's a real bone of contention with me. My motto is, all women should be loved, no matter their size or shape."

The gods?

Ingrid nodded her head with a rapid motion as though she was giving a big "hell yeah" to diversity and healthy body image. Then she shook it off and glared at Khristos. "Okay, buddy, what the hell is happening here? And I warn you—I know people who'll beat the information out of you if you're not willing to give it up."

He shook his dark head of thick, shiny hair. "You'll never believe it."

Ingrid snorted a scathing grunt. "Hah! I've only heard that a million times in the past couple of years. Try me, pal."

"You've never heard anything like this," he assured her in silken tones.

"Don't tell me what I have and haven't heard, Chiseled Man. In fact, I'd lay bets *you'd* never believe what *I've* heard. So get on with it, and while you're at it, step off!" She waved a hand between them, shooing Khristos away.

Ingrid flicked her stare back to Quinn and gripped her arm before she returned her gaze to Khristos. "Okay, so let's get it on here. Out with the explanation. What does this apple have to do with my friend and her sparkly bits, glowing like a diamond in a display case?"

"Well, had your friend left the apple be as I'd asked, those charming traits would have disappeared. They're simply a product of touching the apple and they fade rather quickly, given a day or so."

Quinn breathed a sigh of relief. Okay, so no big Shawna Sutter boobs forever? *Phew.* Because hell on fire, big, big boobies were more work than she was cut out for.

"But alas…" he said with a forlorn, almost comical sigh.

Her antennae went up. Oh, sure. Of course there was an "alas"…an "aside"…a "by the way, your stupid, stubborn friend is a halfwit who just wouldn't listen".

"Alas?" Ingrid asked with a demanding tone.

Quinn held her breath.

He gazed at each woman, driving his hands into his pockets and rocking back on the heels of his casual loafers. "Alas, she broke the skin of the apple with her teeth when we struggled for control."

Ingrid's eyes narrowed and her stance widened. "And that means what, Hard Body?"

Oh, damn. Now he was making that frowny face. That meant bad—so, so bad.

"The explanation's simple. Your friend now has the powers of Aphrodite."

"The Goddess of Love and Beauty?" Quinn managed to squeak.

Khristos winked an arrogant eye. "And all that entails. Clearly, that entails a healthy glow. Know what else it means?"

Ingrid rounded on him, skirting his body in dodgy circles. "Okay, spit it out. What does it mean, Khristos with a K, descendant of Aphrodite?" she asked with a tone of defiant skepticism, leading Quinn to think Ingrid didn't entirely believe him.

But was there any denying what had happened to her?

He planted a deliciously tanned hand on Ingrid's shoulder to prevent her from continuing her dizzying circles. "It means Quinn and I are going to be spending a lot of time together. Do you know why that is, quick-footed one?" he asked, sarcasm lacing his words.

Quinn watched while Ingrid tried to hide her alarm behind the Nina technique. The show-no-fear, take-no-prisoners technique. Ingrid jutted her chin upward and sneered, "Why is that?"

"Because that apple is my curse, and now, because your friend not only refused to return it, but she bit into it, it's *hers*, too. So that means wherever she goes, *I* go. I am the keeper of the apple and all its power."

Quinn's mouth fell open.

This big hunk of a Greek man, with all his ripples of muscle and silky hair straight out of a shampoo commercial, had to go everywhere she went?

Shut up.

It was like hitting the romance Powerball.

If she were still a believer in romance, that is.

Which she was not.

Not, not, not.

But the old Quinn?

She'd find that totally swoon-worthy.

CHAPTER 2

Quinn squinted at this man—this delicious, gorgeous man named Khristos with a K—and shook off the notion of anything romance related. No romance, even if he was a descendant of a Greek goddess.

Logic. That was all that was allowed right now. She might be a dreamer when it came to romance, but almost everything else about her was practical, from her money management right down to how she organized her spice rack.

She used to like to think her practicality came close to outweighing her romantic dreaming, that she'd somehow created a nice balance of the two. But after Igor, she decided romantic was losing and it was time she buck the hell up.

Use your logic and caution, Quinn.

Swallowing hard, she approached him carefully. "Why is the apple your curse?"

Khristos assessed her with a critical eye, crossing his forearms over his chest. "Let me rephrase that. It's not really a curse. Though it sure as hell feels like it sometimes. I'm in charge of keeping watch over the apple. I'm rather more a guardian of sorts."

Quinn bit her knuckle but her eyes were wide as her mind swirled with about a million dreamy scenarios, totally forgetting she was supposed to keep her practical self front and center.

But there was one scenario in particular that stood out. "Oh my God! You mentioned Greek ancestors? Is your ancestor really…" She paused. It was almost too amazing to believe. "Really *Aphrodite?*" The word slipped from her mouth in a hiss before she could prevent it.

He held his hands out, palms up in a gesture of resignation. "Ya caught me. She's my mother."

"Like *the* Aphrodite? Mistress-to-Ares Aphrodite?"

"Now, now," he scolded, his eyes suddenly teasing. "We don't like to talk about that anymore. It's called moving forward and letting go of the past. But yes. That's the Aphrodite I mean."

Quinn almost squealed with joy. It was like a Greek mythology dream come true. Yet, her next words defied her excitement. Especially in light of the fact that the very idea was flat-out crazier than a bedbug.

"She is not. There's no record of a Khristos listed as her son."

He shrugged his wide shoulders and smiled. "Well, if you know my mother's history, you know she…er, wasn't above some bedroom shenanigans from time to time. I cringe talking about it, because really, who wants to visualize their mother doing that? But I'm a result of her shenanigans. Anyway, it looks like she wins this round." He looked skyward. "Way to show me who's the boss, Mom."

Her son? No. This was nuts. He was no more Aphrodite's son than she was…

Are what, Quinn? This from a woman who saw an apple literally plop from a column, shredded a bra like she was practicing for a gig to play The Incredible Hulk and whose skin sparkles?

Quinn licked her dry lips. "Okay, so taking into account this is a little on par with the second coming—"

Khristos clucked his tongue, interrupting her. "I feel like maybe that's a little over the top. Though, knowing my megalomaniacal mother, she'd preen about the comparison. But how about we don't give her that much weight to throw around?"

Quinn shook her head, still trying to process. "Fine. So skipping the comparisons and moving right along past my disbelief, why did she make you the guardian of the apple? For that matter, why would she leave something so valuable at a tourist attraction?"

Because who just leaves the entirety of their power out in the open? It was like leaving an atom bomb at a playground.

"Oh, she didn't just leave it there. Make no mistake. My mother's many things, but careless about her powers isn't one of them. I was a little distracted today. I just set it down for a damn minute, too."

"And how is she going to feel about you slacking off on your guard duties?"

He winced. Beautifully—perfectly, if such a thing were possible. "Well, I'm sure there'll be a conversation."

She almost smiled at the idea of this big man in trouble with someone like Aphrodite. "You think she'll take away your X-box privileges?"

The sun grazed his cheekbone as he hitched his strong jaw. "At the very least, my dessert."

Damn, he was making it hard to keep her focus. "So any special reason why she put you in charge of her powers?"

"Because my mother loves a good joke, and the joke was, let's keep Khristos from ever having a moment's peace."

But wait. The magnitude of what she'd allegedly done began to sink in. Really sink in. Her stomach lurched. "Hold the phone. If the apple has the power of Aphrodite and I broke the skin, which technically means I'm now Aphrodite, isn't your mother going to be really incensed that she's lost her powers because you're a crappy babysitter?"

"That's fair, and I imagine there might be some discontent involved on her part. Maybe even a plague or some locusts, but don't worry. I got this."

"Plague..."

Khristos waved his hand in the air, the long fingers attached to it dismissing the obvious concern in her voice. "Bah. It never lasts long. She's not as good at holding steady as she is one big burst of fury, but it passes quickly." He winked as reassurance.

"I find I'm taking no comfort in this."

"Quinn! What the hell are you doing? Quit talking to him, Miss Stockholm Syndrome!" Ingrid ordered, grabbing her arm, her phone in her other hand.

But Quinn waved her off. "Oh, please, Ingrid. I'm not his hostage, for heaven's sake. Now, shhh. I'm just trying to find out what happens next." She turned back to Khristos with an eager ear. "So what happens next, Khristos?"

Ingrid hopped around as though her mere motion would ward off any evil Khristos harbored. "What happens next is you stop consorting with the enemy, Quinn! I can't believe you're all chatting it up over here with him like he's some guy you met at a damn bar. For the love of crackers, he claims he's a descendent of Aphrodite. Have you lost your mind?"

"I don't go to bars and you know it."

But Khristos just chuckled at Ingrid's assessment. "I find I'm a little insulted by that, Light of Foot. I have no desire to hurt either of you. I'm only doing my job."

Quinn's eyes narrowed, her breathing going shallow again. "Your job in correlation to guarding the apple—define that, would you?"

"Well, where the apple goes, I go. Now that you have the power of Aphrodite, you have to be taught how to use it, and I'm your teacher."

Him? Mr. Long, Tall and Made Out of Granite?

Stop.

Quinn blinked, the heat of the day beginning to sap her energy and what was left of her critical-thinking skills. "You're not serious. *You're* going to teach me how to be Aphrodite? The Goddess of Love? How does one teach someone to be a goddess? How does a *man* teach a *woman* to be a goddess? Don't goddesses wear togas and sit around all day, eating grapes while handing down orders? I can't wear a toga. I work in a secondhand bookstore, for heaven's sake. And while casual Friday is pretty casual at Baby Got Book, I think it at least demands pants."

Before Khristos had the chance to rebut, Ingrid hopped between them, her face red. "Don't you say another word, Quinn. And *you* stay away from her, got it, Khristos, descendant of Aphrodite? I'll handle this from here on out, pal. You just go back to wherever it is you came from."

Khristos closed his eyes as though he were silently asking for divine intervention before he opened them and smiled pleasantly. "I believe I've explained myself. I can't go away. But you handle this however you see fit…Ingrid, is it? I'll wait. The end result will still be the same."

Ingrid glared at him, grabbing Quinn by the arm and smacking into her new boobs as she moved her out of Khristos's earshot. "Put those things away, would you? They're everywhere, for Christ's sake."

Quinn let her hands drop to her sides, slapping them against her thighs in exasperation. "Where would you like me to put them, Ingrid? There's nowhere to put them but in a bigger bra. I mean, look at the size of them. Do you think I'm going to be able to breathe when I'm lying on my back? I'm going to suffocate myself with my own lady lumps. Wait. Maybe Shawna knows. I'd bet she's an expert."

Khristos stuck his face between the two of them, smiling. "Ooo, gossip. Who's Shawna?"

"She's the leggy redhead my ex cheated on me with, and her boobs are enormous. Just like these. Maybe she could offer me some tips?" Quinn said out loud before she was able to stop the words from falling off her tongue.

Ingrid rolled her eyes before giving Khristos a shove with a flat palm to his chest. "I told you to go away! Now do it before I sic my freaky-deaky, very violent friend on you. I swear, if you harm one hair on either of our heads, my friend will eat her way through your colon!"

Khristos made a comically funny sad face. "Already with the threats? Sad panda here. And we've just met, too. I was hoping we could be friends, because we're going to be together for a while—a long while. Plus, I like my colon."

Quinn fought a hysterical giggle when Ingrid hollered up at him, "Go!"

Ingrid grabbed Quinn by the arm and pulled her in. "Look, forget your boobs and focus," she whispered. "I've been down a similar road before with my bosses. There are things I haven't told you yet, Quinn. Things you're going to have a hard time digesting. Things about Nina, Marty, and Wanda you need to know…"

"Cryptic," Quinn muttered, totally missing what Ingrid was hinting at. But it did bring to mind the CIA covert ops secrecy surrounding her job and begged the question: Why wouldn't Ingrid ever let her anywhere near where she worked for their study dates?

They met three times a week outside of a nighttime art history class they took together, and had found, over lattes and scones or tuna subs and green tea, that despite their age difference of ten or so years, and though they had little in common but their mutual love of animals, they enjoyed each other's company. Quinn had witnessed the struggle Ingrid was having in art history, so she'd offered to tutor her.

It would definitely be more convenient for her to meet Ingrid than the other way around. She was done with work by five o' clock, but Ingrid was only just then taking her dinner break. For her to travel all the way to the bookstore was crazy, and Quinn had told her that on several occasions.

But Ingrid always kept her as far away from her place of work as possible.

And that didn't explain how Nina could help now. Unless she was tight with Aphrodite—which of course was ludicrous.

Quinn brushed Ingrid off and squared her shoulders. Maybe it was hysteria or shock or the heat, but she didn't hesitate to wonder out loud what was next. "But Nina's not here right now, is she? I am. Me and my gigunda boobs and sparkly skin—here with you and the man who claims he's got an apple keeping him on a leash. We need to figure out if this guy is for real, right? Because my boobs aren't kidding around. I really, literally grew boobs. So the natural question is, what's next, right?"

Khristos sighed and rolled his head on his neck before answering. "We go back to wherever you live, Quinn. I move in with you, and I teach you the ways of Aphrodite."

Oh.

Simple enough.

Wait. Move in with her? "Move into my apartment with me?"

"You're not moving anywhere, pal!" Ingrid exploded, her face redder than ever. "You're staying right there until I get someone here to help me. Now go over there, and do it now."

Khristos lifted his wide shoulders in an easy gesture of defeat. "Okay, but I'm telling you—"

"*Now!*" Ingrid bellowed, pointing her finger to the steps leading up to the Parthenon, her chest rising and falling with the obvious effort it took for her to yell.

Quinn cocked her head in Ingrid's direction as the dust of crushed rock swirled around their feet. "Why are you yelling?"

"Why the hell aren't *you?*"

She paused a moment. Yeah. Why wasn't she yelling? Or freaking out, for that matter? For that matter, why wasn't Ingrid freaking out?

Sure, she was yelling and ordering this man around as if she knew what she was doing, but she didn't appear any more freaked out than Quinn.

Quinn scratched her forehead. "You know, I don't know. I should be pretty traumatized right now, shouldn't I? I mean, a total stranger appears out of nowhere and tells me I now have the powers of Aphrodite, the Goddess of Love, shortly after my boobs inflate like someone used a bicycle pump on them, to name just one ailment. I should be trussed up in a straitjacket right now, but..."

"It's shock. You're in shock. When something like this goes down, it happens to every...um. It happens."

Every what? Everyone? "So the last time you saw a friend's dirty pillows grow right before your very eyes, they went into shock? Does this kind of thing happen often with you? Because remind me to leave you home if I ever take another post-breakup trip. I mean, what's next? Nicki Minaj's ass?" Quinn teased with a snort.

But wait...

Ingrid took Quinn's hand in hers and gave her a grave look. It was just like the look Ingrid had when she'd found out the One Direction tickets she'd paid three hundred dollars for online were total fakes.

When Quinn had squawked at the amount of money Ingrid had lost, her friend reminded her, with just such a face, that Harry was priceless.

"Look, while we wait for Nina to get in touch with me, there are some things I have to tell you—about my bosses. And I'm just going to say it. You're probably going to freak out, but we need Nina here like *now*, so I don't have a choice but to explain. How she gets here to Greece alone is going to leave you in the fetal position, shitting chickens, but I have to prepare you."

She was hot and tired and this I-know-something-you-don't-know business was old. Quinn threw her hands up in the air, blowing her hair from her face in an exasperated huff. "Okay, you win. Prepare me."

CHAPTER 3

W ell, if nothing else, she now completely understood why Ingrid never wanted her to see where she worked.

Because vampires, and werewolves, and demons, and zombies, oh my.

Quinn stared up at Ingrid while Ingrid stared back down at her, with Khristos still in the distance on the Parthenon steps, scrolling through his phone.

She repositioned herself on Ingrid's backpack, where she sat cross-legged, and held up a hand. Because Ingrid's lips were moving, but the words coming out weren't making any sense. "Stop. Let me process. *Please.*"

Quinn licked her lips and took a sip from her last bottle of lukewarm water. "Okay so, you used to work for a veterinarian named Katie in upstate New York, aka Deliverance-Land—Nina's words, not yours. And one dark and stormy night, while trying to save what you all thought was an injured, escaped cougar from the exotic animal farm down the road from her practice, your veterinarian boss was scratched by the injured kitty and that turned *her* into a cougar too? Am I getting that right?" Because who'd want to screw up that story?

Ingrid bit her lip and winced. "Meow?"

Quinn's eyes narrowed up at her. "Still too soon."

Ingrid sucked in some air. "Sorry. I'm just learning how to prepare someone emotionally for finding out they're paranormal. It's a process. Nina was teaching me, but Marty and Wanda said she's not allowed to help anymore because she's an insensitive cur—Wanda's words, not mine."

"Well, it *was* Nina who said it would be the eff-word stupid to cancel this trip—one I couldn't get a refund for, by the way. Not even when I threatened to slit my wrists with a butter knife right in front of that unshakeable travel agent. Nina said to *not* go to effin' Greece because I was acting like some kind of panty waste over a dick of a man who wasn't any better than the shit on my shoe, was effed up. Imagine my surprise that 'cur' is used when describing her in a sentence."

Ingrid's shoulders sagged. "Okay, forget Nina for a sec. Do you understand what I'm saying to you, Quinn? Really understand? My boss was a regular old human until she was accidentally scratched by the man who's now her husband and she's a cougar—*forever*. She shapeshifts from human form to cougar form. Nina, Marty, and Wanda were the ones who helped her get through the changes."

Quinn's mind whirred like a dervish when she gave Ingrid a dazed look. "Right, and Katie was just over forty when she was turned—so MILF jokes abound."

"You forgot to tack on the 'ha-ha very funny'."

"Slacker be mine name."

Ingrid peered down at her, pushing Quinn's tangled hair from her forehead. "Now repeat after me. Nina is a vampire, Marty is a werewolf, and Wanda is what we teasingly call a halfsie. Half werewolf, half vampire— all of them accidentally turned into supernatural beings by some nutbag event. And I work for them as their receptionist at a place called OOPS. Out In The Open Paranormal Support. They assist paranormal people in crisis, and that's why I know something paranormal has happened to you, and why I tweeted Nina. Because she's an expert on this and she's the only one of the three who can fly. Wanda's tried, but her attempts have had some pretty rough results."

"Right. The crash landing into the hedge maze at Nina's castle."

Ingrid grinned her approval. "Now you're getting it!"

Quinn vehemently shook her head. "Oh, no, no, no. Don't mistake this for getting anything. I'm just repeating what you told me. I still haven't wrapped my head around cougar veterinarian. So forget hedge mazes and castles and zombies. Oh my God. Nina has a vegetarian zombie…"

Ingrid bobbed her colorful head. "Named Carl. He's a great dude. Needy when it comes to a roll of duct-tape, but you'll love him."

Slowly, as the wheels in her head began to grind back into gear, some things were beginning to make sense—a connection of dots, if you will. Like how pale Nina was. "And Nina was already a vampire when I met her?"

"She's been one for seven years now."

"Is that what made her so crusty?"

Ingrid wrinkled her nose. "No. I hear she was always a little cranky, and FYI, I was petrified of her at first, too. I know she comes off as scary with all her swearing and threatening, but she's a total mush."

Quinn massaged the back of her neck. Right. Mushy-mushy. Hah.

She rose, handing Ingrid her backpack. "I'm sure she's very warm and supportive."

Ingrid nodded, pursing her lips. "I'm hearing sarcasm."

"You're not hearing things."

Ingrid made a face, tucking her thumbs into her backpack straps. "Look, she's good to me, Quinn. Nina, Marty, and Wanda pay me ridiculously well, way over the going rate for a receptionist to answer the phones at OOPS. If it weren't for them, I wouldn't have enough money to buy a pencil, let alone pay for my tuition. Plus, it was Nina who suggested you not go by yourself to Greece. She said you looked like you needed a vacation—but you shouldn't go it alone."

Now Quinn wrinkled *her* nose. "Now, now. That wasn't exactly what Nina said."

Ingrid threw up her arms in frustration, her sigh grating. "Fine. She said the last thing you should be doing is hitting Greece alone because the idiot, romantic, rose-colored-glasses wearer that you are, you'd probably end up shackled to some olive farmer as your rebound. Okay? Happy? Despite her forward nature—insensitive, cranky, sometimes crass…okay, *always* crass—even she could tell you looked like hell, and Nina never notices anything about anyone unless it's about her."

Quinn clucked her tongue with admonishment. "Don't forget the label suicidal. She said I looked suicidal." And maybe she had for the first week or so after Igor had told her he wasn't going to Greece with her at all, but leaving her for Shawna.

Red, swollen eyes and the muttered wish to have a bus run you over didn't deserve a label as harsh as suicidal.

Everyone deserved a good cry when their bubble of romance was burst by the pin of infidelity. She'd gotten over the sobbing, gulping, four-bags-of-pork-rinds-in-a-row part of it, and she'd thought she was moving on to something much less pathetic when she'd stepped onto the plane to Greece.

"You still look confused."

"It's a lot to absorb." Her head was spinning from the attempt to absorb.

Ingrid suddenly stuck a finger in the air. "Oh! I have the perfect way for you to relate to this. You know all those Molly Harper books you read about werewolves and vampires and love-sweet-love? It's kind of like that only real."

Right. This was exactly like that. Quinn frowned. "So back to Katie. Repeat the part about why Nina and company had to save her?"

"Remember the bit where I told you bad people wanted to kill Katie and her husband after they found out she was turned into a cougar?"

Panic seized Quinn from the tips of her toes to the top of her head. She gripped Ingrid's arm. "Are you saying someone's going to want to kill me because I bit an apple that tastes like donkey's ass?"

"How do you know what donkey's ass tastes like?"

"I don't. I'm just assuming that ass, in particular a donkey's ass, leaves an aftertaste."

Ingrid kept her voice low, turning her body away from the Greek goodness of Khristos. "I'm not saying anyone wants to kill you. Not yet. I just know from experience, after knowing Nina, Marty, and Wanda for a few years now and hearing all of their client stories, that there's always some bad dude who wants whatever it is the client stumbled upon when they have the paranormal accidents. The last case they had, it was dragon scales. Those scales turned not one, but two people into dragons, and the scales belonged to very bad people, and they didn't like that someone accidentally swallowed them. And then there was baby dragon—"

Quinn's eyes flew open wide in horror, clapping a hand over her mouth. Okay, she'd been willing to suspend disbelief for the most part, but what was next? Were-bears? "Stop it! Dragons? Now you've gone too far, Ingrid. Dragons don't exist. I was willing to suspend my disbelief with Nina and gang, but a baby dragon is too—"

Ingrid squatted in front of her and shoved her phone in Quinn's face. "Don't make me show you, Quinn! I told you I have pictures and everything."

She blanched, throwing her hand over her eyes. "No! No physical proof. Not yet. Please."

Ingrid, peeled back Quinn's fingers from her face, an eyebrow raised. "How could you doubt what I say is true after what's happened to you?"

Quinn sucked in a breath, yanking her hair over her shoulder and rebraiding it. Okay, so fair enough. Nina really could lift a car, and fly, and Marty was a pretty, petite blonde with impeccable fashion sense one minute, a hairy, snarling, jagged-toothed animal on all fours the next. And Wanda? Well, she was a combo pack of both vampire and werewolf.

Composed once more, she let her hand rest on Ingrid's arm, squeezing it. "So just because something's happened to me, you think someone bad is going to want what I have? How many bad guys want bigger boobs, Ingrid?" Ridiculous.

But Ingrid shook her head vehemently. "Oh, no. No, no. That's not the entire story. I can guarantee you that much. He said you have the power of Aphrodite. That's huge! And I've seen things because of Nina, Quinn Morris. I've seen some scary things and I don't believe this Khristos is telling us the *whole* truth about that stupid apple. There's more. I just don't know what. Which is why we need Nina. She'll beat it out of him if need be."

Perfect. That was exactly what she needed to top this trip off. Nina. But she kept her lips pressed together.

Or at least she really tried to. "Do you think it's wise to consult—"

Ingrid threw up a finger under Quinn's nose. "Do not. Do not say a single word. Nina's the expert on this, and we're going to listen to her advice. We're in a foreign country, with a crazypants guy who says he's a descendant of Aphrodite instead of doing what we said we were coming here to do. Flipping Igor the bird while you text him pictures of you slugging back ouzo belly shots off some slick Greek dude's hard abs. So shut it."

She tried really hard to do as Ingrid asked, but honestly, could one call the most gorgeous man on earth crazypants when there was a Nina? "I think you're being incredibly unfair, Ingrid. Why is it so crazy to believe this man is the descendant of Aphrodite if Nina can be Dracula's kin?"

"She's not Dracula's kin. Now knock it off and let me handle this. Caution is the better part of valor. Don't speak to him; don't even look at him while I keep trying to get in touch with Nina. Understood?"

"Okay. I'll just be over here looking at my new taters while I *sparkle*. In the shade, where the sun isn't eating a hole in the top of my head." She pointed to the steps of the Parthenon where the sun had begun to move away.

"Okay, but I have my eye on you, Quinn, and you, too, Made Out of Marble Man!"

Khristos tipped an imaginary hat in Ingrid's direction and smiled at Quinn when she sat down near the column farthest away from him.

They sat silently for a moment, her absorbing and processing this madness; him, hands folded around his knees, staring off into the distance.

Digging in her bag, she rooted around for a bottle of water. "Damn," she mumbled.

"Problem?"

Quinn pushed herself back against the columns, trying to make herself as small as possible before she answered, a little freaked out now that Ingrid's story was beginning to sink in. "No more water," she croaked, her throat dry and sore.

He nodded his head. "I can help." Lifting an arm, he began to snap his fingers when she shouted.

"No!"

Out of the clear blue, a bottle of water appeared, with delicious drops of condensation gleaming in the burning sun as they slid down along the plastic length of it. He rose and offered it to her, his brown hand strong and wide. "Drink."

When she hesitated, he moved and sat down next to her.

God, he smelled heavenly. Like the earth on a spring day and Tide. Yet, she cringed farther against the column and closed her eyes. "You just made a bottle of water appear with the snap of your fingers. I think you have to go away."

He scoffed, all sexy and rumbly-tumbly, as if she'd just accused him of trying to poison her. "Now, Quinn, what could I possibly do to you with a bottle of water?"

Hello. Big, big boobies here.

She popped her eyes open and looked at him with a scathing glance. "You, who claims to guard an apple that gave me boobs the size of fresh cantaloupes, and made a bottle of cold water appear out of thin air, are asking me what you could possibly do to me? In fact, I just asked Ingrid what's next? Nicki Minaj's ass?"

His laughter rumbled deep and low, echoing throughout the Parthenon in a delicious vibration that shot straight up her spine. "I promise you the water won't give you Nicki's ass. Though, gun to head, if I were going to give you someone's ass, I prefer J-Lo's."

Her look must have been one of horror because he quickly added, "Kidding." He unscrewed the top and handed it to her. "Drink."

Licking her dry lips, Quinn couldn't resist. She took the bottle from him, giving him one last look of hesitation. "If I come out of this looking like one of those *Real Housewives* who use so much Botox they look like merely going to the ladies' room is a surprise party, I'm going to put your apple in a damn food processor."

Khristos mocked a wince. "So many threats today from such tiny women. The female force is mighty in your circle, huh? Now drink before you dehydrate."

Putting the bottle to her lips, Quinn took a small sip, letting it sit on her tongue to decide whether it tasted funny before she could no longer resist and chugged it, finishing it off. Handing it back to him, she smiled. "Thank you."

"Another?"

At first her eyes narrowed in skepticism, but then she gave the front of her shirt a subtle glance and threw caution to the wind. "Please."

Khristos snapped his fingers and yet another bottle appeared, as enticing as the first. He popped the top once again and smiled, easy and light. "So tell me about yourself, Quinn Morris. What are you doing here in Greece?"

Licking my wounds? Plotting my ex-fiancé's death? She looked off into the vast horizon of blue and white puffy clouds. "Vacation."

His dark eyebrow rose. "Really? How does this Igor factor into your vacation?"

Shame flooded her cheeks crimson. "You heard?"

"I did. The jerk."

Anger spiked along her spine, and she wasn't sure if it was still over Igor breaking her heart or that Khristos had heard her humiliating story. "He'll get what he deserves. Mark my words."

"Revenge can be very sweet."

Suddenly she was tired of mucking about. She didn't want to talk about Igor or Shawna or her embarrassing confession. Not if those words Ingrid had bandied about just moments ago had any validity.

If he was going to kill her for the apple thing, then she wanted a head start. The best way to get an answer was just to confront him. "Let's stop pussyfooting around."

Khristos cocked his beautiful head. "Okay. No more pussyfooting."

"And I want honesty when I ask this very sensitive question."

He nodded, his thick hair falling over his eye, making him look even more rakish than he had at first glance. "You got it."

"Are you going to kill me for biting your apple?"

"It was an accident, right?"

"If you would have just let go of my hand..." She stopped justifying and shook her head. "Yes, it was an accident."

"Then this time I suppose I can let you live. But I don't spare lives often. Remember that as we take this journey, Quinn Morris," he said, but his amber-brown eyes were teasing.

She smiled. For the first time in days, it wasn't just for the sake of everyone around her. "Okay, good. So that's settled. Now, I don't want to waste any more time freaking out about this and panicking. I've heard when something paranormal like this happens, there's a lot of that."

Straight from Ingrid's mouth, she'd heard it. Crying, whining, mourning your old life were all symptoms of the change—symptoms that made Nina want to throat punch the OOPS clients.

She did not want to be throat punched by Nina. She was a lover. Not a fighter. Okay, a former lover, but she'd still never be a fighter.

Khristos raised an eyebrow again, a clearly skeptical one. "You've heard? What kind of human are you?"

She shrugged her shoulders as her dilemma began to sink deeper and deeper into her brain—the ramifications of it all were beginning to wear her down. "The kind who likes to be prepared. So what's next?"

Ingrid interrupted any hope he had of answering when she made a beeline for Quinn, her eyes blazing and angry. "Didn't I tell you not to talk to him? You!" she yelped at Khristos. "Back off!"

Khristos sighed and slid back over to his side of the steps and leaned back on his elbows "Apologies," he said with a smirk.

Ingrid's phone dinged, making Quinn jump up and peer over her shoulder. While she kept one eye on Khristos, Ingrid held up her phone. "Finally! I've been trying to get a signal forever. So I gave up and tweeted Nina. Go figure Twitter works but I can't dial internationally. Read."

OOPS: @ingridbelieves Did u fucking say she's sparkling?

Quinn nodded her head at the phone. Fucking yes, she did.

Ingrid watched Khristos while she tweeted, *Ingrid Lawson Ingridbelieves: @OOPS Yes! Something's happened. Man—big man involved. Help now. Come pls!*

OOPS: @Ingridbelieves R u telling me I should leave my man and kid because the nitwit is glowing? Did u eat moron 4 breakfast?

Ingridbelieves: @OOPS She also has cans the size of water balloons. Come pls!

OOPS: @Ingridbelieves LOLLOLLOLLOL!

Quinn frowned then stuck her tongue out at Nina's tweet. "How are my big cans funny? This is not funny! He's claiming I'm the Goddess of Love. After this past week, where I've decided love blows some hefty chunks, I don't think I can hold up my end of the bargain. So tell Nina to stop mocking me and do her job, which is to help someone in paranormal crisis."

She couldn't even believe she'd just repeated those words. But help was help.

Ingrid's fingers flew over the keyboard on her phone. *Ingridbelieves: @OOPS Come pls. He says Quinn's Aphrodite!*

OOPS: @Ingridbelieves The Goddess of Love?

Ingridbelieves: @OOPS Yes! Batshit, right?

"Khristos? Is that my favorite Greek ever?"

Quinn and Ingrid both whipped around at the sound of a familiar voice.

Nina used the word "favorite" in a sentence—referencing another person? One of these things was not like the other.

Khristos shaded his eyes and gazed into the far corner of the Parthenon. "Nina Statleon? Is that you?"

Quinn's burning eyes went wide. "You know her?"

Nina's form blurred momentarily as she moved from the far corner of the ruins to right in front of them in the blink of an eye. Her long dark hair poking out from beneath her hoodie, her usual dark sunglasses on her nose, sporting a white strip of zinc oxide for added sun protection.

She eyeballed Quinn's breasts and whistled. "He sure does, Boobs. Dude, how ya been?"

"Get over here, you!" Khristos said with enthusiasm, opening his arms to Nina—to *Nina*—and she went right into them, as if hugging was her favorite pastime.

He chuckled as he squeezed her hard and let her go, smiling down at her. "If it isn't my favorite vampire! I'm really good, lady. Damn, when was the last time we saw each other?"

Nina pushed her hoodie from her head with a wide grin, unzipping it to reveal a black T-shirt that read "I'm A Delicate Fucking Flower".

A grin. Nina was grinning. Not scowling. Oh, the world really had tipped on its axis.

"Gods versus Vampires picnic of 2012. Remember that shit? Took Apollo out like he was GD wearin' lace panties and a bra. Good times, my friend."

Khristos barked a laugh, his head falling back on his shoulders, revealing a strong neck, thick with cords of muscle. "That's right! That was one helluva play you made, too. Talked about it for days."

Nina slapped him on his broad back while an astonished Ingrid and Quinn stood frozen and watched. "So what's goin' on here, man? Ingrid tells me Boobs McGee is Aphrodite? Seriously? Like she didn't have big enough rose-colored glasses sitting on that snooty nose of hers? What in the ever-lovin' hell have you done, Khristos?"

Khristos stood back and jammed his hands into the pockets of his trousers. "Me? I didn't do a thing. She did. She nicked the apple with her teeth, and you know what that means."

Nina lifted her dark sunglasses and rolled her eyes, the strip of zinc oxide beginning to melt on her nose. "The golden one? Aw, duuude."

Khristos threw up his hands. "Honest to God, I look away for one minute and bam. It's partially my fault. I was a little distracted—"

"With a hot, leggy blonde, no doubt?" Nina asked, her grin facetious as she moved to the shade beneath a column.

Khristos rolled his eyes, but his face split into a gloriously handsome grin. "I tried to tell her not to touch it, but she wouldn't listen."

Quinn knew she should speak up, say something in her defense, but she still wasn't over the fact that Nina knew this man.

"What the hell was the apple doing here in the first place?"

Khristos looked up at the column and shrugged. "I only set it down for a minute. We had some kind of weird tremor, right, Quinn? Maybe a mini-earthquake?" he asked her. "And it fell on the ground and she grabbed it up."

Quinn's mouth dropped open.

Khristos shook his head. "Never mind. She's still a little shell-shocked. You know, the whole body change? I know it's a delicate subject with women, but as I explained earlier, you know what the gods were like back in the day, right? Ample bodies and lush curves were all the rage. Anyway, the apple fell from the column and then, well, you know the rest."

Nina nodded then nudged Quinn with her shoulder. "Did he tell you not to touch the apple, doofus?"

Quinn frowned, not liking the ugly guilt she was experiencing. "Well, yes...but I thought he was nuts. I mean, I thought maybe the apple was some rare artifact he was trying to steal. I tried to get it away from him, but in our struggle, I nicked my tooth on it. I thought by keeping it from him, I was saving all of Greece!"

"See?" Khristos said, hitching his angular jaw in her direction.

Nina nodded, her next words laced with typical Nina sarcasm. "Job well done, Indiana Jones."

Oh, blame, blame, blame.

Nina brushed her hands together as if she were over this. "Then we're good to go. And thank Christ, too. I thought I was going to have to spend another piece of my damn eternity codling one more cockadoodie whiny woman. But you can take it from here, right, Khristos?"

Wait. Nina was just going to leave her here with her big, big boobies and an utter stranger-slash-alleged-god who said he had to teach her how to be Aphrodite?

Aw, hell no.

She was terrified of Nina. Every time she ran into her when she and Ingrid had a study date, she literally shook in her shoes and avoided her like the plague or, if forced into her company, sat quietly as Nina scowled at her.

But what if Khristos wasn't being completely honest, like Ingrid said? What if, even though he knew Nina, she didn't really *know*-know him?

Did you ever really know a person? Wasn't it true that when serial killers were revealed, all the people who knew them in their everyday lives were all in total shock because they never suspected a thing?

Nina was a beast, but she was the beast Quinn knew, and if something went awry, she wanted the vampire on her side.

Which meant—let the begging and scraping commence.

CHAPTER 4

Nina stopped dead in her tracks and gave her what Quinn decided was the scariest face ever. "Stop hanging on to me like I'm the last prom date on planet earth, for crap's sake! He's not gonna eat your face off, but I will if you don't get the eff off me."

Quinn backed off but still hovered at Nina's elbow. Somehow, Nina seemed like the best bet. She'd lost count of how many times Ingrid had reminded her of what a badass Nina was.

"How do you know he won't eat my face off?" she asked as the group made their way up the sidewalk to her small basement apartment.

Upon Quinn deciding her trip of a lifetime was officially over due to her new powers—and the discussion had with Khristos about how she couldn't be trusted to know what true soul mates looked like in her fragile, heartbroken state—Nina demanded they come back to New York immediately and consult with Marty and Wanda before Khristos took over.

So now two things weighed heavily on her mind. What exactly did Khristos mean when he said she wouldn't know two soul mates if Cupid threw them at her? And how they'd gotten here—without an actual plane—was still hard for her to form complete sentences about.

"FYI, speaking from my vast experience in face-eating, faces can be a little bony. I prefer other parts of a body, like a nice, fleshy upper arm," Khristos growled from behind her, his tone teasing.

Quinn jumped, tucking her light sweater around her as though the flimsy material would protect her from this hulk of a man. Gone was her bravado, now replaced with sheer terror. Ingrid had filled her head with so many vivid images of demons and Hell and vampires running amok, Quinn couldn't shake them.

She stopped by the big maple tree just before her apartment building and turned to face him, keeping Nina close. "Listen, I don't know what goddesses teach their offspring, but where I come from, my mother taught me never to trust strangers, and as far as I'm concerned, you're a stranger. I don't care if you come with a recommendation from the Masters of the Universe and the FDA, you're still a stranger to me. As a result of your stranger-ness, I now have lady pillows like a porn star and I glow. So, until I feel more comfortable—back…off!"

Khristos didn't seem at all offended. In fact, he merely chuckled and motioned for her to go ahead of him. "My apologies. I thought Nina was a good enough reference."

Stopping when they reached the stairs leading down to her apartment, Quinn dropped her carryon bag, letting it thump with a satisfying crunch to the hard, semi-frozen ground. "I hardly know Nina, and what I do know of her is enough to give me nightmares for a hundred years."

Had she said that out loud?

Nina popped her lips, her eyes narrowing under the fluorescent street-lights. "I'm sorry, Lite-Brite, but wasn't that you back in the Parthenon, clinging to me like some damn leech, begging me not to leave you alone with big scary Khristos? I'm all the nightmare you got right now. If I were you, I'd shut that yap of yours, and I'd shut it now." She leered down at Quinn, making her shiver a cringe.

Yep. She'd said it out loud.

Honey. You get more flies with honey than vinegar, Quinn, her Aunt Rachel had always said. Reaching up, her fingers shaking, she patted Nina on the shoulder before snatching her hand away. "That was rude of me."

"The rudest," Nina said before growling at her and snapping her teeth.

Headlights shining in her eyes as a big SUV drove up forced her to squint and back away from Nina.

Ingrid clapped her hands in delight. "It's Marty and Wanda!"

Nina rolled her eyes before slapping Khristos on the back. "If you thought this one was a pain in the ass—wait. Marty and Wanda are the champions of ass pain."

But laid-back, easygoing, hotter-than-hell Khristos rocked on his heels and smiled. What was with all the smiling? "Can't wait."

Marty and Wanda fell out of the car in a cloud of hair and perfume, rushing to Ingrid and scooping her up in a hug. Their eyes, sympathetic with only hints of shock, locked with Quinn's.

And then they were scooping her up, too, in vanilla-scented hugs and bangle bracelets clacking in the howling night air. "Oh, Quinn!" Marty said, rubbing her arm with a gentle hand. "How are you feeling? Do you need to talk about it? I wish Ingrid had contacted us instead of Elvira here. We're far more sympathetic to the changes you'll experience, and well, we don't swear nearly as much."

Nina leaned down and looked Marty in the eye, flipping her middle finger up into the air. "Oh, eff you, Pretty-Pretty Princess. She's here, isn't she? Not a hair on her head out of place and her boobs even managed to stay inflated, all nice and poofy, just like I found her. I'd say that was damn well the best display of sympathy ever."

Wanda sighed, poking Nina with a gloved finger between her shoulder blades. "You. Quiet. Now." Reaching for Quinn, she hooked her arm through hers and smiled.

Wow. She was pretty—for a halfsie.

"I'm Wanda Schwartz-Jefferson, and we're here to help. Now, let's get you inside where you can warm up and we'll chat over some tea, yes? You drink tea, if I recall what Ingrid said correctly, right?"

As Wanda led her down the flight of stairs to her apartment, Quinn couldn't help but find her strangely soothing, in her slim-fitting taupe trench coat and silky turquoise-and-brown scarf. She smelled of good things—warm, kind things—and Quinn was instantly drawn to her.

Quinn nodded, reaching into her purse to dig for her keys, to no avail. "I can't find my keys." But she sure knew how to find an apple.

Nina groaned. "Move," she ordered, parting the group and skipping down the steps to grab the handle on her door.

The other two women yelped, "No, Nina!" just as she mutilated Quinn's doorknob with her long fingers.

Mutilated. As in, pulverized with a mere turn of her wrist, the heavy metal so twisted, it dropped and fell to the ground with a loud clang.

Oh, cripes.

Nina's defiant black eyes found Quinn's as though she were daring her to complain. Her raven eyebrow rose while she waited for Quinn to react. When she didn't—because hello, throat-puncher alert—Nina grinned and said, "After you."

She traded off clinging to Nina for clinging to Wanda. If nothing else, she was softer for the clinging, and she didn't gnash her teeth at her.

Pushing her way through the door, she flipped on the lights to her very tiny living room and sucked in the familiar air of home, her eyes scanning the pastel colors and bleached white walls. She'd worked hard to make this space hers, using her favorite colors—pale blues and white—and decorating it with all the things she loved, like roses and hydrangeas and sheer curtains with lace.

"Jesus. Did Barbie die and leave you all her shit?"

Naturally, someone like Nina would find her tiny abode, decorated in various shades of white and muted blues, distasteful. She probably had deer antlers and beer mugs hanging from the walls of her castle.

Marty rasped a sigh as she pulled off her ankle-length coat in royal blue, and hung it up on the coatrack in the corner. "Not now, Night Dweller. Quinn's had a long day. Go make that tea or something. Can't you see the poor woman's teeth are chattering?"

Her teeth were indeed chattering, the harsh winds of mid-fall in Manhattan a far cry from the heat of Greece. Quinn spread out a shaky arm. "Please, make yourselves comfortable."

"On what? The Barbie couch? Can I sit next to Ken?" Nina asked with a cackle.

Wanda unfurled her scarf and shook it at Nina. "Knock it off. Not everyone finds BOGO velvet wall art from the flea market and lava lamps appealing. Now go make tea, so the rest of us can help Quinn sit and catch her breath."

Marty wrapped an arm around Quinn's shoulders and squeezed. "It's so nice to finally meet you. I know Ingrid kept you at arm's length because of…well, you know—us, but we've heard so much about you and how you've helped our Ingrid out in your art history classes. It's nice to put the face to the topic of many conversations."

Quinn nodded. She could only imagine the conversations her stupidity over Igor and love and romance had evoked. Ingrid was always mocking her for it. Turned out she was right.

Suddenly exhausted, all she wanted to do was climb under her fluffy comforter and sleep off this Nina-lag. "It's nice to finally meet you, too," she mumbled, leaning into the warmth of Marty's side and letting her lead her across the room.

Marty smelled as nice as Wanda, and she dressed as if she'd fallen out of a copy of *Vogue*, with her skinny jeans, royal blue knee-high boots, and dolman-sleeved purple and pink sweater. Her hair glistened all shades of blonde under the dim glow of Quinn's end table lamps, falling down her back in beachy waves.

Her hands were gentle when she drew Quinn to the couch and sat her down, tucking the blanket around her and ordering Ingrid to find some warm socks for her sandaled feet.

In a sleep-deprived haze, she let these people she didn't know tend to her, forgetting they were historically considered heinous creatures and thinking only that she could sleep for days with this kind of attention paid to her.

When a firm hand, warm and gentle, reached for her foot and unhooked the buckle to her sandal, she didn't open her eyes. She knew it was Khristos, but she almost didn't care.

Almost—except for that tingle running along her calf as he eased her fluffy socks up and over her ankle.

He leaned into her then and whispered, "Rest. I'll be here when you wake up, Quinn."

And somehow, that was strangely comforting.

"Who is this smooshy face?" she heard Nina's husky voice ask in a tone that almost sounded childlike and sweet. "Oh my goodness, I can't believe who's such a sweet, sweet girl!"

Quinn's eyes flew open, scanning the room. Buffy and Spike. How could she have forgotten about her cats? But it didn't seem to matter, Nina clearly had it all taken care of as she scratched Spike's hindquarters and rubbed her cheek against Buffy's head.

"I told you—total mush on the inside," Ingrid commented, nudging her shoulder with a grin.

Quinn pushed her hair from her face, assessing her surroundings. She was still on the couch. Rubbing her temples with the heels of her hand, she groaned. "What time is it?"

Ingrid patted her hand. "Midnight."

Quinn sat forward with a jolt as everything came rushing back to her, but suddenly Marty was there, holding a cup of steaming tea and a grilled cheese sandwich, a warm smile on her red lips. "It's okay, Quinn," she said softly. "Everything is okay. Ingrid called your cat sitter to let her know you were home and as you can see, our resident Mistress of Evil-slash-marshmallow has everything under control. Now drink your tea and just relax." She patted her thigh, and set her tea and sandwich on the end table before wandering off to Quinn's kitchen, the heels of her boots clacking over the bleached white flooring of her living room.

Khristos was there suddenly, too, standing in front of her before sinking to his haunches, his face maybe even more beautiful in the glow of the lamp. "Better now?"

God. That voice. His voice did things to her stomach, warm and squishy things she rebelled against almost instantly. He was not allowed to give her warm squishies, and while this circumstance was indeed right out of a piece of fiction, it wasn't romantic at all.

He had to go.

"I'm fine. Look, I don't need a babysitter. You can go home, wherever that is." Where did a Greek goddess's son call home anyway?

"Um, no. I can't just go home and leave you with the power of Aphrodite, Quinn. It doesn't work that way. It's an enormous responsibility, putting people together for life."

"That's why they have this thing called divorce. On the off chance you make the wrong decision." Such an ugly word. As a child of divorce, and a nasty, knock-down drag-out one at that, she'd promised herself when she married it was going to be forever, no matter what it took to keep it together.

Not that she believed in forever anymore.

Khristos clucked his tongue. "First lesson, and it's a hard-and-fast rule. Never use the 'D' word. Aphrodite creates true mates for life."

"You sound like an infomercial. Next you'll show me how to cook an entire chicken in under ten minutes while you Oxy Clean my whites."

He chuckled, low, deep, husky. "Matchmaking is nothing like cooking chickens, but it is a delicate matter, Quinn."

She gaped at him. "Clearly, because your gods decided it was a smart idea to leave all the power of the most famous goddess ever in an apple in the Parthenon where just about anyone could get their hands on it. It's obviously ultra-delicate."

"And here we go," Nina cooed to Buffy, one of Quinn's late-night alleyway rescues from a Dumpster.

Quinn cocked her head in Nina's direction, and she almost didn't care if she bit it right off. "What is that supposed to mean?"

Nina's eyes narrowed, glittering and fierce. "It means you're finally hitting the grief crap. You know, the five-stages thing? Whining, crying, anger—which is usually first. I don't know. It's some bullshite Marty and Wanda feed everybody while they're going through the change. We have a pamphlet on it. But they never give it to anyone—because that makes sense, and who the hell would wanna make sense when they can jump into your personal crap feet first and wallow in it with you?"

Quinn frowned, not understanding.

Nina rolled her eyes. "It means any second now, you're gonna be a motherfluffin' train wreck." She looked down at Spike and grinned. "But don't worry, little man. I'll protect you from your crazyface mother."

Was she any of those things? She hadn't stopped to think about ramifications and everything that went with biting the apple. What *were* the ramifications, anyway?

What Khristos had said back at the Parthenon made no sense. How could he help her be the Goddess of Love when, if history served her correctly, the Goddess of Love didn't do much but create havoc and make men fall in love with her?

Was that a job? Would she now be a savvy player in the game of love? Because hold the phone. That could mean Bradley Cooper, her Mr. Darcy in her mind, was ripe for the picking. Why stop there? Why not have a whole passel of hunks? The Avengers, perhaps—or a Thor-Loki-RDJ triple-decker sammie?

Squee.

Quinn reared upward, putting a hand on Khristos's shoulder and moving him for a clearer view of Nina, gritting her teeth at how firm he was beneath her palm. "But I feel fine."

"But you won't once the crazy starts. So save it, Glow Stick, and get the frick on with it so we can move to the next phase. I have a gazillion things I'd rather be doing. Like watching paint dry or having my fingernails pulled off one by stinkin' one."

Wanda zipped into the room, scooping up Spike and shaking a finger at Nina with a scowl. "What Nina means to say is, there will be phases to this change, Quinn. Phases we're quite sensitive to, and happy to help you through. That's what we do as paranormal crisis counselors."

Nina shook her head, the dark curtain of her silky hair brushing her pale cheek. "That wasn't what the flip I meant to say at all, Wanda. What I meant to say, and I'm always happy to make crap clear—"

Wanda smooshed Nina's lips together with two pink-tipped fingers. "But it *is* what you meant to say, Vampire. In fact, that's all you're going to say until I tell you to say something. Remember how you were working on not swearing because it's unhealthy for little Charlie? Work harder."

Quinn was baffled. "Who's Charlie?"

Wanda's face broke into a beaming smile as she continued to hold Nina's lips together. "Nina's little girl."

"*You* have children?" Okay, so to be fair, it shot out of her mouth before she had the chance to stop it, but she prayed for some slack from Nina—or at least only a light punch to the throat.

Ingrid clamped a hand over Quinn's mouth, too. "I'd stop now if you value your guts staying on the inside."

Quinn instantly backed off, brushing Ingrid's hand away. "I'm sorry. I didn't know vampires could have children. It caught me off guard."

Wanda nodded with a curt bounce of her elegantly coiffed head. "And Nina accepts your apology, don't you?"

Nina swatted Wanda's hands away and growled, flashing her fangs.

Oh, cheese and rice. *Her. Fangs.*

And then Wanda leaned in close and growled back an order. "Nod your head or I'll rip it clean off. Understood?"

Nina obediently nodded her head, but she didn't like it, if the flare of her nostrils and her clenched fists were any indication.

Setting Spike back on Nina's lap with a scratch under his chin, Wanda smiled. "See? Nice vampire is nice. Now, onto what Khristos was saying about being Aphrodite. Please. Finish. I'll keep Nina in line while you do."

He sat on the edge of her coffee table and looked directly into her eyes, taking one of her hands in his. "As I said, I'll move in here with you, and we'll begin immediately."

But she snatched her fingers from the warmth of his palm. How was she going to breathe with this man in her apartment? "Why does the way it works have to include you staying here? You can see how tiny my apartment is. I only have one bedroom the size of a broom closet. Where would you sleep? Can't we do like a nine-to-five thing? You know, like school hours?"

"Oooo, I hope they cut your carrot sticks into shapes and make happy freakin' faces out of your fruit for snack time at Goddess School, Lite-Brite," Nina crowed sarcastically.

"Nina!" Marty hissed, coming around the corner of the kitchen and back into the living room. "Don't make me snatch that tongue of yours from your head."

"Fuuu…" Nina's lips thinned in exasperation. "*Fluff* you, Blondie. Fluff you so hard."

Marty winked and snickered. "Fluff this. Now be quiet and let Khristos explain."

"I can't leave you alone, Quinn. Especially not with the way you're feeling about love and relationships at this point."

"Ah. Does my utter disdain trouble you?" Because it should. Which just might be her permission slip out of this crazy gym class.

"In a startling way."

All of this was becoming too much. Her senses were preparing for a crash—just like Nina predicted. "I don't understand what being Aphrodite even means. Doesn't she just make people fall in love with her beauty? What does it have to do with other relationships? She's not a matchmaker. I thought Cupid handled that?"

Khristos grinned. "Here's a little inside dirt on gods and goddesses—something you won't find in your books. They have minions. Cupid might shoot the arrow, but Aphrodite's the one who tells him when and where. She's an expert matchmaker and when her true matches fall in love, it's forever. It's her contribution to procreation."

Quinn took another long, deep breath. "So what you're saying is, I decide who falls in love and who doesn't? And what does her contribution to procreation mean? Am I responsible for matching people so they can have children and thus future generations will continue to repopulate the world?" That was crackers. Total crackers.

How could she be responsible for something so enormous? Her? A nobody ex-dreamer who worked at a bookstore? What if she did it wrong? What if she put two people together who ended up miserable?

"It's like a dream job come true, huh, Boobs?" Nina snorted. "You with all your floaty dreams about love and the sky raining rose petals. You're a shoo-in. See? No bad guys. No need for a good rumble where I gotta get in the mud with some freaky-deaky demon. Which means I can go."

Demon?

But Quinn popped up from the couch without a second thought, her hand outstretched. "No!" she shouted, knocking over the cup of tea in the process. Nina leaving left her utterly panicked. "Please don't go. I...I don't know him. I mean, I know *you* know him, and I'm not saying that your friendship vouch isn't solid. I'd never doubt your word because you leave me so terrified I want to hide under my covers, but I'm feeling very, very uncomfortable with a strange man in my apartment."

Surely she'd pay for this moment of weakness in the way of endless snark and Nina's cackles, but she didn't care. If what Ingrid said was true, and Nina was the muscle of the group, then she wanted some muscle. It might sound silly to someone as confident as Nina, but she wasn't going to stay with a man she didn't know without a buffer of some kind.

And it had nothing to do with the fact that he was hotter than lava. Nothing.

Especially a man who'd likely inherited his mother's gift for making women hither and yon fall in love with him.

No, ma'am. Not on her new no-romance watch.

Not to mention, she couldn't forget what Ingrid had said about there always being some kind of danger in these cases of accidental turnings.

41

Did she really want to face some big angry god or goddess alone without some kind of plan B?

What would she defend herself with? Her vast jugs and miles of charm?

Nina let her head fall back on her shoulders with a groan of pure displeasure. "Oh, come *on*, Whiny Pants. It's GD matchmaking, not brain surgery. It's not like you accidentally got some rare super power the entire dark side wants. It's hooking people up, you twit. Like this is totally your gig, Lady Lumps. Think of it as one big episode of *The Bachelor* where every day somebody gets a stupid rose."

So many surprises tonight. "*You* watch *The Bachelor?*" Quinn squawked.

It was one of the shows she'd vowed to give up on the mental list of things she'd made as she'd packed her bags in a flurry to come home from Greece while Nina barked orders about sharp objects and no more than two ounces of fluid per flight.

"Yeah. When these two fuc...*nitwits* make me. I do a lot of Monday-night shifts at OOPS, and they always force me to watch under the label 'girls' night.' There's popcorn and wine and all sorts of shiz I can't eat or drink. There's crying and wadded-up tissues and big, girlie sighs when those heifers are chosen like cattle at a 4H fair."

Marty sighed a raspy escape of air. "We come to keep you company. That we happen to watch *The Bachelor* while we do it is pure coincidence. And I hate to say it, Quinn, but I agree with Nina. This is your thing! Your moment to shine. If what Ingrid tells us is true, who knows more about romance than you?"

Oh, just everyone on the planet? She knew when to quit, and after Igor and the humiliating debacle of his infidelity with Shawna Sutter, it was blatantly obvious she didn't know real love from a boil on her ass.

Dropping back to the couch, Quinn shook her head. "I think my record stands for itself at this point. I can't find my own soul mate. How can I be trusted to find someone else's? So maybe there's a way we can pass this power off to someone else. Maybe knock down a better candidate and make them bite the apple? I'll hold 'em down if you steamroll." She held up a fist to Ingrid to encourage her help. "You in, buddy?"

Khristos slid forward on the coffee table then, bracketing her face with his big hands. "Quinn, look at me and listen to my words. There is no handing this off to someone. This is *forever*. The second you nicked that apple with your teeth was the second you gave up your mortality and became Aphrodite. Period."

Mortality? "I'm immortal now, too?"

Khristos nodded his dark head. "Just like Dracula."

"I don't like this turn of events."

"I don't get this sudden change of heart. Back in Greece, you were all eye of the tiger."

That's because Ingrid had been right. She'd been in shock. Now that shock had worn off, and quite frankly, she wanted out.

"Your motherland does something to me I can't quite explain. Plus, I'm sure I had a touch of heat stroke. I mean, my boobs did inflate. All that pumping me up must have in turn deflated my brain cells. Something clearly had to give. But I'm back on my turf now and my turf says I'm the minimum wage of Aphrodites."

"On the contrary, darling," a disembodied voice scolded, though it was tinkly and light.

Quinn's heart began to race as her eyes scanned the room. The air grew still again, much like it had back at the Parthenon. Which meant she was in line for a Nicki Minaj ass.

Immediately, she was on her feet and tripping over Khristos's shoes to get to Nina. Scooping Buffy and Spike up, she huddled them close and hopped in Nina's lap before wrapping her arms around her neck and burying her face in the vampire's thick cloud of hair.

And then the voice spoke again while the air crackled with fissions of electric blue and pink and the room rumbled all around them. "You will perform your duties as Aphrodite, Quinn, and you will perform them well, or my son will suffer the wrath of the gods!"

CHAPTER 5

Ah. There she was. He'd known it wouldn't be long until word made it to her that her power had been taken.

Perfect.

"Get off me, Lite-Brite or I'll give you a real reason to freak," Nina ordered, attempting to pull out of Quinn's hold on her. "Jesus H, you're like a damn octopus."

Nina lifted Quinn up off her lap and stood her in the corner of the room, but Quinn wasn't letting go. She clung to Nina's hand, her legs visibly shaking as the other women rushed to her side.

Khristos looked heavenward, hands on hips, ready for third-degree verbal lacerations from his mother's sharp tongue. But he wouldn't allow her to frighten Quinn. This wasn't her fault.

"Mom, knock off the big, scary disembodied voice thing, would you?" he ordered. "Delicate flower here. If you want to rumble, show yourself. But you'll do all the rumbling with *me*."

Silence. Deafeningly so.

He was getting the silent treatment—which was just as well, considering the vocal treatment involved things breaking and sometimes a slight shift in Mt. Rushmore. But it also meant she was pretty damn pissed. And to be fair, she should be.

She'd just lost the power to do what she loved to do best. Meddle. Mythology told the story of Aphrodite, the master at evoking love and lust in men, and while that much was once true, the game had grown cold for his mother—whose real name was Esther-Lou.

She'd mellowed over the centuries, and what she really loved was helping people find love and happily ever afters—likely because she couldn't find one of her own. But she loved love in all shapes and sizes. Especially if you took into account the amount of Hallmark movies she watched as a barometer for her sentimental streak.

Yet, she'd been talking about retiring for years now. She was tired. She'd complained just last family dinner about it. She wanted to travel, maybe find a nice condo in Boca to settle down in. Relax, sit by the pool, read a book without the constant interruption of matchmaking.

But what she wanted most was for Khristos to settle down and give her grandchildren. Making him guard the apple was her way of sticking it to him for remaining a bachelor for so many centuries.

She'd often said he'd bucked responsibility his entire life, using his charm and good looks to go about his merry way without being caught up in the net of a relationship. Guarding the apple was, according to her, a last-ditch effort to teach him a lesson in accountability.

And he'd done a damn good job of it for hundreds of years.

Until Quinn.

And a distraction on his part that, despite what Nina had joked, wasn't a leggy blonde. Add to that what he'd chalked up to a small seismic occurrence he couldn't explain, and his perfectly good union of man and apple had ended.

However, his mother didn't like having things taken from her before she was ready to give them up. She hadn't planned on losing her powers by having them ripped right out from under her. They were supposed to be handed down to Iris, the Goddess of Rainbows, who was chomping at the bit to take over.

Which meant now *two* women would want his head on a platter. Two volatile, chaotic, very angry women.

"Was that really your mother?" Quinn finally squeaked.

Shit, shit, shit. She was frightened, her pretty eyes wide, her hand shaking as she stuck to Nina like glue, and it saddened him. She'd had a tough go with this prick Igor. He wasn't so much of an asshole he couldn't see that. He'd heard the story while she'd confessed her love woes to the apple.

So what choice did he have but to tell the truth?

He moved toward Quinn slowly, his eyes on her face. "Yes. That was my mother, and I promise, she'd never hurt you. I wouldn't allow it."

Quinn's head poked out from behind Nina's back, her wide eyes just peeking an inch over the vampire's shoulder. "But she does hurt people? Is it a practice she makes a habit of?"

He closed his eyes and breathed deeply. This was his fault and his fault alone. He had to remember that and remind himself patience was a virtue—one Quinn and her fears would likely sap the life right out of.

But he had no one to blame but himself for this quandary, and he'd do whatever he had to in order to help her be the best Aphrodite she could be.

If she'd just get out of her own way.

"No. She doesn't make a habit of it. I promise you, everything will be fine."

Quinn licked her lips, her face pale, her grip on Nina of the Kung-Fu variety. "What did she mean, you'd suffer the wrath of the gods?"

He jammed his hands in his pockets and wondered if she had any whiskey stashed somewhere in that tiny kitchen of hers. He was going to need it. "Don't worry about it."

"So she's into idle threats, too?"

"No. There's nothing idle about my mother."

Quinn snorted as though she understood. "I can relate."

"My mother will cool off."

"You didn't answer the question. What did your mother mean by the wrath of the gods?"

He chose to remain silent. She didn't need any added pressure to a situation that was already stressful.

Quinn cocked her head, the lovely cascade of her chestnut-brown hair falling from her braid and sweeping over her shoulder as she pushed her way past Nina with a confidence she hadn't displayed as of yet. "Does it mean you're due for some kind of punishment if I don't do this and do this right?"

If daily floggings and jail time on Mt. Olympus could be considered punishment, then yes—he'd be punished. In fact, he might still be punished even if Quinn managed to pull this off to the gods' and his mother's satisfaction. But he wasn't going to tell her that. Not with her in such a skittish state, and he didn't want anyone's pity. Instead, he shut up.

But suddenly, there was a fire in her shiny new violet eyes. "You're not answering the question. Will you get into trouble if I don't do this?"

"There are many definitions to the word trouble, Quinn."

She approached him, her pretty face a mask of concern. "You *will* be punished! I can tell. What is it with your people? They're a vengeful bunch, huh? I get unrequited love, but wow, the whole Narkissos thing? Pretty harsh, don't you think? And what about Prometheus? Did he really deserve to end up chained to a rock and have his liver pecked out by an eagle every night for simply having the audacity to create fire?"

Khristos nodded his head. He'd be amused at her knowledge of the gods if the truth weren't so painful. "In all fairness, Zeus has begun to show some remorse for his over-the-top behavior in sensitivity training. Unfortunately, I still can't get Echo or Nemesis to relent. Nymphs are the worst. It's like talking to a brick wall."

"You're joking now, but you won't be LOL-ing if you're chained to a spinning wheel of fire for eternity!"

He wiggled a finger at her in admonishment to lighten the mood and hopefully ease her rising panic. "I kinda have to side with Zeus on that one, Quinn. I mean, Ixion was willing to hit that beast of a woman Hera even after a good old-fashioned warning from Zeus. It's not nice to touch someone else's merchandise."

Quinn winced, her cute nose wrinkling. "Is Hera really that awful? Because I often wondered if the myths weren't embellished just a teensy bit."

"She's a nightmare of a horror."

She sucked in her cheeks—adorably so, and planted her hands on her hips. Gone was the meek, sad-over-her-recent-breakup Quinn, and in her place was the warrior who thought she was saving a rare Greek artifact. "Forget that. Is that really the point here?"

Nina gave Quinn a small shove between the shoulder blades. "What is the point, Lite-Brite? Because if you don't make it soon, I'll wring it the eff out of you. Are you in or are you out?"

She flapped her hands at Nina, dismissing her without even realizing she was brushing the vampire off—which in his estimation was a good sign she'd rally if the going got tough, because sometimes in matchmaking, it did.

"The point is, will these gods dole out some sort of excessive punishment if I refuse to participate? And I want the truth, Khristos. Don't sugarcoat—just straight-up honesty, please."

As he watched her make a demand of him, watched her eyes flash and her full lips move, he realized she was only *perceived* as weak, and not just by others but also herself. On the inside, this woman had the 'nads of a gladiator if she was willing to attempt to keep him from the wrath of his ancestors.

And she wasn't just stronger than she thought, she was compassionate. She didn't know him, yet he saw the fear in her eyes when she realized he could end up punished severely. That trait would go a long way in her matchmaking.

But if the gods chose to punish him for his carelessness, they wouldn't care what the explanation was. They were all burn-him-at-the-stake overkill now, ask questions later.

Quinn would eventually find out about it, and for some reason, he didn't want her to think poorly of him for lying.

"That is a possibility," he finally said, because it was the truth.

Quinn rolled up the sleeves of her sweater, her mouth set in a line of determination. "Then consider this Aphrodite thing on."

A hand brushed the hair from her face; the fingertips were callused, the touch gentle. "Quinn," a voice, thick and deep, rumbled in her ear.

Yes, sexiest man on the face of the planet? "What?" she groaned.

She had a goddess hangover the size of Yankee Stadium. As she peeked at her alarm clock, she realized why. She'd had only two hours of sleep. Two hours of restless, haunted-by-horrible-dreams sleep.

The apple, in all its bitten glory, sat on her nightstand. Still just as perfect and gold as it had been before she'd gotten on her high horse and had chosen that brief moment in time to finally take control of her life.

After deciding she was all in last night, she'd handed out blankets and as many pillows as she could find to everyone and gone to bed, determined to keep Khristos from doing time. While she lay in bed, what she'd done began to really sink in and she'd come to the conclusion she was mostly to blame.

Distracted or not, it didn't matter what Khristos had been doing at the time the apple fell from the column. She'd refused to heed his words, his very clear warning. She'd stomped all over his wish for her to give it back because she was too busy playing Joan of Arc.

Thinking about it now, it made complete sense that he'd been so evasive when she'd demanded to know why he thought it belonged to him.

Because seriously, who'd believe it anyway?

"Quinn," he said again. "It's time to begin."

She shivered, burrowing deeper into her comforter and trying to ignore the un-ignorable.

Khristos. And being Aphrodite.

The Khristos who'll be punished severely if you don't damn well get up, Quinn. Think Actaeon, for example. Do you want this man, whose apple you defiled because you all of a sudden found your backbone, to end up eaten by a wild pack of dogs?

No. She didn't want that.

She sat upright with a jolt, not even thinking to take the comforter with her—now that her jugs were enormous, none of her nightgowns fit properly, which left her spilling out of them.

But Khristos averted his eyes like a consummate gentleman. He smiled at her as perfectly as if he hadn't had the exact amount of sleep she'd had. "It's time to rise and shine, Goddess of Love. The Love Boat leaves in an hour. So up and at 'em. C'mon, lets hit the showers and *carpe diem!*"

Her stare was blank when she looked up at him, pushing her long tangle of hair from her face. "I take it you're a morning person?"

"I'm a whatever-I-have-to-be-to-keep-my-butt-out-of-the-pokey person."

God. The guilt, followed by the flashes of visions of heinous Greek punishments. "Right. I'm on it. Just give me twenty minutes." She scrambled upward, this time remembering the comforter, and rose to a standing position. But her bedroom was so small, there was little choice except to end up almost touching.

Her heart pounded hard in her chest as she sucked in her stomach. Wow, he smelled good. In fact, if she were to have a picture in her mind of what a god would look and smell like, Khristos with a K certainly fit the bill.

"There's coffee right there on the nightstand. Marty made it, and Wanda baked some cinnamon rolls."

"They actually stayed the night?" All but begging Nina to stay after Aphrodite had shown up, she'd also requested Marty, Ingrid, and Wanda stay, too. She'd even offered to pay them for their services. Not that they would hear of it—except for Nina, who named her price at two-point-two-million. The point-two being for her hoodie fund.

There was something about them as a group, something she innately trusted—*needed* at this very moment in her life—and she was afraid if they left, she'd miss something she couldn't define or find the right words to describe.

Warmth spread throughout her limbs. These people didn't know her, even if they'd talked about her with Ingrid. Yet, they'd targeted her fears and offered a soothing balm of comfort to ease them all because of their relationship to her friend.

They were really good at this OOPS thing.

Khristos nodded, sticking his hands in the pockets of his pants "They did. I only know of them through Nina, but they're exactly as she described. Well, almost. I don't find Marty at all offensive when she recommends colors that are in my color wheel." He yanked a hand from his jeans and circled his face just the way Marty had last night when she'd explained what a color wheel was.

Quinn giggled. "I can't believe she owns Bobbie-Sue Cosmetics and her husband owns Pack Cosmetics. Talk about the Jets and the Sharks."

"They're good people. They'll protect you from me."

Her cheeks went bright red; she felt the flush of them. "I…I'm sorry. It's just that—"

"That I'm a stranger. I'm not offended by that either. Anyway, wasn't sure if you were a *New York Times* reader or whatever, but I know you love to read, if the mountain of books versus actual food in your kitchen pantry is any indication. So I went out and bought a slew of reading material, just in case it's what you do in the mornings." He pointed to the stack of newspapers he'd set right under her white lamp with the ruffled lampshade.

He was so nice. So considerate. Sweet, in fact. Her heart clenched, and then she froze and took a deep breath.

This would not happen. No way was she going to let any warm feelings for this man creep into her heart. Absolutely not. He was her teacher and she was his student.

Grasshopper and sensei. Coach and football player.

"Do you have to call in to work? Will anyone worry if you don't show up?"

Ugh. Work. She loved her job because she could drown herself in books. But how would she ever explain her hooters? Thankfully, she had plenty of time to figure it out.

"No. I had a ton of vacation saved up. The plan was to spend two weeks in Greece and then come home…" Engaged and wildly in love. "And spend the next couple of weeks looking for an apartment."

Together. Jesus, she was an idiot. Had she even consulted Igor about any of the dreams she'd spun in her head? Had she ever once considered he'd say no to her proposal, let alone agree to move into a new place with her?

"Good to know."

"I have another question. If I'm in charge of all this matchmaking and procreation and whatever else I've managed to commit myself to in my absurd efforts to save your homeland, how do I do it? I mean, do goddesses of love ever sleep? How can I be everywhere? I'm not just the Goddess of Love of New York, am I? Did I only win that tiara at the pageant—or am I holding the world crown?"

"You've got the world crown, but eventually you'll be able to do this in your sleep—literally. Your command to make a match will happen as effortlessly as you breathe."

"Then why do I need these lessons you keep insisting I need?"

"Honestly?"

"No. Lie to me. All the best messes in history come from a well thought out lie."

"Fair enough. Because you're rusty and very unclear about what makes a good match. You need to experience a few before I hand over the reins completely."

"So you have the reins right now? Like this second?"

"Even as we speak. Look at me, no hands," he joked.

"Then why can't you be Aphrodite and I'll just go back to being boring Quinn Morris from the bookstore?"

"Because you bit the apple, and my reign can't last forever if I'm doin' time."

"I swear I'm going to do everything in my power to prevent that."

"Then hustle, Aphrodite."

Instead of lingering, she squeezed around his big body. As she did, she remembered the disembodied voice of his mother from the night before and swallowed hard. "Have you heard from your mother?"

He knelt and scooped up Spike, setting him on his shoulder and scratching his ears. "Not a peep."

"Which means she's really, really mad. I know when my mother's beyond angry and well into homicidal, she gets eerily quiet."

He rose again and shrugged his shoulders. "Homicidal's probably a kind adjective where my mother's concerned. But I don't want you to trouble yourself with any of that right now, Quinn. She's mad at me, not you. Right now we need to teach you how to make solid matches that will last a lifetime."

"Because those happen so often." She winced the moment the words shot out of her mouth. Bitter Spice had arrived at the party.

He cocked his deliciously dark head and smiled. "You're just sore from an ugly breakup right now, Quinn. But you won't always be. Trust me."

When he said the words "trust me" her knees trembled a little. Then she shook it off. She was all out of trust at this point. Igor had taken the last ounce of trust she had in her judgment and smeared it all over like finger-paint on her broken heart.

She felt foolish now for all the times she'd berated her mother for man hating, for all the times she'd defended Team Soul Mate. Her mother really was right. Soul mates didn't exist. Real, deep, abiding love and forever were enormous jokes.

"Trust you? Here's a thought. If the whole soul mate thing is real, why haven't you found yours then?" Yeah. Why hadn't the matchmaker's son made a match? She looked up at him, searching his amber-brown eyes. Damn, he was amazing to look at. Even in the bright light of early morning.

He winked when he looked down at her. "I guess it's like the shoe-maker's son. Everyone in the village has shoes but him?"

"FYI, the village has DSW now. I think you haven't found your soul mate because you're too fond of leggy blondes. Not that I blame you because honestly, who isn't?"

"Not everyone likes leggy blondes, Quinn. Your scorn for Igor's rearing its ugly head. Besides, I thought Shawna was a redhead?"

Quinn bobbed her head as she dug a pair of jeans out of her dresser. "That she is. A redhead with all the trimmings."

And if that sounded bitter—tough titties.

It wasn't that she couldn't see the appeal to leggy and gorgeous. On the contrary. She totally understood how Igor might find the jeans Shawna spray-painted on and the navel ring that lay against her lean abdomen just beneath her belly shirts appealing.

If she were to push that sex-bomb theory to the limits of the anger it brought, she could even see how thirty-six double-Ds might appear more exciting than her mere thirty-four Bs

Without question, Shawna was young, supple and beautiful. Young, supple, beautiful, and dumb as any inanimate object you could buy at The Dollar Store.

To be left for someone who pronounced the goddess Persephone's name "Per-sef-phone" or who mispronounced the word disoriented, twisting it to "disorien-tay-ted", was like a slap in the face. A hard one.

Khristos put his warm hands on her shoulders as she looked through her closet for a scarf. "Slow down."

A warm heat traveled up her spine and stopped right in her chest. "Pick a speed. First we have to seize the day, and now you want me to slow my roll. Which is it?"

He turned her to face him, Spike still perched contentedly on his shoulder, his face buried in Khristos's neck. "You're frazzled. When you're frazzled, it means you're overwhelmed, and if you're overwhelmed, you'll be too focused on your anxiety to open up your heart and make proper matches."

Her shoulders slumped. "How am I supposed to know who's a good match and who isn't, anyway? Is it a feeling? A vibe of some kind?"

"There are all sorts of things on the checklist for a successful match, and sometimes, you'll match people knowing they won't be together forever. You just have to know when to make a match like that for the greater good."

Her fist tightened on the comforter still wrapped around her. "You're a bundle of contradictions. Am I making matches for life or just for temporary flings?"

"Sometimes you'll make a match to teach a lesson."

"Like?"

"Like, sometimes someone is so hell bent and focused on what they *think* they want in a partner, they don't really know what they need to be fulfilled in a relationship—even when it's right under their noses. It's your job to show them what's all wrong by allowing them to stumble."

Oh, she was good at that. Queen Stumbler, at your service.

Taking a step back from him, mostly to ease the warmth he created in her belly, she waved an ironic finger. "Now *that* I can do. I know heartache and a bag or ten of Lay's Sour Cream & Onion potato chips. After all my failed attempts, I have some skill in the what's-all-wrong-in-a-relationship area."

"The best way I can describe what happens, and these are my mother's words, is this: You know the feeling you get right in your chest when you see the person you love? Or hear their voice, or know it's them calling you on your cell? That's love, Quinn. You'll feel that and much more, but that's the *Reader's Digest* version of it."

In her chest? Her chest was many things these days, but it had never had any special feeling. Yet, he naturally assumed she was familiar with this feeling. Probably because of Igor and her confession of love. But maybe she really had no clue what falling in love truly felt like.

Maybe how distraught she'd been over her breakup with Igor had nothing to do with love and everything to do with pride.

"I promise to remember to check for that feeling in my chest."

He chuckled, silky and low, his hand lifting to stroke Spike's spine. "That's the spirit."

A loud bang on the door made her jump. "Hey, Ta-Tas! Would you get the hell in the shower and get this damn show on the road? I should GD well be sleeping right now. But instead, I'm playing bodyguard to you, whiny pants. Now make haste, Chariots of Fire—your ride leaves in twenty, and if you're not in it, I'll find your scrawny as…er, butt, and run you over with it!"

Gathering her clothes, she slipped past Khristos and headed for the door. "Coming!" she shouted as she popped open the door to find Nina, pale, beautiful, a heavy stripe of zinc oxide over her nose, her brow furrowed. "Sorry. I'll hurry. Swear it."

Nina flashed her fangs and snapped her teeth as Quinn zipped past her to the bathroom and shut the door behind her with a heavy sigh, closing her eyes.

"I don't hear the water running, Glow Stick! Lickety-split!"

Nina's voice from behind the door made her push herself forward, dropping her clothes on the back of the toilet and tearing off her nightgown.

She looked down at her breasts.

Yep. Still like cantaloupes.

Jesus, they were ridiculous—too big for her body, and a complete distraction. Were they always going to be like this? How was she ever going to explain them to everyone at the bookstore? Her mother? Her father?

Her gynecologist?

But there was one saving grace—she could still breathe when she lay down.

Which meant Shawna Sutter wasn't going to suffocate herself to death right next to Igor on the fuchsia sheets he and Quinn had bought together at Bed Bath & Beyond.

More's the pity.

CHAPTER 6

"Christ, you blow slimy chunks at this," Nina said on a yawn, leaning back and crossing her long legs on the bench they sat on in Central Park. She made the most beautiful portrait, sitting under the harvest colors of the trees with her long, dark hair and pale skin.

"It's a good thing validation isn't something I need today," Quinn said, tightening her scarf around her neck.

Nina tilted her sunglasses forward. "Just keepin' shiz real, Love Maker. We've been here six damn hours and nothing. Maybe your Aphrodite radar is on the clink."

Quinn blew warm air into her fists and shook her head with a firm back and forth. "*No*. Khristos said I'd feel it, and I felt something and that something led me here." She just couldn't be sure if it was what she was supposed to feel.

This feeling, this gut instinct, happened shortly after they'd left her apartment. It was warm, imminent, and tinged with urgency, and like nothing she'd ever felt before. But the feeling, rather like an odd homing device, had demanded she sit here.

Right here. With Nina, while Ingrid and Khristos went off to find some coffee with the strict instructions that she act on nothing.

"It's probably all that hot air you got keepin' those hooters of yours inflated."

"Or the sting of your sharp tongue, perhaps?"

She rolled her eyes at the vampire and once more tried to zip up her faux leather jacket. She hoped being Aphrodite came with a clothing expense account, because if this kept up, she was going to have to go shirtless.

"I could go home," she offered. Nina had razzed her from the second they'd left Quinn's apartment and she hadn't let up.

Quinn instantly scooted closer to her, gripping the vampire's icy-cold hand and ignoring Nina's flinch. She held it against her cheek and gave Nina her best Bambi eyes. "Please don't do that, Wicked One. I can't stop thinking about what Ingrid said about how there's always a bad guy who wants what the newly turned paranormal client has. I can't think of anyone who'd want to lug these cans around—because heavy. But I'm not sure I want to find out if that's true without you there to help."

Nina snatched her hand away and flicked Quinn's hair. "Ingrid knows the score. She's seen some pretty ripe shite after Katie."

Her heart sped up. "Right. She told me about her old boss, Katie. So all of that really did happen? There really is that breed of bad guys in situations like this?"

She knew her voice quivered, and she hated it, but she wasn't ashamed to say she was a total chicken. Wings and all. She hated horror movies, hid under the covers and stayed there whenever Igor had indulged in his love of them by watching a marathon filled with gore.

"Yes, Lite-Brite. There are really bad guys. Lots of them. There's a Boogey Man, too."

She crooked her neck to look at the vampire, her lips pursed in disapproval. "You stop. You've gone too far. There is not."

Nina leaned forward, letting her elbows rest on her knees. "You're glowing and I have a zombie named Carl. Are you really gonna poke holes in my flippin' words?"

Oh, my Jesus. There was a Boogey Man. "This is crazy."

Nina nudged her with her shoulder and snorted as if the Boogey Man was one big joke. "He's an okay dude. Just misunderstood, and if you don't get on with this shi...*crap*, I'm gonna text his ass and tell him to make a camp under your Barbie bed."

She closed her eyes and gulped. She didn't ever, ever want to meet the Boogey Man. In fact, today, she rued the day she'd met Ingrid.

But Nina gave her a light thwack on the shoulder. "Stop freaking out, Princess. I won't let anything happen to you."

Instantly, that warmed her. "Why are you doing this?"

Nina scrunched up her pretty face. "Because you're Ingrid's friend and she asked me to, dipshi...*dork*. She's a good kid. I want her to be happy. If babysitting you makes her happy, then I'm all in. It's not like she hasn't taken a hit for us. Not to mention, she won't let us pay her tuition for college. She said she'd earn it by working for us. Also, you helped her pass the first semester of art history, and even though you two schmoes are like ebony and ivory as far as age and anything in common go, you work. She told us you do. That's why."

Nina's loyalty to Ingrid stole her breath. For all the times Ingrid had taken a stand for Nina, for all the times she'd defended her poor language and cantankerous behavior, she hadn't been kidding when she said you had to witness Nina at her best. That was no exaggeration. Her best was like no other.

"You offered to pay her tuition?"

"Yeah, we did. Not that she'll let us. She wants to do something with her life, and she wants to damn well earn it. I want her to have what she wants because somebody has to be her GD cheerleader. So I snatched Marty's worn-out, Mesozoic-era pom-poms and Wanda's stupid-ass skirt, and this is me all cheerin' her on."

Quinn cocked her head, dipping her chin into her scarf. Ingrid didn't talk a lot about her home life. In fact, looking back, she'd talked more about the women of OOPS than anyone else. "What do you mean somebody has to be her cheerleader?"

"Jesus, you're nosy. Ingrid doesn't have any biological family. It's just us, and Katie and her husband and kids. She's just a kid, and no way in hell was I going to let her move to New York without someone to look out for her. So we look out for her. *I* look out for her. That's why I wanted to meet you after she told us you'd offered to tutor her for free. No one does jack for frickin' free."

Except Nina and gang. How wonderful to have these people in Ingrid's corner.

"I didn't know," she murmured, still astonished someone so outwardly callous felt something so deep.

"You don't need to know anything else other than because *she* asked me to help you, I'll do it. That doesn't mean you and me are fuc—" She paused, clenching her teeth to keep from using foul language. Also another testament to how big Nina's love could be. "It doesn't mean we're friends. So knock that girlie crap right outta your head or I'll knock you on your ass."

Quinn smiled when she shook her finger in reprimand. "I thought you were trying not to swear?"

"Ass isn't a cuss word. It's a donkey's GD—"

But Quinn suddenly wasn't listening. There it was again. That feeling.

And it tugged her—yanked her *hard*, up and toward an enormous oak tree where leaves fell in soft multicolored flutters to the ground and a couple stood, leaning against it, holding each other close, almost as though they were posing for a picture.

They were beautiful together. Long, lean, perfectly dressed against the backdrop of the overcast day.

"Hang the hell on, Love Maker!" Nina ordered, her feet sounding right behind Quinn. "Khristos said to wait for him!"

But she couldn't. Whatever was propelling her forward gave her feet a life of their own. Her sneakers thumped against the concrete even as she heard Khristos and Ingrid yell her name.

But it was all a little hazy and muted. Instead, she heard two heart-beats—*heartbeats?*—crashing out of sync until the sound of them morphed together and synchronized. And it was all she could hear, rhythmic, steady, as she pushed her way through a small crowd of German tourists to get to these two beautiful people.

But what would she do when she got to them? Didn't Hot Greek Guy say Cupid had to shoot the arrow to make it official? How did one call upon Cupid? Did he have a phone number? A Twitter account?

"*Quinn—waaaait!*" Khristos barked.

Her mother had always said she wasn't a very good listener because her head was so high up in the clouds.

Lately it seemed a lot of the things her mother had once told her were all coming to fruition.

Ingrid handed her what was left of the coffee after it had sloshed from the cup as she'd chased after Quinn. "You're a crappy listener, Quinn Morris."

She puffed her cheeks out and took the cup, wincing when Khristos glared down at her before he began to pace again.

Oh, she was in trouble. So much trouble. "I did say I was going to suck at this, didn't I? My head's all a mess."

"And I did say to stay put until we returned, didn't I?" Khristos asked, the tic in his sharp jaw pulsing beneath the dark stubble.

Remorse stung her gut. "I don't know what made me do it. It felt so right. The rest just happened."

Oh, had it ever happened. Just not in the way or with the finesse she was sure Aphrodite would have lent to the situation.

Ingrid plopped down next to her and patted her thigh in comfort. "I don't think that photographer really meant it when he said he'd sue your oversized boobs right off your scrawny chest. He was just talking smack because he was mad. Don't worry, Quinn."

According to the ultra-swanky fashion photographer from some magazine whose name she couldn't pronounce, she'd ruined his ultimate shot.

Of the couple who were *not* supposed to be together eternally.

The absolute perfect shot. The one they'd waited all day for. The one they needed to have in by tonight so this ultra-swanky magazine could go to press.

She bit the inside of her cheek before she said, "I knocked over his camera. I had no idea a camera had so many working parts. You think it was expensive?"

Ingrid wrinkled her nose and waved a dismissive gloved hand. "Bah. He threw some numbers out, but I bet it's all just bullshit. You know those creative types. They all think they bleed diamonds and shit Dolce & Gabbana. He probably lives in some crappy apartment in Brooklyn with his mother and her poodle."

Ingrid's attempt to make her laugh wasn't working. "That number he threw out was five thousand dollars." Quinn blanched. She didn't have five thousand pennies—not after that trip to Greece.

"Well, yeah, he did. But all's not lost. You did make a friend. That hot model who looks like he stepped right out of a Hugo Boss commercial was willing to pay good money to get his hands on whatever lotion you use to make you sparkle. He was pretty nice, right?"

"He was gay, Ingrid. *Gay*, and I matched him with a straight female model—*for life*." Oh, Jesus and a fucked-up mess, she'd really done it.

"But Khristos fixed it. It's all okay now."

She snorted her disgust. "I could have ruined his life, Ingrid! What if Khristos hadn't been here? Because the time will come when he's not. Poor Rolando could have ended up forever in the closet, unsure why he was madly in love with a woman he wasn't even a little attracted to. And let's not forget, Shay-Shay—"

"La-Tee-Shay, remember? It's part of her first name and her last name all mashed together as one. Her agent told her to do it so she'd get noticed. She was pretty, huh? But not as nice as Rolando. Kinda snippy, in fact."

"Not the point, Ingrid! As if she doesn't already have enough self-esteem issues about her age—even if she's just barely twenty, but she could have ended up with a man who physically wouldn't want her *ever*, but who she'd love desperately anyway. In her mind, that's like death!"

"But you set her straight. You gave her a good talking to about the importance of all that inner-beauty stuff and how someone should love your bones, not your shell—"

"For which she reminded me of what a hypocrite I am when my *shell* probably cost a few grand at the plastic surgeons, if you'll recall," Quinn said, pointing to her chest.

"Oh, what does she know? You'll make a good mother someday, Quinn. That speech you gave her was, bar none, one of the best I've ever heard about healthy body images. Ya done good."

She let her head hang in utter shame. "They looked so perfect together, Ingrid. So right. And that feeling—I can't explain it, but it was so...*urgent.* Like if I didn't get my ass in gear, the world was going to fall down around my ears."

Ingrid nodded her head, the spikes of her multicolored Mohawk bouncing. "A romantic notion from a diehard romantic, if I ever heard one. So see? Your romance bone isn't broken after all."

"After what just happened, I wouldn't rule out an amputation."

"This from the woman who started the Romeo and Juliet Club on campus."

"And we now have two proud members." She held up her frozen fingers for emphasis.

"After a year of its existence," Ingrid reminded.

"Some things take longer than others to grow." Okay, so her Romeo and Juliet Club hadn't been a huge success. It was just another reason why this Aphrodite job wasn't her bag. She wouldn't know romance from her elbow.

Khristos rubbed his jaw and loomed over her. She'd watched him attempt to gather his patience while he'd paced back and forth in front of them for the last half an hour.

But his attempt to soothe her was valiant. "Your aim is off just yet. You'll get better, but you have to listen and wait for me before you act. You absolutely can't be impulsive about this, Quinn."

She rose, putting her hand on his arm, instantly reacting to the strong muscles of his forearm beneath his down jacket. "I'm sorry. I'm really sorry. But kudos. You were amazing out there."

Ingrid bobbed her head and patted Khristos on the back. "Not a lie, dude. You were like Tyrell Owens. That zigzag move you made to catch an invisible arrow none of us could see but you—ah-maze-balls."

Nina snorted. "Too bad you didn't use that shite at the last football game, eh, buddy?"

Khristos's NFL moves reminded Quinn of something pretty important. "You know what's been troubling me?"

"Your impulsive asshattery?" Nina crowed.

Yet, that was a fair assessment of her behavior and she wouldn't deny it. "Not just that. How did you see an arrow? I didn't see an arrow. What happens if I can't ever see the arrow? And how did Cupid know where to shoot the arrow? It's not like I gave him a signal. I don't even know who he is. So how could he have known?"

The man who'd been sitting on a large rock across from them, his face buried deep inside his jacket, a paper bag with what she suspected was booze sticking out of his pocket, rose and approached them, his round body propelling him forward.

Maybe he was one of the bad guys Nina had assured her existed?

She hopped behind Khristos, but he pried her fingers off his arm and squeezed them, shooting that warm zing along her hand. "It's okay, Quinn. He's a friend."

"Sorry, Boss," the man said. "I got all caught up in her excitement and I lost my damn shit."

Khristos chuckled and slapped the round man on the back. "No worries. It's all handled now. So, introductions are in order. Cupid, meet Quinn, your new boss."

He held out a doughy hand in her direction. "Nice to meet you. Usually, I'm a better team player. Next time I'll chill before I spill. Promise to do a better job of having your back."

This was Cupid? This gruff, unshaven man with a distinct New York accent was Cupid?

His eyes, sparkling blue and amused, set in a pleasingly round face, twinkled as he grabbed her hand and pumped it with a wide grin. "You're wondering where my diaper is, right? Fuck if I can get rid of those damn pictures. Google Images has not been my friend. Hallmark cards either. I don't know whose stupid-ass idea it was to cover my junk up with a diaper, but there you have it. Branded for life. Anyway, I hear we'll be working together from now on. Nice to meet you in the flesh."

Quinn's mouth hung open, but she quickly snapped it shut when Nina slapped her on the back. "Say hello to the nice guy who shoots the arrow of luurve, Lite-Brite. It's polite to fekkin' make nice with your coworkers."

She squared her shoulders and nodded. "I'm sorry. I was just surprised by—"

"Me without a diaper," he finished for her on a chuckle.

Yep. Right on the money. "Ye...yes. But it's nice to meet you, and my apologies for my premature match. It just felt so right."

He held up his hands and grinned. "I get it. Love's a powerful thing. Just ask your friend Nina here. She fought hard enough to make a WWE wrestler proud, but my arrow always wins out in the end. It's like Khristos said, your aim was just off, but you'll get better."

Nina grinned and gave his thick neck a squeeze. "Good to see ya, C."

Khristos gave Cupid a hard handshake. "Thanks for that save, buddy. If you hadn't yelled at me to go left, we'd have been screwed. Couldn't do this without you. Now *you*," he said, turning to Quinn, "come with me." He held out his hand to her.

She took it hesitantly, letting the warmth of it seep into her skin.

He led her to almost the exact spot where the photographer had posed Rolando and La-Tee-Shay and pointed to another couple just beyond the tree where she'd all but knocked them over.

He pulled her closer, forcing her to smell his yummy goodness mingled with the crisp air of fall. Quinn gritted her teeth to quell the butterflies flitting about the lining of her stomach and chalked them up to never having had a man as incredibly good-looking as Khristos so near.

"Look over there, Quinn," he said, his tone hushed and gruff.

She followed the line of his finger and saw an elderly couple with their backs to them, probably in their mid-eighties, judging by their hunched figures and silver hair. The man sat on a thick plaid blanket beside the woman who was in a wheelchair, his hand, aged and gnarled, entwined with hers.

He looked up at the woman then; his gaze was tender, almost fragile, but the love shining from his eyes was so real it pierced Quinn's heart. So real and so full of complete adoration, for the second time that day, her breath was stolen.

The woman leaned over the arm of her chair and smiled back at him. The profile of her face, silhouetted by the setting sun, was just as full of love when she pressed a kiss to his lips and cupped his jaw with a hand that had a dried carnation attached to its wrist.

Quinn's heart melted right in her chest when the man rose and tucked a blanket just underneath the woman's chin with such a fiercely protective gesture, her knees shook.

A tear stung her eye and her throat tightened. She gripped Khristos's arm. "It was them, wasn't it?"

"Yes," he murmured. "They were your target. But you were only off by a hair."

Her heart pounded as guilt pricked her very soul. "What would have happened if you hadn't intercepted and saved the day?"

She knew she shouldn't ask. The answer would likely haunt her dreams, but she had to know.

"You don't really want to know, do you, Quinn? It's all good now. That's all that matters."

"No. I really do want to know, to serve as a reminder of how I could blow this whole thing sky-high. Call me a masochist, but maybe it'll keep me on my toes. Because I couldn't bear it if these two people had ended up apart when they so clearly adore one another." Her words hitched, forcing her to clear her throat.

Khristos turned to face her, his eyes, glinted with amber flecks, searching hers. "If I hadn't intercepted, Bart would have lost his courage for the second time in their lives and Alice wouldn't be wearing that carnation around her wrist—one he'd dried and saved all these years. That was her engagement ring, so to speak."

She clenched her fists and eyes together to keep from crying out an apology to them. "What do you mean by the second time?"

"Bart and Alice knew each other a long time ago. They were almost married straight out of high school, but Bart was drafted and her father didn't approve of him anyway. Alice's father made that very clear to Bart. He told Bart he'd kick her out of the house and she'd have to fend for herself while Bart was serving in the military overseas."

Parents, they could really suck. No one got that better than she did. "How awful."

"So instead of proposing the way he'd planned, he let her go rather than ask her to choose between him and her family. He feared her father really meant what he said and she'd be left with nothing."

Her heart ached for them. "Wow. Talk about a painful sacrifice."

"The sacrifice of real love."

"What happened to them all that time in between?" All that lost time.

"In the interim, of course, each moved on and married and had families. They hadn't seen or heard from each other since their high school graduation. Until their fifty-third high school reunion just this past year, where they reunited and fell in love all over again."

The romantic in her was all ears—ears and floaty hearts and bouquets filled with colorful flowers. "So what's that got to do with chickening out *again?*"

Khristos's face softened, the hard lines easing. "Bart's dying, Quinn. He has another year, maybe two to live, but he was afraid to burden Alice with the news. Her health is fragile, too. Both families are against them marrying, and Bart almost let his children's wishes run roughshod over the last bit of happiness he'll have before he leaves this earth. Today, he was going to break off their relationship. If Cupid hadn't hit him with that arrow, he might have missed a second opportunity to say to hell with the naysayers and propose to the woman he's loved for more than fifty years who doesn't give a fig, as she says, that they only have a little time left—Alice just wants them to spend it together. Bart just needed a nudge in the right direction, and you'll learn to feel that over time. It'll become instinct."

A rush of warmth stung her heart—one she desperately wanted to fight, but Bart and Alice were living proof that, at least for them, true love did exist. They'd proven real love could weather fifty years.

"What would have happened if Bart hadn't proposed today?"

"They both would have died brokenhearted."

Quinn gulped, hard, loosening the scarf around her neck. She needed to understand the dynamics of this, the repercussions if she mistakenly did something wrong. Knowing she could muck this up made her all the more determined to get it right in the future. So there'd be no Bart and Alice's left in her clumsy wake.

"So the earth won't stop revolving if a match isn't successfully made, yet, I feel like there's a 'but' attached to that."

He rolled his wide shoulders, but his eyes were shadowed. "Most times not, but sometimes, one match sets off a chain reaction that can reverberate for lifetimes to come. This time, it was just two people who want to finish out their lives as partners. And sometimes, Quinn, that's just as important as procreation of future world leaders."

Quinn swallowed hard again, her chest so tight she almost couldn't speak at the near disaster Khristos had saved them from. "Thank you," she whispered at him.

He looked down at her and smiled, that warm, easygoing, "don't worry about me having my liver eaten straight from my gut night after night while I'm tied down to a boulder" smile and squeezed her shoulders. "That's why I'm here, Quinn. To help you learn when the timing is right."

She fought another rush of tears—for Bart and Alice and the time wasted apart all those years due to a disapproving parent, and for the sacrifice Bart was willing to make to be with the woman he loved no matter what anyone else said.

Khristos cupped her jaw, and lifted her chin. "C'mon. We've been out here for hours. Let's go back to your place and have some dinner, and then we'll give it another try. You just have to loosen up and interpret the varying vibes of matchmaking."

She moved a step back, because having him so close made her lungs scream for air. "If I get any looser, I'll end up matching armed robbers to bank tellers. You're not wrong when you say this feeling I'm supposed to get needs some honing. All I could hear was two heartbeats, and the crashing of them in my ears was so loud, I just figured…" She shrugged, still horrified by her near mishap.

Khristos grabbed her hand again and chuckled as he led her back to Nina and Ingrid. "You know when we really need to worry?"

She blanched. "When?"

"When you mistake some indigestion for true love. That's always an epic disaster."

As their hands swung between them, and they crested the small hill to see Nina and Ingrid chatting with Cupid, Quinn barked a laugh, her head falling back on her shoulders. "Note to self, no spicy food until my craft is perfected."

Khristos chuckled, too, the vibration of it settling in her ears, warm and easy.

And that was just a little nice.

CHAPTER 7

"Are you ready, Quinn?"

Content from one of the best meals she'd had in a long time, Quinn nodded and hid a burp. Though the warmth of the beef stew Darnell the demon had made had since dissipated in her stomach, the sentiment behind it hadn't.

When they'd arrive back at her house, it was full of people. A man named Archibald, dressed formally in a black suit, silver vest, white shirt and ascot, had waved them to a long table wedged into her tiny living room that had magically appeared in her absence.

On it were bowls and spoons, and napkins folded into small swans. Archibald had apologized for the lack of proper cutlery, but he'd made the trip all the way in from Staten Island at Wanda's request and decided a more formal place setting would only deter him from his duties—which was to ease Quinn's load.

He'd greeted her with the same kind of warmth Wanda and Marty had, whisking her off to a place at the table, where he'd poured her a glass of wine and said, "Do rest, Miss Quinn. Goddess work is hard work. Matchmaking must be fraught with pitfalls sure to test the merits of one's heart, and surely you're exhausted from your first day out? Now, we've taken care of everything. Supper simmers as I speak, and your sheets are freshly laundered and pressed, awaiting your weary head at days end. I've watered and fed Buffy and Spike, whom, if I do say so myself, are a delightful couple, even though guilt burdens my heart, as I was Team Angel. And please, don't trouble yourself until you've settled into your new role in life. I'm at your service for as long as needed."

And then he was off, calling to Darnell—who was in the kitchen making fresh bread—to ensure he'd taken butter out of the fridge so that it would soften enough to spread in time for dinner.

"Quinn?" Khristos interrupted the pleasure brought by the memory of all these strange new people, sitting at a table she didn't own, all eating together. They'd laughed and chatted and passed bowl after bowl of food, all while she'd watched in silence.

Yet, secretly, she reveled in their friendships and wondered why she'd spent so much of her time with her nose in a book instead of forging friendships of her own.

Because books never left you. That's why. It was as plain as the nose on her face she had hang-ups where relationships were concerned. Fictitious families never let you down—all you had to do was turn the page for the happily ever after. In the end, the heroine never fell in love with the wrong hero the way Quinn had done repeatedly like some broken record.

Rather than create real-life connections with real-world struggles, she stuck her nose in a book and ignored everything else to the point of isolating herself with her ridiculous expectations.

It wasn't absurd to think Igor should have been faithful. It was ridiculous to have turned him into something in her mind he absolutely wasn't interested in being. Hindsight, and the past few days had taught her that.

But she was done with that. Everything she did from here on out was going to be steeped in realism so real, they'd dub her the realest Aphrodite ever.

Khristos grabbed her hand from across the table of the diner they sat in and squeezed it. "You in there?"

Her eyes were heavy now, but she'd had that feeling again shortly after they'd eaten, and she was pretty sure it wasn't indigestion. That feeling had led them here, to a diner, where, with Khristos's guidance, she'd pinpointed the difference between an urgent need to match and the quest for a true match.

If what she felt was what Khristos described, then the unsuspecting couple was somewhere in this vicinity, though the diner was almost totally empty.

She snatched her hand back, almost knocking her coffee over. No more hand holding. No more warm fuzzies and crushing on Greek gods who liked leggy blondes. Real people who wanted realistic things didn't let men like Khristos into their realms of possibility.

"Sorry. I'm just tired, I think. That stew was amazing, and I overate."

"No joke. But that's not even the half of it. Wait until Arch breaks out his pancetta-crusted tilapia. Nothing compares to that man's cooking."

She found herself wishing she'd be around long enough to do that. After Khristos was gone, and everyone left to go off and continue leading the lives she was coming to envy, it would be just her and Buffy and Spike again. That felt cold and lonely compared to the warmth these people had thrust upon her in such a short time.

"So you've known Archibald a long time?" They'd seemed like old friends, laughing and talking about past get-togethers during the course of dinner.

"Yep. Since he was a vampire and I was just a kid. He's a good guy and his game-day feasts, especially his artichoke dip, are what dreams are made of."

She smiled absently, running her finger over the rim of her coffee mug, tamping down her envy. "I'm still trying to wrap my head around this paranormal thing. Hearing the word vampire as though it isn't crazy is still a bit of a struggle."

"You'll get used to it."

"So tell me about you. What do Greek gods do all day long?" *Attend orgies?*

"I'm not a god. I'm just a descendent of one."

"But it has its perks."

"If by perks you mean guarding an apple with the power to make or break humankind, sure. It's very perky."

Was that bitterness she was hearing? Or boredom? She couldn't read his tone well enough to know just yet. "You're being very vague. Why is that, Khristos with a K? C'mon, you can tell me. Do you organize orgies? Iron togas? Make head wreaths out of olive leaves? Sip ouzo while beautiful women pop juicy olives into your mouth all day long as you bask in the glow of Mt. Olympus?"

He cocked a dark eyebrow at her and wiggled it. "I handed over orgy organization to a lowly serf years ago. After a while, when you've seen one orgy, you've seen them all. Togas get all tangled up around your feet if you're not careful, not to mention a stiff breeze can present a problem. I hate olives and I prefer whiskey. Jack, to be specific, just in case you pick my name out of the hat for the white elephant this Christmas."

"So you don't have a job?"

"My job is to guard the apple."

"And that's it? Who pays your bills? Wait, do descendants of Greek gods have bills?"

"Don't be ridiculous. Of course I have bills. How do you suppose we keep the Parthenon up and running? You don't think sweeping off all those steps just happens, do you? It's a collective god effort."

He was mocking her, and the edge to his tone was growing harder by the second—which meant back off. What difference did it make what he did with his days anyway? It was none of her business.

She sat back in the booth and slammed her flappy lips shut. Keeping her distance from Khristos was the smartest thing to do. The less personal they became, the less trouble she could find herself in. She wasn't going to let his classically handsome face and incredibly hot body, with abs that rippled beneath his stupid sweater that also accented his eyes, sway her either.

They could just sit in silence for the duration as far as she was concerned. Rooting around in her purse, she felt for the current book she was reading, soothed by the cover and the cool feel of it beneath her fingertips.

As she was about to pull it out and bury herself in it, Khristos surprised her.

"So can I ask *you* a question?"

"I refuse to take over the organization of orgies. I have to have boundaries. Togas are out. I'm too pale to wear white successfully. But I love olives, and while ouzo isn't really my thing, I'm all for making head wreaths from olive leaves. I was hell on wheels in my last craft class."

Khristos snorted. "No orgies. Noted. But my question is a little more personal."

Oh, so now the hunky god wanted something from her that he, himself, wasn't willing to provide? Huh. She folded her hands on the tabletop, watching the play of the neon signs flash over his face. "And that question is?"

"Igor. How did the two of you end up together? You both seem a pretty unlikely pair."

How did he know anything about Igor other than what she'd shared out loud at the Parthenon? "How do you know what Igor is or isn't like?"

"Because I do my homework, and you became my homework when you bit the apple. I needed to understand your state of mind, and how it came to be, in order to understand how to proceed. Being as you're freshly broken up, it sometimes creates havoc with oversensitivity. No slight to you, it's just how the heart and mind work."

Her cheeks grew hot at the memory of all she'd confessed to that stupid apple. "He came into the bookstore where I work a lot." Like every day for two solid weeks, watching her, flirting with her, asking for suggestions about books she liked.

"And?"

And she thought her daydreaming days had ended when she'd found Igor. He read Shelley and Keats to her while he peered at her over horn-rimmed glasses and she rested her feet in his lap, sipping Bordeaux.

They'd watched *Wuthering Heights* and *Gone With the Wind* together on Saturday nights, rebuffing loud nightclubs and crowded restaurants for crackers with Brie and strawberries dipped in chocolate while the strains of Chopin or Beethoven could be heard from her CD player.

They drank wine and talked classic literature while Rachmaninoff and Paganini dusted her cloud of love with the magical arrows of Cupid.

She rolled her shoulders. "And I dunno. He was smart and funny and well versed in all sorts of things I'm interested in, I guess."

"So you had a lot in common?"

Had they? Looking back now, she wasn't sure if he'd just pretended to have a lot in common with her because he wanted in her drawers. If Shawna was who he'd turned to, a woman she had absolutely nothing in common with aside from gender, how much did Igor really enjoy *Wuthering Heights* and listening to Paganini?

"I thought we did. Maybe in hindsight we didn't." This was uncomfortable and embarrassing, but it wasn't as if he didn't know the whole story anyway.

Khristos nodded, sipping his milkshake. "Nope. You didn't. But he let you believe you did and you went along for the ride."

Anger spiked along her spine at being exposed. "And you know this how?"

"Because Igor transforms himself every time some pretty woman catches his eye. You could have been into breeding scorpions and sword swallowing, and he'd have said he was, too. In the end, it all comes crashing down around his ears because he's not really into sword swallowing. In fact, it bores him to tears. His reasons for beginning a relationship with you or anyone have little to do with anything other than the desire to have sex. At first, anyway. You saw the signs, you just chose to ignore them."

"Scorpions have breeders?"

He rolled his eyes in that adorable way he did when she was pushing him over the edge of his patience. "Don't avoid what's unpleasant by deflecting. You know exactly what I mean. You didn't feel Igor there," he said, pointing to the area where her heart pounded erratically. "You felt him in your pretty head."

Quinn snorted. "So you're saying he pretended to like poetry readings and quiet nights by the fire because he wanted my smokin'-hot bod, and I let him because I wanted him to be someone he's not? I think you can clearly see there's nothing smokin' about me unless you count my new melons, which I hope you're going to talk to someone about deflating. Like, soon? Please? Bras cost the earth for a double-D."

Khristos grabbed her fingers, forcing Quinn to look at him, leaving her uncomfortable with the depth of his gaze. "Don't underestimate your feminine wiles, Quinn. You have plenty of those. That's not what I'm saying at all. What I'm saying is, Igor doesn't know what he wants specifically—what he *does* know is he just doesn't want to be alone."

She cocked her head and paused. What Khristos said washed over her in waves of truth. It explained why she spent so much time convincing herself Igor loved her, even though he'd declared as such. She'd never felt terribly secure when he assured her he felt the same way. Maybe because his words had never really rung true?

Ow.

That hurt—to be duped, to be used. "So he spent all that time with me, pretending to be something he wasn't, just to avoid being alone. Perfect. I love the idea that I was a some kind of placeholder for Shawna."

"You weren't a placeholder for her, per se. Shawna could have been anyone, Quinn. She could have been your next door neighbor."

"I bet Lydia would've loved to have known that."

His adorable face scrunched up in a "huh?" look. "Who's Lydia?"

"Our old next-door neighbor. She's eighty-three, watches *Judge Judy* at ear-shattering decibels and loves pickled gefilte fish."

"You love to avoid, don't you?"

Quinn put her hands to her chest and mocked surprise with the bat of her eyelashes. "Me? The woman who's been looking for her Mr. Darcy since she was old enough to know what the words 'unrealistically' and 'romantic' meant? That's just plain silly."

But suddenly, Khristos wasn't joking. His face took a harder turn. As though he needed to drum into her head why she'd been so wrong about Igor. "My point is, Shawna could have been anyone. You were a placeholder until he figured out what he wants—and he was *yours*, by the way."

She didn't like that. She didn't like it at all. "Igor's a jerk."

He pushed his milkshake aside, wiping his mouth with a napkin. "Igor's just confused."

"Are you defending him?"

"Someone has to. I mean, the guy went to poetry readings for you. I'd rather watch paint dry than sit through something like that. But I won't do something I'm completely disinterested in just to avoid sleeping alone. If I'm honest, I feel a little sorry for him. He was pretty lost for a really long time."

Was? Her cheeks went hot, her jaw tight. "Oh, and I suppose now he's not lost because Shawna and her ripped body and skimpy clothing helped him find his way?"

Khristos stared at her for a moment before he answered. "I don't know if he's still lost. But forget Igor. What I'm saying is, he was the wrong man for *you*, Quinn. I am absolutely *not* saying his infidelity was okay or fair to you. But in the long run, you're better off because Igor doesn't know what he wants in a life partner. You do."

"The hell I do. I don't know what I want, because when I think I *have* what I want, what I want turns out to be a fat lie."

"All the romantic notions aside, like sunsets and picnics in the park while the breeze blows through all that luscious hair of yours, you want two things, Quinn. You want unconditional acceptance, and a real man with unshakeable morals."

He thought her hair was luscious?

Knock that right off, dreamweaver.

Her heart crashed against her ribs. Yes. That was what she wanted. "Well, I didn't get that, which is why I stink at this Aphrodite thing thus far. And isn't what I did the same thing as what Igor did? I allowed myself to ignore the signs he was wrong for me because I didn't want to be alone?"

Khristos shook his head. "You're not afraid to be alone, Quinn. You've done that before and you were perfectly happy with your life and your books. A little lonely? Maybe. A little isolated because you live in those books you read so many of? Maybe. But you weren't miserable. Igor is miserable. With himself, with his life. His validation comes from the coup of getting the girl. Once he has her, and she's not what he'd hoped, he strays because he's always searching instead of finding out what it is he wants. Instead of learning to like his own damn company. And yes, you were happy with Igor for a time, but you didn't love him the way you want to love a man, the way you should love a man, and you never would have. Eventually, you would have been discontent and grossly disappointed."

"Well, how nice. Got a big fat bow you can slap on that evaluation of my love life?"

He looked perplexed and it showed when he frowned. "Don't take insult, Quinn. I'm just trying to help you get over your breakup."

"Phew. You're a real soother, huh? Next time, just hand me the gallon of ice cream and skip the assessments. It would be kinder."

Still, he persisted as though he just didn't get how insensitive his words came off. "I'm just trying to help you understand how this works in correlation to you."

Using the heels of her hands, she pressed them against the table and stretched her arms. "Right, so we can hurry things along and you can get back to your playboying. Forgive me in all my novice for holding you up."

"No. That's not it at all. I'm telling you this for the future. So you know what you need to look out for. You want a man who challenges you. Not a man who conforms to your idea of what the perfect mate should be—because that's not a man. Men—good, honest men—stay true to who they really are."

She bobbed her head, grabbing her hat and her purse, her lips tight. "Thanks for all the man-fo. Look, I don't think we're going to get anywhere tonight. The feeling I had after dinner is long gone, and if you don't mind, I'm really tired. So I'm just going to go home and get into bed and ponder all the things you tell me I want. I'll see you back at my place later."

She slid out of the red-and-white vinyl booth and snatched her jacket from the hook, trying not to stomp off like a two-year-old having a temper tantrum. Swinging open the glass door, she padded down the steps, her anger fueling each stride.

She wanted a man who challenged her. Really? She jammed her arms into her coat, making a face of disgust when she couldn't zip it up over her stupid, oversized hooters.

As she made her way out of the small parking lot and onto the curb, she thought ugly thoughts. Thank God for Khristos and his analysis. How had she gotten to the ripe old age of thirty-five without it?

What hurts more, Quinn? The fact that he's spot on, or the fact that you weren't smart enough to figure it out for yourself and a man who bed hops had to tell you?

Dragging her purse over her shoulder, she simmered as she walked beneath the heavy, cloud-covered night, going over Khristos's words about Igor and his desire to have anyone beside him in his ugly bed with the equally ugly leather headboard, as long as that someone had a pulse.

In the height of her reflection, she almost mistook the sound of someone crying for street noise. But the rawness of it caught her ear and made her pause. Her eyes scanned the street, not terribly well lit, and quite honestly, it was stupid on her part to be walking alone.

Sticking her hand in her purse, she felt for her pepper spray. She'd lived in the city all alone for a long time, petrified a moment like this might come along. Her breathing slowing as she tipped her head and heard someone gasp for breath. And then sobbing. Sobbing so real, so gut-wrenchingly heartrending, her own heart clenched.

Quinn swiveled her head and that was when she saw the man on the bridge, just across the street. He was so small, his dark shoulders hunched and shaking as he straddled the steel edge of the bridge. As she drew closer, a glimmer of the puddle of his tears shone on the guardrail from the light of the full moon, making her fight a loud intake of breath.

She jammed her knuckles into her mouth. No. No, he wasn't going to...Was he?

Everything stopped for her then. All motion, all sound. There was nothing but this man and his rasping sobs, wrenched from his body as though someone were physically pulling each one from his chest.

His breaths came in short, cloudy puffs against the deep black velvet of night, and his muttered apologies came out in fits and spurts of jumbled, agonizingly stark words like "done" and phrases of the "I just can't do this anymore" nature, startling her to the core.

Her heart fell to her feet, her stomach churned with fear. Yet, his figure, so diminutive against the enormous backdrop of the New York City skyline, cried out to her—screamed for her to do something, anything.

And then she heard the heartbeat—just one, a single rapid fire of pain and anguish. This made no sense. How could he be the person she was supposed to be finding true love for? It was clear he wanted out of life, not a life mate.

Quinn's throat clogged up as she remembered Khristos's words about not rushing—to wait for him before she did anything rash. But she was torn as the heartbeat grew louder. What if she waited and he pitched himself into the murky waters of the Hudson? She'd never be able to live with herself if she didn't offer help.

And then she thought, fuck this business of being Aphrodite. She didn't know why she was here at this very moment or what the shit kind of match she was supposed to make with someone who wanted to end their life, but not a chance in hell was she going to let this guy plunge off this bridge.

Instantly, she had a choice to make—approach or call 911. Slipping her hand inside her purse, she rolled her fingers over her phone, locating it, but another heartbeat interrupted the action she planned to take.

A heartbeat smaller, much smaller than what she'd heard before and assumed belonged to the man on the bridge. It was erratic and quick, as though the owner was panicked or afraid. She took quick steps to get a closer glimpse when someone grabbed her arm and slipped a hand over her mouth.

Instinct told her to fight as her heart fought to get out of her chest until the owner of the hand said, "Do you hear it, Quinn?" Khristos whispered in her ear, an urgent demand.

She stilled and leaned back into Khristos with a nod of flooding relief that he wasn't a bad guy out to kill her. Gripping his wrist to pull his hand from her mouth, she pushed at it. "Let me go! I have to help him!"

"*No!*" he ordered in a hiss against her ear. "I need you to trust me, Quinn."

She struggled against Khristos. Trust him? "He'll die! I won't let that happen!"

"Trust me, Quinn. Trust me and listen. *Listen.*"

Her panic subsided as the smaller heartbeat took over, thrumming, melding with the larger, more powerful one...and then something else.

A third heartbeat? She strained against the grip Khristos had on her, as though leaning into the night would make the listening easier.

"Listen, Quinn. *Feel* it. Close your eyes, lean into me and feel it."

Quinn did as he instructed, forgetting that his chest was rock-hard yet inviting, forgetting that his embrace left her unafraid and comforted. Instead, she did what he requested. She felt.

Felt the thrumming in her veins, a sweet pulse of joy that grew stronger.

Felt the release of helplessness and, in its place, hope. So much hope it almost doubled her over, blooming into her chest like a flower opening under the warmth of the sun.

Squeezing Khristos's arm, she whispered, "Ohhh..."

His chin fell to the top of her head, where he let it rest. "Hang on to it, Quinn. Ride it out and listen."

Stealing a slow breath, Quinn cocked her head and heard another voice coming from the area of the bridge—a female voice, soft and lilting. "It's a kitten! I knew I heard meowing. Aw, c'mere, little guy. Oh my God, you're freezing!"

The man on the guardrail looked up, and for a beat of a moment, his face was as clear as if Quinn were standing right in front of him. His eyes glittered from his tears, his gaunt cheeks chapped with two bright spots of red, the despair written on his face clear—and that was when he hesitated.

And it was when she knew, when she felt what Khristos has described. This feeling, this pull wasn't urgent at all—it was *right*. It fit like a lost piece to a puzzle.

It simply *was*.

Quinn stopped breathing altogether as she clung to Khristos to keep from running to the man's aid—to allow whatever was supposed to happen, just happen.

This little woman, bundled from head to toe in a puffy jacket and boots, had managed to stop his momentum as she held up a tiny white and black kitten. Violent shudders wracked its freezing body as she cupped it close to her chest and stroked its head.

The man's grip on the guardrail loosened and he looked down at the woman without qualm. He cleared his throat. "Is he…is he okay?"

The young woman looked up then, her profile sloping and soft, her hair falling along her back in raven swirls highlighted in blue, and she smiled up at him—a smile that was filled with sincerity…with understanding… with rare kindness. "I think he will be. Would you mind holding him while I dig around in my purse for my hat? I'll tuck him into it and he'll be right as rain until I get home." She held up the tiny ball of shaking fur, as the man slid effortlessly from the guardrail, taking the kitten, his eyes meeting the woman's.

"Now, Quinn. Call for Cupid *now*," Khristos murmured, and this time, it was an urgent demand. "Close your eyes and picture his arrow."

Biting the inside of her cheek, she listened to her instincts, saw this imaginary arrow in her head in the way she'd always daydreamed, and mentally summoned Cupid.

Just as the image of the arrow faded from her mind's eye, Khristos squeezed her shoulders. "Look quickly, Quinn!"

Her eyes popped open, and in that moment, the most magical moment she'd experienced to date, she saw the arrow, soaring over the midnight sky like a firework, illuminated in a haze of shimmering white and pink. It landed in its target, disappearing into the left side of his chest then exploding in a fountain-like shower of sparks and color.

As the sparks framed their images, the woman held out her hand to the man—a simple gesture, but one filled with so much faith, Quinn had to keep from shouting at him to take it—take it and run as far and as fast as he could.

Please, God. Please let him take her hand. Quinn didn't understand the compelling nature of her request, there was no rhyme or reason to why she was sure it was crucial this man agreed to go with this woman, but she knew it was—to the depths of her soul, she knew.

And he did, gripping it tight in a shaky grab of flesh meeting flesh, and then the tiny woman said to him as though she had no clue he'd been about to take his own life, "It's pretty dark out here. Would you mind waiting with me while I call a cab?"

The man nodded, his mussed hair spiking in the cold wind picking up from the water. They trailed off hand in hand, winding their way down along the bridge until they were gone.

And suddenly, Quinn felt at peace, at total ease. She relaxed back into Khristos's grip and sighed a happy sigh at this turn of events. An event she hadn't just read about in a book. This had really happened, and she'd been a part of it.

Scenery is fine, but human nature is finer, flitted through her head.

"Nice job, Quinn. Well executed shot, too."

She mentally sent up a thank you to Cupid, blowing a kiss to the heavens. Then she turned to Khristos and smiled, fighting tears, forgetting she was angry with his assessment of her life. "That was amazing. The most amazing thing I've ever witnessed."

He chuckled, his laughter filtering to her ears, warming her. "It can be pretty incredible, and you made it happen."

But then a thread of fear shivered along her spine. "Why was he considering taking his life?"

Khristos's voice grew distant as he looked past her head and out into the expanse of the city's skyline. "I don't know all the particulars on this one, Quinn. I just know, in this case, he needed someone. That someone was the woman who found the kitten. The right woman to help him through whatever it is he's going through. He's going to be fine now. *They're* going to be fine and so will the little guy."

Quinn breathed a sigh of relief and happiness, still caught up in the joy of the moment. "How utterly and extraordinarily beautiful. Two random strangers cross paths, and poof—magic."

Running a finger long the line of her nose, he smiled and nodded. "Yep, poof."

Complete joy swept over her at this miracle that had occurred right under her nose, making her forget everything but this very second, one she would always cherish.

"Thank you," she whispered in awe. In her excitement, Quinn wrapped her arms around his neck and hugged him close.

She didn't mean to shudder a breath of contentment when his scent reached her nose. She didn't mean for her hands to curl into the hair at the nape of his neck, or luxuriate in the thick softness of it against her cold fingers. She didn't mean to sigh when his large body met hers.

And she definitely hadn't meant to graze his lips—his firm but soft lips. But graze she did when she began to pull away from his embrace and their mouths brushed.

The sweet sting of longing jolted her with a sharp tug, and then Khristos's lips covered hers, his hands winding around her waist and up along her back until she was molded tight against his tall, well-muscled frame.

For the briefest of seconds, something deep inside Quinn shifted, rooted around for a new place to settle, making her pulse race and her mouth open wider, accepting the silky taste of his tongue.

Her nipples tightened, tingling with need. The rigid outline of him, pressing at the apex of her thighs, made her breathing hitch.

He was all man, all hard, all everything.

If ever there was a perfect kiss, this was it. Soft, hard, deep, and delicious.

Her eyes would have rolled to the back of her head at such bliss—but in her almost swoon, her foot slipped off the curb and she fell backward.

"Quinn!" Khristos yelped as she began to tip sideways in what felt like a slow-motion action.

Which was odd, she thought on her way down.

It had been an amazing kiss, but one worthy of leaving her flat-out on the pavement in face-plant fashion?

Not quite.

Though, she'd be willing to try it again—just to test the theory.

CHAPTER 8

"Sweet baby J in a manger, what did you do to the matchmaker, my friend? Love hurts, huh?" Nina asked, her fingers dabbing at the scrape on Quinn's forehead with an antiseptic wipe as though she were swatting flies.

But Quinn wasn't complaining. At least Nina wasn't choking her out. That surely meant a friendship with the vampire was in the offing.

Wanda brushed at Nina's hands with an impatient flap. "Be gentle, Nina! You're not washing the tires on your big rig, for heaven's sake!"

Nina threw up her middle finger in Wanda's direction, along with the antiseptic wipe. "Oh, put a sock in it, Nightingale. I'm helping. You said help, didn't you? This is me being all sensitive over a minor boo-boo."

Marty plopped down on a chair next to Quinn and shooed Nina away with disgust—a tone Marty took often with Nina, but Quinn realized was always tempered with love. "Go help Carl. Last I saw him, he lost his hand again. Now move, and let the experts do their thing."

The vampire made a face of disgust. "Carl!" Nina shouted, her husky voice making Quinn's aching head wince. "Carl? Where the hell are you, buddy? You know what I said about hiding. You can only do it when we're playing a game with Charlie. Olli-olli-oxen-free, pal!"

Quinn gripped the edges of the chair she sat in and tried not to think about Carl the zombie or where his hand had gone. Or that he was a verified zombie. Or that he needed duct-tape with him at all times to keep his essential parts from falling off.

Marty rolled up the sleeve of her sweater and ran gentle fingers over Quinn's elbow. "I think we're going to need more Band-Aids. Arch? Band-Aid, stat, please!"

She felt so fussed over, so nurtured, it was almost overwhelming. From the moment she'd hobbled into her apartment, still brimming with people, they'd all worked as one. Everyone had a job, from Arch right down to Nina, and they all knew their roles.

"I'm okay, really, Marty. I can do this. I've been single and taking care of myself for a long time. I don't want to put you out. Don't you have a little girl and a husband you should be with?"

"I definitely do, and I love them more than I love my shoes and my false eyelashes—"

"Which is a huge admission for our ass-sniffer here," Nina crowed with a chuckle.

Marty shook her head, the jingle of her bracelets clacking together in a symphony of silver and gold. "But we all need something that fulfills us outside of our families, right? Something just for us. Doing this, OOPS, I mean, helping people who are scared and unsure in a world that's far scarier than the human one, is what I love."

Marty's words made her chest tight and her eyes well up. She was a hot mess of emotions tonight, a myriad of oversensitive nerve endings and feelings she didn't know how to absorb.

As a result, her words stuck to the roof of her mouth like peanut butter, but she needed them to know how much she appreciated everyone setting their lives aside for her because she was such a chicken. "I'm so grateful to Ingrid and you and Wanda and everyone else. Even Nina. I…"

Marty's perfectly made-up eyes twinkled as she lifted Quinn's leg and tentatively touched her ankle. "If you didn't let us help, it'd be an arrow to our hearts, kiddo. Where would we be if we didn't have someone to take care of, Wanda? And you don't have to do anything on your own anymore if you don't want to. You have us. Like it or not. Now lean back and relax and let us mother hen you to death. It's what we live for."

Wanda chuckled, pressing some antibiotic cream to Quinn's road-rashed cheek. "We do, indeed. So tell us what the heck happened, for gravy's sake? You look like you went a couple rounds with Holyfield, honey."

Quinn shook her head in a slow motion of total confusion and shrugged her shoulders. "I don't know. One minute I was kis—Um, fist-bumping Khristos over my first matchmaking success, the next I was rolling around on the concrete like a plastic bag, blowing in the wind."

Which was so damn strange. She remembered her foot slipping from the curb, something she was going to attribute to the wow factor Khristos's kiss had evoked, but she had no clue how she'd managed to hit the ground with such force. Enough force to cause her to skid along the concrete, scraping her until she was raw and bruised.

Marty stopped pressing an ice compress to Quinn's ankle and sighed a breathy sigh, giving her hand a light squeeze. "Khristos told us all about your awesome matchmaking. How incredible and heroic and so dreamy!"

Her heart warmed all over again just thinking about the moment that arrow hit that man on the bridge. It humbled her, left her in awe. "It was magic. Like no other kind of magic." Ever.

Wanda held up the peroxide and dipped another cotton ball in it with a smile. "Love in all its perfect imperfection. We're so proud of you, Quinn. Way to really make a go of this crazy turn of events in your life!"

Quinn's heart literally glowed at Wanda's warm approval. All these feels were beginning to make her question everything in her life. She'd never needed a cheering section before this Aphrodite thing had gone down. Yet, hearing she'd done something well, hearing it out loud, was becoming addictive.

Ingrid flew into her apartment, the door slamming behind her with a klunk. "Oh my God, Quinn! Are you okay? I left class the second I got Nina's text. I would have been here sooner, but the stupid subway was all backed up." She dropped down next to Quinn in a chair and reached for her hand with a wince.

She smiled at Ingrid. "I'm okay. I really am. Just a little beat up."

Ingrid dropped her backpack at her feet and leaned in to examine Quinn's roughed-up face. "You have a hella shiner. I thought you said you were going to take care of my girl, Khristos?"

Khristos ran a hand through his dark locks and shook his head in wonder. He'd been hovering over her before the women had shooed him away in order to allow them to do their thing, but he was never very far.

"I don't know what happened, Ingrid. It's like Quinn was just telling Marty and Wanda. One minute we were celebrating, the next, it was as if an invisible hand shot out of the dark like a bat outta hell and pushed her. The force of it knocked her to the ground." His tone implied worry and concern.

He'd only apologized a hundred times on the piggyback ride home he'd given her because he was certain she'd sprained her ankle.

Quinn avoided looking at him, but only because she was so deeply ensconced in having Wanda and Marty patch her up. Yes, siree—that was exactly why she was avoiding looking at him. These women were fascinating. "But I don't remember feeling like I was pushed…"

"That's because you weren't standing in front of you. It looked like someone steamrolled you from the left. I know that's crazy, but that's how it looked from my perspective."

Nina strode back into the living room, now awash with more bodies than Quinn ever thought was possible to fit into this small space. She held up a hand and a roll of duct tape.

Oh, Jesus and some adhesive—she held a hand.

"Did you say it looked like someone pushed her, dude?"

Khristos nodded, his face a mask of concern. "With force."

Nina's shoulders slumped when she moaned. "Aw, fuck."

"Aw, fuck, what?" Quinn asked. "Aw, fuck" couldn't be good.

Marty waved an admonishing hand at her. "Language, please, Dark One. I swear, it's like you don't even try. Charlie's going to end up in detention at daycare before she can even walk."

"Blow me, Girdle Queen. This calls for an 'aw, fuck'. I knew it. I GD knew it. Every time I damn well think we got shit all sewn up, we got a big, fat black fucking hole."

Quinn suddenly couldn't breathe. "Knew *what?*"

Nina glanced down at her, her coal-black eyes somber. "Bad guys, kiddo. I'd bet a month's worth of my blood supply."

And just when everything was going so swimmingly.

Khristos forced his hands to stay in the pockets of his jeans rather than check every square inch of Quinn's battered body. He fought even glancing at her lips—full, ripe lips that had been perfect against his.

He pulled Nina to the kitchen instead and looked her dead in the eye. "I'm worried you might be right."

She rolled her eyes in return. "I'm always right, dude. I can smell bad from a hundred miles away. I don't want to eff up Guru of Love's mojo, so I'll keep this between you and me for now, but shit ain't right. What's your take?"

Was it fair to keep the possibility of danger from Quinn? She should always be aware, but Nina was right. It would create havoc with her intuitiveness, which, given the situation, could change the entire future of the world.

"Tell me your thoughts and we'll make a decision based on them."

"I think you know the answer to that, dude. Mini-goddess has got little bones—little, breakable bones. She came out of that fall like she went a round in a street fight. It hurt me to look at her, and I don't feel much of anything since I was turned, physically speaking. So the question is, who'd want to hurt the love guru? You think your mother would do this? She didn't strike me as a total bitch when I met her, but what the fuck do I know about you crazy motherfuckers? I mean, you guys don't shit around when you're hacked off. What kind of guy turns a chick into a cow because he doesn't want to get caught slammin' her behind his wife's back?"

Khristos shook his head, racking his brain. "My mother's many things, spiteful on occasion, even vengeful, but to physically hurt someone isn't her style, Nina. Iris was my mother's choice to receive her powers, but Iris is the Goddess of Rainbows. She'll be bent out of shape when she finds out she's not next in line, no doubt, but she's not violent. It's not like *Thunderdome*—not these days, anyway."

She ignored his joke and looked right at him, her eyes full of concern. "Then we have a problem, my friend."

Fuck, fuck, fuck. He was really worried they *did* have a problem because the power of that blow had knocked Quinn's small frame over and she'd crumpled like a rag doll. No one in sight, and absolutely no reason for her to have fallen with the amount of force she did.

His centuries-long life had passed before his damn eyes when she'd been pulled from his arms and knocked to the ground. He'd never moved as fast as he had when he'd seen her beautiful face scrape the harsh black pavement.

He'd let himself get carried away with that kiss, with her curves finally pressed into his willing hands, with her soft lips moaning against his—and he was paying for it.

Nina slapped him on the back. "Look, I know you're kind is pretty tough, and you can make shit appear out of thin air or whatever. I'm not knocking your manliness, buddy, but you and your lady love didn't get any superhuman strength or speed or any of the things me and those two nuts in there have. She has hearts and flowers and fucking unicorns on her side. That means she's vulnerable, and I ain't likin' that crap. She can't protect herself if we're dealing with some deity who's a badass with lightning bolts or cows or whatever you nutbag bitches can come up with. So we got your back. She's Ingrid's friend, and I promised I'd make sure she was safe. No more matchmaking alone without me, Darnell, Marty or Wanda, got that?"

Nina was right. He had no powers other than immortality, the ability to know true love, and making things appear and disappear. He wasn't a god, his skills were minimal, but if it came down to it, he'd damn well use everything he had in him to keep Quinn safe.

"Fair enough."

Nina yanked at the duct tape, pulling a piece off as she leaned her hip against the gray-and-white granite countertop in the kitchen. "Where is your mother, anyway? You'd think she'd be tweaked as hell right now, all ragin' at you for taking her toys."

"Yeah. You'd think that. Strangely, not a damn word. It's as if she fell off the face of the earth." He'd tried like hell to get in touch with her. He'd Facebooked, tweeted, texted, called.

But she was unreachable, and no one, not Zeus, not his batty wife Hera, none of her closest god friends knew where she was. Since her powers had been transferred to Quinn, she was *persona non grata*.

Nina put a hand on his shoulder, forcing him to look at her. "Is there something you're not telling us, dude? Because look, I get this is an inconvenience for you. I know you're rather be doin' belly shots off some hot stray goddess than skippin' around the city, playing *Love Connection*. But is there anything else about the apple we should know? Some rare legend? Some stupid, frigged-up rule no one knows about but your mom? It's happened to us more times than I care to count. So don't fuck with me now. Your best bet is to just spit it out. Don't make me play a game I don't have all the rules for, cuz old friends or not, I'll fuck you and all your organs right the hell up."

Nothing. There was nothing he could think of, *no one* he could think of who'd knock Quinn on her ass in order to become Aphrodite.

Her ass.

Shit, he had to stop thinking about that particular part of her body, along with her smile, and the way she got that wide-eyed look when she was staring off into space, trying hard not to be the daydreamer she was.

He liked that she was a dreamer. He didn't meet many women who weren't so entrenched in their past bad relationship experiences that it colored everything they did. And in most cases, they had every right to those feelings.

He liked that she had a picture of her and a cardboard Mr. Darcy sitting on her dresser. He liked that she liked frilly ruffles, and lacy clothes, and anything ultra-feminine.

He hated Jane Austen's work, but he loved that Quinn loved it. Because that was who she was. Not a chance in hell would he sit around and read Keats with her, but he'd certainly smile while *she* did as he watched a game or caught up on his Grisham, if it made her happy.

There was an innocence to Quinn's outlook, and though she was still stinging right now from her breakup with a wishy-washy mockery of a man, her vow to be more realistic was all a sham. He liked that she kept trying, even when she didn't realize she was.

She'd always gasp at the wonder of love and its many miracles just the way she'd gasped over the magic of the arrow tonight. She might be fighting it right now, but it would always be in Quinn's nature to keep reaching, to keep hoping. She just had to learn the difference between hope and a lost cause.

Which Igor had been. Stupid, too, if he were pressed to label.

Her joy, her happiness…it did something to the inside of his chest. Something he wasn't sure he wanted floating around his insides as if it belonged there.

He just had to stop thinking about the kiss; if he could do that, it would be all right. It was just a kiss. He'd kissed plenty of women. Quinn was no different.

Oh, stop now. She was so different.

"Khris?" Nina prodded.

"No. There's no secret, no hidden issues that I know of personally, attached to that apple."

Nina pursed her lips and scanned his face. "Okay. But I'm telling you—"

"I know, I know," he said on a laugh. "You'll kick my sorry, powerless ass. Loud and clear."

He definitely got it. He just hoped he was right.

Carl sat across the table from Quinn and smiled, his grin lopsided, his face greenish in cast as Nina reattached his hand to his wrist. When she was done, she ruffled his dark hair and smiled. "Good job, buddy. You sat really still this time. Now, no more taking off like that, got it? Big, scary city out there, and if something happened to your wandering butt, I'd be heartbroken, okay?"

Carl nodded and thumped the table with his hand then he turned his gaze back to Quinn.

Who tried to keep it together. Because *zombie*. Like, real zombie. Sitting-right-in-front-of-her, happy-as-a-clam zombie, completely unaware he was about as hard to digest as finding out there really was a Santa Claus.

But to look at Carl, to see him up close, well…he really was darling. Gentle as a lamb as he stroked Buffy's head, who'd decided Carl had the best lap ever and had curled herself right into it as though she never planned to leave.

Archibald brought a plate of broccoli with a napkin and set it beside him, straightening to gaze down at Carl and give him a look of reproach.

"All right, young man, enjoy your snack, but in no way should you consider this a reward for your poor behavior. I'm absolutely doing this against my better judgment. You will be the death of Grampa Archibald, Carl. If anything happened to you while you were out carousing as though zombies are not something the great people of New York City would burn at the stake, I'd never forgive myself. You must stop making me fret like that."

Carl lifted his lips in his adorably lopsided grin and reached upward, patting Archibald's chin in an obvious apology.

Archibald grabbed his hand and squeezed it. "Don't you try to soften me up either. Next time you behave poorly, there will be no *Goodnight Moon* for you before bedtime. Understood?"

Carl bobbed his head and nabbed a piece of broccoli, driving it into his mouth and chomping, green stems falling to his shirt where Nina had tucked a napkin into his collar.

Ingrid set a steaming cup of tea in front of Quinn and sat next to her at the table. She leaned forward and nudged her with a shoulder. "You okay?"

"*Zombie.*"

Ingrid giggled. "Yep."

"He's so—so—precious," she whispered in pure wonder.

"That he is. And he's amazing with the kids."

"This week has had more fangs and fur than a mash-up episode of *The Vampire Diaries* and *Teen Wolf*."

"And how do you feel about that?"

Quinn gave her a skeptical sidelong glance, leaning her head on her hand. "Are you shrinking me right now, Ingrid Lawson?"

"I'm just checking on your emotional barometer. It's in the pamphlet, if you want to read it. I brought one with me from the office. According to the bosses, you should be having some serious swings in your emotional state. You know, the five stages thing Nina talked about. I just want to keep on top of it. So how do you feel?"

How did she feel? Earlier she'd been euphoric. Sharing that moment with Khristos and two people who had no idea anyone else in the world existed in that moment in time was amazing—fulfilling.

But now? Now she was projecting into the future, when she'd have to explain to her parents and her coworkers she was responsible for helping to repopulate the world.

How did you sit someone down and tell them you couldn't come to work today because you had to make sure the world kept evolving—forever?

Hey, Mom, what did you do today? Wait. No, don't tell me. Bet it doesn't beat what I did today. Know what I did today? I ordered Cupid to shoot glow-in-the-dark arrows at people who are soul mates. You know, those things you staunchly disregard as real?

Worse, she worried about when she'd have to do this on her own without someone to share it with. What fun was helping true love along if you didn't have someone to share it with?

"Quinn?"

She patted Ingrid's hand. "I'm hanging in there. Everything's going to be okay." Okay, okay, okay. She'd only told herself that a hundred times since the day began.

"I heard you were a real superstar today."

She shook her head as she sipped her tea and tried not to think about the kiss. "It wasn't me, really. It was mostly Khristos."

"But I heard it was a total save. Like, you saved someone's life, Quinn! That's incredible, and awesome, and you should be proud. Give yourself some credit. So, this must also mean you're less butthurt about Igor? Maybe some of those old feelings about everlasting love are coming back?"

After the eye-opening conversation she'd had with Khristos, where she'd had her poor choices laid out in front of her and really examined— um, mostly no. "You know what I've decided after tonight? I've decided that eternal love is for *some* people, and it's beautiful. God, it was so beautiful, Ingrid. But I learned something about myself this fine evening as well. Something valuable." And while she hated to admit it, Khristos's words had clicked.

Ingrid grabbed a cookie from the plate Archibald silently set on the table and took a healthy bite. "Tell me," she ordered as she munched.

"I discovered that it isn't that the men I pick suck ass, per se. *I* suck ass at the picking. I've invested a lot of time in putting on my blinders. On overlooking some of the things I knew were clear signs that Igor and I weren't a good match, but ignored anyway because I was sure, in the big scheme of things, he was my Mr. Darcy. That I could turn him *into* my Mr. Darcy."

"Signs like…?"

Quinn sighed and leaned deeper into her hand. "Like when Igor told me he loved me. Sure, he said it, but I never felt secure in it. Not even a little. Despite what I portrayed outwardly. That's because I wanted it to be true in my head, but I guess I knew it wasn't in my heart. I just couldn't admit it. Apparently, I have a gift for picking men who'll be whatever I want them to be just to keep from being alone, and then they realize what

I want isn't what they want and they skip off to someone with big guns and abs I could bounce a quarter off of."

"Wow. That's deep, my friend. But you seem like you've come to terms with it. Though, I still say, it doesn't mean it can't happen to you."

Quinn shrugged, wincing when she tried to stretch out her arm. "But maybe it's just not for everyone. I mean, this Aphrodite thing is about repopulating the world, right? But some people choose not to procreate for whatever reasons. If everyone procreated we'd have far bigger problems than we already do, don't you think? I've made my peace with the idea I just wasn't meant to be part of that particular bigger picture."

Ingrid rolled her tongue along the inside of her cheek, her patience clearly waning. "Look, Igor *is* the shit on your shoe. He didn't even have the decency to break up with you properly, Quinn. You're a nice lady. He's a dicknuckle of a man. It shouldn't sour you forever." She waved her hands in a dismissive motion. "That's beside the point. The point is, despite our complete lack of almost anything in common other than English Lit, and considering our age difference, I still know that a bad breakup takes time to get over. I'm not so young that I don't get—"

"Why are you always harping on the fact that I'm almost old enough to be your mother?" Quinn planted an indignant hand on her hip with a grin. "I'm so tired of hearing about your youth, I could cry. I'm thirty-five, not three thousand-five. Yes, I decided to continue my education a little later in life. So. What?" Quinn waved her finger under Ingrid's nose to make her point.

Ingrid gave her a look of outrage, her heavily made-up eyes wide. "I'm not making fun of you. I'm stating a fact. It was me, wasn't it, who clunked Thor Benson in the head for making fun of your age?"

That was true. Ingrid had. Right after their fellow classmate Thor, who shouldn't have been given vocal chords, let alone a high school diploma, had called her a wannabe MILF.

Okay. Unfair call. She was picking fights in her touchiness after the diner revelations. "Yes. It was a nice shot, too. Perfectly executed."

"He deserved it. He doesn't even know how to spell MILF, let alone identify one. He said to tell you hello, too."

She'd forgotten all about her class. "What did you tell everyone?"

"That you had a boob job and you're recuperating."

Quinn snorted. "You didn't."

"Nah, I didn't. I just told them you had to cut your trip short because you were the new Aphrodite, Goddess of Lurve, and your plate suddenly became full and especially sparkly."

Quinn giggled. "Thanks for covering for me. I'm not ready to explain about Igor yet."

"So seriously. Are you really, really going to let that douchenozzle crap on your future dreams? Don't you think it's time to let the failures go?"

Youth, in all its impatience, thy name is Ingrid. It had nothing to do with letting go. It had to do with a dream dashed, and coming to terms with the dashing.

"Look, Miss Youthful and Resilient 2015, you're young, maybe too young to have experienced real betrayal. So while Igor is a piece of limp wiener, we *were* in a relationship for over a year. Maybe at your age that's no big deal, and maybe the day after you found out the man you thought was your soul mate cheated on you, you'd skip right off to the next available guy with tickets to a Justin Bieber concert. But at my age, a year *means* something. It's time invested, and it still stings a little. I'm gun-shy now. And it isn't much about Igor anymore. It's about all of my failed relationships as a whole."

"Hey, Old Maid," Ingrid prodded, swatting at her arm. "First of all, no way I'd date a dude who liked Bieber. Second of all, I'd mourn my lost relationship for at least a week before I even considered dating anyone else. I might even go two weeks, and I'm not saying you shouldn't be angry and bitter over all that time invested. Not at all. I'm just saying, never give up. It's what you told me when we had to write that stupid essay about some ancient artist's perspective of his death. Remember how I struggled with that? Christ, I wanted to raise him up from the dead just so I could kill him all over again."

Quinn sighed, but she shot Ingrid a fond smile. "One essay and several drastically bad life-choices are exactly the same."

"You're breaking me," Ingrid said mournfully, letting the cookie drop to the plate.

Quinn patted her hand and wiped the side of Ingrid's mouth free of crumbs. "Don't be broken. I'm not." And that was the truth.

Carl stood up suddenly, pushing aside his chair and grabbing a big tote bag from under the table. He stooped in an awkward half-bend of knees and pulled out a book.

Holding it up, he grinned crookedly at Quinn and held out his hand, now duct-taped securely to his wrist, the shiny silver metallic catching the overhead light.

Quinn cocked her head in Nina's direction.

Nina smiled, and when that smile was in direct relation to someone she loved, it was the most amazing, serene sight to behold. She was so beautiful when she wasn't threatening to turn your liver into pâté.

Nina ruffled Carl's dark hair like a proud parent. "He wants to read to you, Lite-Brite. Carl's an intuitive little dude, and he must sense you're sad about all this love goop. He loves to read. Reads everything he can get his hands on. It makes him happy. He thinks it makes everyone else happy, too. Don't you buddy? It's his way of cheering you up."

Quinn smiled up at Carl then, her heart tight and melty in her chest. "I love to read, too, Carl. It's my absolute favorite pastime."

Carl grunted and stuck his hand back at her with that grin even the hardest of hearts couldn't deny.

Quinn took it, letting Carl lead her to her bedroom, where he sat on the edge of the bed and patted the place next to him.

And there she sat, on her frilly romantic bed with the plump white and blue lace pillows, right next to a vegetarian zombie who clumsily nestled *Goodnight Moon* on his thighs and grunted out words to her.

And it was the second most amazing thing that had happened to her today.

CHAPTER 9

T he doorbell, tinny and obnoxiously loud, had Quinn literally falling out of her bed, stumbling over Carl, who'd fallen fast asleep after they'd read together.

Buffy and Spike stirred only briefly from their spot on the pillows before yawning and settling back in, curling together in a warm ball of contentment.

Grabbing her bathrobe, Quinn made a break for the door in the hopes whoever it was, holding their finger to the damn doorbell as if they were demanding entry to Heaven, wouldn't wake Nina.

Because she did not want to be the one who ruffled those bat wings.

But it was already too late. Nina held the door wide open, the freezing rush of air whooshing around Quinn's ankles.

The vampire folded her arms over her red thermal shirt with black bats on it, crossing her long legs covered in matching thermal underwear, and cocked her head in Quinn's direction. "Ding-dong, parental unit calling," she growled.

Oh no. No, no, no.

"Quinn?" Her mother rushed in, pushing her way past Nina to stop directly in front of Khristos, whose big body was sprawled awkwardly on her couch, sound asleep. His beautiful face took her breath away, relaxed and serene as though his liver wasn't in dire danger of being pecked out.

His muscled arm was flung over his forehead in abandon, and his chest, covered in a T-shirt, lifted in a slow, mesmerizing rhythm of rippled goodness.

Her mother stabbed a finger at Khristos without saying a word, her disapproval ringing in the still apartment air as surely as if she'd expressed it verbally.

Nina strolled up behind her mother's left shoulder, the floppy bunny ears on her slippers bobbing up and down. "Cat got your tongue?"

Her mother's eyes went wide at Nina's presence. "What is *this?*"

"Hot dude."

"Explain!" Helen Morris demanded.

Nina scratched her head, "Um, hot dude I'd consider hittin' if I didn't have my own hot dude at home?"

"Why?" she spat, adjusting her yellow and blue fanny pack around her waist.

The vampire frowned. "Why is hot dude on the couch?"

When Helen didn't answer quickly enough for Nina, she said, "Look, lady, are we free associating or playing charades or somethin'? Because it's damn early for me, and I don't have a pen and paper. There's a hot dude on your kid's couch. He's a nice hot dude, by the way. If you're lookin' for anything more in-depth than that from me, you'll have to come back in about five hours when I've fed...er, myself and showered."

Her mother's lips thinned when she crooked her neck and looked up at Nina, her sharp green eyes assessing the vampire. "And *who* are you?"

Nina grinned. "Me? Not the hot dude, that's for sure."

"Nina!" Quinn hissed in reproach, tightening the belt on her robe. "Mom, why are you here? Why didn't you just use your key?"

Her mother planted her hands on her hips and narrowed her gaze. "Well, the row of shoes outside your door was an indication you might have guests. I didn't want to just barge in."

"Since when?"

Her mother's eyes flashed all kinds of warnings. "I think explanations are in order, young lady. You're still supposed to be in Greece, but instead you're here with a houseful of strangers. What's going on, Quinn?"

"Mama bear's bowels are all twisted up," Nina remarked, poking her finger in Quinn's shoulder. "Looks like someone's in for a lickin'."

Archibald flew around the corner from the kitchen, a plate of fluffy eggs in his hand, his usually perfect hair mussed. "Forgive me, Miss Quinn. I didn't hear the doorbell!"

"*Who—are—these—people?*" Helen screeched, her face turning a blotchy red, the color creeping down over her neck.

Khristos popped upward at her mother's howl, losing his balance and promptly falling off the couch, knocking the end table lamp to the floor. He sat straight up and wiped the corner of his mouth free of drool.

Marty and Wanda flew out from behind Arch, dressed as though they'd never slept, and rushed toward Helen, surrounding her with clouds of perfume and immaculate fashion sense.

Marty held her hand out with a warm smile. "You're Quinn's mother? I'm Marty Flaherty. It's so lovely to meet you! We were just getting ready for some breakfast. Won't you join us? Arch? Would you set another place at the table?"

Wanda wrapped her arm around Helen and purposely directed her toward the table. "And I'm Wanda Schwartz. We've heard so many wonderful things about you from Quinn!" she cooed.

Quinn's heart pounded in her chest as she offered her own hand to Khristos and yanked him upward, attempting to avoid his eyes. This was so, so bad. How was she not only going to explain all these people in her apartment, but her gigantic cans, purple eyes and glow-in-the-dark skin?

And Carl? Oh, Jesus and some duct tape. How would she ever explain Carl, who was still fast asleep on her floor, a blanket tucked under his chin?

Khristos bounced his head from side to side, massaging his neck. "How do you feel today? Did you get a good night's rest?"

She ached from head to toe. Sometime during the course of the evening, Nina had explained her own ability to self-heal as she'd dropped an ice pack in Quinn's lap. She wouldn't complain if that had been one of the super powers bestowed upon her. It had to be more useful than enormous lady lumps.

He looked down at her and winced, trailing a finger across her bruised cheek before she took a step backward to avoid his touch. "I can't apologize enough, Quinn. If I could take your place, I would," he rumbled, deep and low.

God, did he have to be chivalrous and hot? She brushed it off. "I'll heal. Nothing some aspirin and antibiotic cream won't mend."

"So Mom's here. She seems nice."

Quinn's fists clenched at her side. Not just because her mother had arrived in all her angry disapproval, but because even in the midst of chaos and morning breath, Khristos was delicious, and he sent a ripple of hot awareness along her spine just to remind her.

"Let me just give you a head's up about Helen Morris. If you think your mother's difficult? Think a hundred times as difficult minus the orgies and ability to see an invisible arrow. She doesn't need to turn you into a cow to make you pray for death."

"Aw. She doesn't look so bad. She's the size of a minute, Quinn," he said on an affable smile, flashing his toothpaste-commercial white teeth.

"Ah, but her opinion's the size of the population of China."

He winked, all charming and easygoing. "There isn't a woman on the face of the planet I can't win over. Don't worry."

Quinn leaned into him, despite her better judgment. Yeah, yeah, yeah. He was hot. Indeed, he was probably a real lady killer. But he was in for a big whack to his self-esteem with her mother.

"Listen, if you want your ego to remain healthy, run. Run far, run fast, because if anyone can trash your record, it's Helen."

She knew well how hard her mother could be on a person's self-esteem, how critical, how utterly infuriating—all part of the reason she'd spent so much of her childhood and teen years buried in books.

He rested a hand on her shoulder and gave it a squeeze, shooting her another one-hundred watt smile. "Trust me. I got this."

Khristos yanked the door shut to her apartment and leaned against it with a shudder as Nina skipped up the steps in front of them to survey the street.

Quinn gave him the I-told-you-so look. "I warned."

"And I was an idiot not to heed. Jesus, she's brutal—a warrior disguised in pink mom jeans and a turtleneck with sheep on it. She looks so innocent. Who'da thunk a woman the size of a teacup poodle could fit so much venom in that small a space?"

She pulled her gloves on and laughed. "I tried to tell you. I know you have your Casanova on level ten, but my mother's immune to all men. It doesn't matter how good-looking, how smart, how *anything*, she wants nothing to do with them."

Khristos held out his arm, offering it to her once they'd made their way up the stairs when Nina gave them the thumbs-up. "You're not kidding. I pulled out all the stops, too. Every last one. Centuries worth of tried-and-true methods all hacked to pieces by a gladiator."

Quinn giggled as she had to decide whether taking his arm was healthy for her state of mind. "I gotta give it to you. That was a smooth move, chatting her up about the rare Mauritius kestrel. How do you know so much about birds? How did you know she even *liked* birds?"

Khristos wiggled an eyebrow. "I saw a text from her to someone named Maude about their Bird Enthusiasts Club meeting next week. And then I googled so fast, I almost broke a finger."

She patted his arm as they strolled down the sidewalk with Nina trailing behind them. "Ah, Maude. The only friend my mother has. You still get an A for effort. That bit about how the sheep on her turtleneck accented her eyes just might've worked if you hadn't tried to take it to the next level."

Khristos grimaced. "Yeahhh. I should have known to stop at sheep and not get carried away with the whole pink-galoshes thing."

"But you were right—they did match her lipstick."

Nina pushed her way between them and cackled. "Your mom is like a fucking ray of GD sunshine. Christ, she beat player here's ass down like she was the hammer and he was a nail. That crap about his cheekbones being the sharpest thing he owns was the shit."

Now Quinn winced. Her mother had gone for Khristos's jugular from the moment he'd sat down next to her. Every word out of his mouth, she'd made a point of shooting down like she was the supersonic death ray and he was the army of supervillains.

She'd whipped him with her words while she'd poked and prodded Marty and Wanda about their relationship to Quinn—and all during the course of just one meal that had lasted no more than thirty minutes.

She'd held her breath the entire time as Marty explained they were having a book club sleepover to console Quinn after her breakup with Igor.

Which then sent her mother off on another tangent about the unreliability of men and somehow kept her so occupied, she didn't seem to notice Quinn's breasts.

Breasts she'd taken great pains to wrap an Ace bandage around to flatten them out. She'd also borrowed one of Khristos's sweaters, at least three sizes too big for her, in order to camouflage them.

Her lightly tinted sunglasses had mostly kept her eyes hidden, heavier than usual makeup had covered her bruised face, and she hadn't even had to explain away her glittery skin due to her mother's laser focus on angry rants about that anus-head Igor.

"I can't even believe you told her you were gay."

Khristos chuckled. "Are you kidding me? I'd have told her I was the Zodiac Killer if it meant she'd sheathe those claws."

"Bravo then, because it did make her pause," Quinn commented as the wind began to pick up. Khristos had been very clever, smart, funny, but her mother would have none of it until he'd dropped that bomb right in the middle of her second helping of eggs.

"Listen, if she thinks all men are out to get you for one thing, and one thing only, I don't want her uncomfortable. We have to do this, Quinn. In light of the fact that our situation is urgent, knowing you're out with me and thinking I'm some kind of rebound after Igor would only upset her. She's your mother. I don't want that."

So the playboy was decent, too. These little insights into his personality were so enlightening, coming from a man who was, according to Nina, known worldwide for his talent at wooing women with a prowess so strong, it'd make your libido spin.

She shrugged, fighting off the warmth his sensitivity to her situation created, and sighed as they came to the crosswalk. "She's not upset about me or my feelings. She just loves to carry on about how awful the opposite sex is. Give her a platform, and she's on the highest tier, waving her hands in the air. I don't think she's ever gotten over my father leaving her." Like *ever*.

Khristos shook his head, the ends of his dark hair just peeking out beneath his knit cap. "She loves you, Quinn. Not a doubt in my mind. It's her way of protecting you even if comes off a little Femi-Nazi. I'm not sure what her reasons are, but she has them."

"A little? Did you hear her, Khristos? Like, really hear her? She doesn't just take an inch; she takes the hundred-yard run. She's a zealot with a cause. All she needs is a tinfoil hat and a pitchfork.

Nina scoffed, pushing her glasses up her zinc-slathered nose. "I'm here to tell ya, I don't give a shit what her reasons are. She's a shark. It's a beautiful thing to witness, friends. So damn beautiful, if I wasn't the baddest ass we got, I would have opted to go to the bird sanctuary with her instead of playing bodyguard to Lite-Brite here. Marty and Wanda always get the good shit."

"I don't even know why she's here. She drove in all the way from Jersey, still thinking I wasn't even back from Greece yet. Something's up. I just don't know what." Her mother didn't love the city. She didn't love it when Quinn had decided to move here after college, and she continued not to love it almost fourteen years later.

She'd considered Quinn's move to Manhattan flighty and irresponsible, full of whimsical dreams that would never come true.

And okay, she'd mostly been right. Most of her dreams hadn't come true. But she was happier away from the oppressive blanket of negativity her mother smothered everything with. It gave them distance, and time for her to store up her energy for their next visit.

"Well, she's here, and I'm gay for the moment, and I'm good with it."

Nina knocked shoulders with Khristos and cackled. "You're a chicken-shit."

"I prefer to call myself testicle-saver, thank you very much."

"You got a cape?" Quinn teased, basking in the warmth of his lighter banter.

"If it means your mother's teeth won't be in my ass, I'll even wear tights."

Quinn laughed until she remembered something Nina had mentioned. Something she'd avoided or purposely tuned out the night before in order to keep her sleep nightmare-free. "Question?"

"Go," Nina prompted as they stopped in front of an art store where classes were being held and, allegedly, where someone, somewhere, needed Quinn's power.

"The bad-guy thing. Tell me about it. I can take it."

Nina's face changed, going from taking intense pleasure in the wrath of Storm Helen and the path of its debris to serious. "Look, kiddo. I'm not gonna lie, this whole paranormal thing is fraught with danger. Not always, but sometimes. Do I think someone might wanna kick your scaredy-cat, teeny-tiny ass? I dunno. Can't say for sure until we dig deeper into this thing. But I do want you to pay attention. All the GD time. I'll always be right here. So will Khristos, no matter what. But sometimes, shit happens that we don't know about. And that's just the truth."

Visions of supervillains danced in her head, supervillains like the one Katie, Ingrid's old boss had experienced, and it made her shiver. "So there could be someone out there, someone who actually wants to be Aphrodite?" Who?

Khristos's lips thinned. "I don't know that for sure, but it's like Nina said, better safe than sorry."

"So they'd have to get the apple from me in order to steal my powers, right?"

Khristos's face became grave. "No. You took the power from the apple, Quinn. The power's in *you* now. The dynamics of the apple have changed."

She scrunched her eyes shut and clung to her scarf. She was pretty sure she knew what that meant, but because she was taking this stab at hitting things head-on these past few days, she was going to ask anyway. "So that in turn means what?"

Nina gripped her shoulders and looked her dead in the eye, almost making her tremble at the somber glaze of her stare. "That means in order to get the power from you, they have to kill you."

Wow. Those crazy Greeks. Totally cutthroat, huh?

"Look!" Nina yelled her success from across the room, holding up her hands covered in paint. "I made a still-life blob!"

Quinn fought a cringe. They'd been in this terminally long, therapeutic finger-painting art class, trying to get in touch with their inner turmoil for over an hour, and nothing. No vibe. No warm fuzzy. Nothing.

Where the hell was this match?

The instructor, dressed to play the part of the Guru of Peace and Light, who wore a white cotton caftan and matching pants in all his yoga-like Zen, nodded as he strolled through the aisles of easels where fingers flew in a flurry of color.

His hands were steepled beneath his chin, his lined face serene. "Do you *feel* it, my friends of the earth and sky? Feeeeel the power of your strokes. Become one with the paint, soar to the clouds. Let it guide your hands along the journey that is your quest for deep inner peace."

"Is that like *Vision Quest?*" Quinn asked out loud.

Khristos snorted, using a knuckle to roll another color onto his canvas. "I don't think Madonna has anything to do with this."

She looked at her canvas and then to Khristos, who'd quite successfully painted what looked like a sunset. If you tilted your chin up and moved your head to the left, anyway.

"I think whatever intuition you had this morning was a mistake because not only am I not feeeeling the connection to the paint, but my journey is neither deep nor peaceful. I don't know about you, but any two people in the world who find this class even remotely therapeutic deserve each other. They don't need us for the matching."

Khristos smiled, sliding his stool closer to hers and leaning in so close, he made her dizzy. "Aw, c'mon, Quinn. Haven't you found the core of your discontent? I think it's right there in that odd combination of squares in bright Big Bird yellow and spicy-brown mustard."

She gasped and tried leaning away. "That's not a square. It's a picture of my old swing set from when I was a kid." God, she'd hated that thing. It wasn't that she didn't enjoy the outdoors and all its magical sound and movement. She just didn't enjoy it on a stupid swing in the height of winter.

But her mother had been convinced part of Quinn's withdrawal into a book had to do with her lack of friends, and she was certain adding a play set to their backyard would bring everyone in the neighborhood over, just begging and scraping to be her daughter's friend.

Instead, it only made Barry Womack, who lived two doors down, laugh and point at her when she'd taken a tumble from the slide and couldn't get back up off her ass, what with so many layers of clothing on to keep her warm.

She kept people away from her mother and her bitterness because it humiliated her, and as she looked back on that time in her young life now, she realized she'd just kept right on isolating herself.

Khristos paused and pursed his luscious lips, so near her ear she wanted to scream at him to move away, with all his magical raising of her hormone levels. "Oh, yeah. I see it now. That's the slide, right? Are slides so square?"

She rolled her eyes and swished a finger through the rectangle of color. "No, that's the stupid monkey bars where my mother was convinced I should be getting some fresh air instead of staying buried under my covers reading Judy Blume."

"Monkey bars are at the core of your discontent? You're deep as the ocean, Quinn Morris."

She made a face at him in mock exasperation. "Not the monkey bars, per se. Just a time in my life I was discontent because my mother is the exact opposite of me."

"Wow."

She put a hand on her hip in defensive indignation. "Wow, what?"

"Wow, those look nothing like monkey bars."

"I agree," the lady to the left remarked, batting her eyelashes at Khristos in that coy way females did when they wanted to catch a man's attention.

Oh, because Mother Earth here knew the first thing about painting monkey bars accurately, in all her flowy robes and open-toed sandals in the height of a thirty-degree spell of cold weather?

But Quinn put on a smile anyway, only due to the fact that she shouldn't care if the woman was trying to catch Khristos's attention. He was free for the catching. She turned to address her.

Then the woman looked at her hard. "Has anyone ever told you maybe you went a little overboard with the colored contacts? They're not realistic at all."

Has anyone told you I could match you with an orangutan? "They looked different online," Quinn muttered.

"Also, whatever you're putting on your skin to make it glow like that? Can't be good for it. I'm a dermatologist, in case you doubt."

Quinn clenched her teeth. "Got a little carried away with the lotion. It'll wash off."

The woman glanced Khristos's way again and gave him a dreamy smile. "Do they get any hotter than that? Is he your boyfriend?"

Khristos shook his head and gave her one of his perfect, toe-tingling smiles. "Nuh-uh. I'm gay."

The woman's shoulders slumped. "Of course."

Quinn was determined to keep it cheerful while she waited on her matchmaking sign. "What are you painting?"

"This idiot's demise." She pointed to a man to her immediate left, just two seats down from them, who was neatly dressed in a plaid collared shirt with a knit sweater over top.

Khristos cocked his head to the right as he scanned the woman's painting. "But what a brilliant use of color. Who knew demise was so neon green?"

"Those are his brains, which I plan to dance in when this ridiculous blind date is done with." She turned to the man and grinned.

The man, dressed in the absolute antithesis of everything earthy and green, whipped his neon-blue, paint-covered finger in the air. "Not if I get there first."

Quinn blanched, feeling an odd solidarity with this woman and her failed date. "So, I take it, it's not going well?"

The woman, maybe forty-five or so, rolled her quite lovely hazel eyes almost to the back of her head. "Are you kidding me? I put out fifty bucks apiece to get into this class and all he's done is complain."

The man, sandy-blond with the beginning touches of gray at his temples, arched an eyebrow straight upward. "I thought that was what we were supposed to do in this touchy-feely, overpriced hotbed of neuroses— express our discontent?"

"On the canvas, not with your open mouth, and you can leave at any time."

The man balked. "And not finish my masterpiece of discontent? Don't talk crazy like that. It'll make me question my very reason for getting up this morning. Not on your life."

The woman shook her long head of hair, hair that almost touched her waist. "I was so hopeful. My girlfriend said we'd be a perfect match, and who knows you better than your best friend? But we're nothing alike. I'd have more in common with a breast implant salesman," she whispered from behind the hand she'd cupped over her mouth.

Something inside Quinn clicked at that moment. A connection to this woman's deeper sadness, one she didn't always show to the outside world.

"Still in the same room with you! Have ears!" the man yelled out.

Quinn put a hand on the woman's forearm and nodded. "I totally get it. I was in a relationship like that, too. But you know what? It's better to know now rather than get in any deeper. Trust me when I tell you, one drastically cut-short trip to Greece where I thought I was going to end up engaged at the Parthenon and my entire life in complete chaos later, and I only wish I'd realized on our first date how wrong he was for me. Phew, was he wronger than wrong. Could've saved almost six thousand dollars if I'd just paid attention."

Khristos nudged her with a light elbow to her still-smarting ribs. "*Quinn...*" He muttered what sounded like a warning under his breath."

She flapped an absent hand at him. "Hush. Girl time. Bonding over stupid man choices. Go paint some more discontent." She turned back toward the woman, giving her back to Khristos. "Anyway, I understand and I sympathize. I've personally given up on finding the one and decided to focus on me." Quinn squeezed her arm again and smiled her reassurance.

"*Quinn!*" Khristos hissed.

The man snorted. "How did you manage to find another granola-loving, tree-hugging woman in a sea of all the women in New York City, right here in this class?"

The woman pushed her stool out and stood up, her rounded body rigid. "You know what? If you're not careful, I'm going to drown you in that sea, you uptight, pompous, overblown bag of Abercrombie & Fitch!"

Quinn raised a fist in the air, cheering on this brave woman in solidarity. "You tell him, sister! Don't settle for second best!"

The man almost knocked his easel over when he pushed his stool out, too, and stomped over to them. He glared down at her, and if she were honest with herself, he was quite handsome. He'd aged well.

"Second best? Why don't you stick your nose in someone else's trail mix and mind your own business, lady?"

Khristos was on his feet in mere seconds, setting her behind him in an act of protective measure. "Okay now, buddy. Let's all just cool off. Quinn didn't mean to interfere."

Quinn poked him in his broad back. God, touching him was like touching a wall of sumptuous granite. "I did too!"

"*Quinn,*" Khristos warned, his voice rising.

She pushed him out of her way and stood on tiptoe, her finger under his nose. "Don't you 'Quinn' me, buddy. She's doing the right thing by nipping this disaster in the bud. I mean—"

And that precise moment was when it hit her—so hard, she almost fell into Khristos and took out her easel of discontent. But it wasn't like the night before, that incredible, warm certainty.

It was jolting and fast and almost painful in its intensity as it grabbed her intestines and tugged with such ferocity, she lost her breath.

"Quinn!" Khristos grabbed at her as she began to fall forward, her knees buckling.

She looked up at him in helpless question, everything else in the room blurring but his face. "Cupid?" she asked, almost unable to get the word out from her lips at the pain tearing her apart.

Nina was there, too, in a flash of movement and hoodie, bracing her from behind, her hands surprisingly gentle as she cupped Quinn's elbows and supported her. "Kiddo?"

But everything else had faded away, everything but the pain and the certainty of this match. "*Cupid!*" she whispered on a groan as another stab of searing-hot pain ripped through her.

The man and the woman had moved just behind Khristos. She caught a brief glimpse over his shoulder of their faces, full of concern

They stood together, her shoulder touching the top of his chest as they each scrambled for their phones. But her hands shook, and his phone was out of charge, according to his yelp of dismay.

So he took the phone from her and held it steady as she peered over the top of it and ran her finger over the screen, their heads now touching. While her fingers flew over the phone, he looked down at her and inhaled, his once hard-as-chips-of-ice eyes gentle and almost surprised.

When the last gut-punch of agony grabbed her and tossed her insides like a salad, she clenched her teeth together and gave the order on an urgent whisper, "*Now!*"

Like an old friend, trusty and steadfast, the arrow arced over the couple's heads and tagged each of them in the heart, melting into multicolored sparkles.

Love bloomed—perfect and everlasting, making them both look into each other's eyes in wonder.

And even through the haze of shooting, fiery jabs of pain—it was beautiful and deep and real. So real, Quinn could almost taste the sweet tang of it on her tongue.

Well, then.

Namaste.

Namaste.

CHAPTER 10

Khristos carried her out of the art class with Nina hot on his heels, his heart pounding in his chest. He held her close to him, as though trying to absorb her pain. If he just kept her as close as possible, he'd somehow take the distortion of her beautiful face from agony to that impish smile she lavished on people with such generosity.

The one that made his chest tight and his fingers itch to run through her hair.

"Did you make sure they didn't call 911?" he asked Nina.

"I got it all covered. I told them she's off her meds, and that's why she fainted. They're so diggin' each other, it's a wonder they even managed to see the fucking phone."

Quinn's head bounced upward. "I heard what you said to them, Nina. You said I had irritable bowel syndrome."

"Oh, shut your piehole, Goddess-Lite. I had to think fast."

Quinn began to squirm against him, her once limp hands struggling to brace herself into a sitting position. "Put me down, Khristos! I'm okay now. Whatever it was passed."

Whatever it was. What the fuck was it?

No match had ever gone down like that. There was no pain involved in it—no suffering. He knew firsthand how the emotions felt. His mother had taught him well to know all the signs, see and feel all the highs and even the lows.

But none of them damn well hurt. Not the way they'd appeared to hurt *her*. Last night, she'd been smacked into the hard pavement and she hadn't made a peep.

She might declare she was a chicken, but not when it came to pain—which meant, whatever happened back at that studio had to have been pretty bad.

"Did you hear me, Khristos with a K? Put me down!"

"I'm not putting you down until we're back at your place. So suck it," he said.

She twisted his nipple through his jacket. "Khristos! Put me down!"

He stopped in the middle of the busy sidewalk, Nina reaching over him to tighten Quinn's scarf and make sure her hat was covering her ears. "Okay, but if you face plant again and get any more scraped up than you already are, I'm not responsible for what your mother's going to do to me. You don't want her to chew my face off, do you?"

"Jesus, kiddo. What the hell? You scared the shit out of us."

Quinn hit her feet and wobbled a little, reaching for the brick wall of a store. Then she straightened and batted her eyelashes at Nina. "I scared you? You of the big muscles and cold, black heart? Know what that means, don't you?"

"It means if you do it again, I take you out and I don't have to worry about it anymore?"

Quinn grinned, but it was weak, and he sensed it. She tugged on a strand of Nina's long hair. "It means I've grown on you. Maybe it's only like mold or whatever bacteria, but I've grown on you. You really are a marshmallow just like Ingrid said."

Nina growled under her breath and tipped her sunglasses down her nose so Quinn could see her eyes. "Walk, or I'm going to eat your skinny little bird legs right off your body and pick my teeth with their bones."

Quinn reached upward with a notable shaky hand and patted Nina's lean cheek. "Clearly someone didn't paint away their discontent."

Nina moved in closer and flashed her fangs. "*Move* or I'm hiking your featherweight ass over my shoulder like the sack of potatoes you are."

But Quinn only chuckled. "If only my scale said featherweight. I might be short, but my hips don't lie."

Nina pointed in the direction of home. "*Now.*"

"On it, Boss."

As Quinn turned to make her way down along the sidewalk, Khristos cupped her elbow, unable to let her too far from his grasp.

Yet, her excitement was uncontained. "So, OMG, right? Who knew those two should end up together?"

"Sometimes, the most unlikely people, people who appear so ill-suited it makes you cringe, are true soul mates. I tried to tell you."

"Was that the part where you were clenching your teeth and you had that tic in your jaw?"

He laughed as he navigated them through the crowd. "Somewhere around there. You were so busy sharing your bad experiences and bonding, I worried you'd talk yourself out of their match. You have to be careful not to let your experiences cloud your judgment, Quinn. It's important. Those two are going to do great things together for children in Doctors Without Borders."

Her sigh was one of happiness, her eyes full of that special brand of Quinn wonder. "How unbelievably romantic."

Then she stopped dead, her eyes wide in revelation. "I'm just like my mother. Oh, criminy, I'm just like her. Bitter and preachy," she said on a groan.

He grabbed her hand, not just because she needed a reminder of how different she was from her mother, but because he liked how it fit in his. "No. You're not that bitter. That takes time, and long, dark nights spent raging against life instead of living it. You have plenty of hope left in you, Quinn. I promise."

She sagged against him. "My mother drives me crazy, but I hate hearing she was in such a dark place. If there's one thing I want, almost more than I want a family and all the stupid things people razz me for wanting, I want her to find some measure of happiness."

"She can find her way out of that dark place if she tries." And she could. If she'd just open up to Quinn.

"I like your mother's dark place. Nay. I fucking love it. It's balls-to-the-wall stunning shit," Nina interjected, her hand at Quinn's back.

"But it's not healthy," Quinn reminded Nina. "I know you love all her sarcasm, but you also know complete happiness. I know you do. I see it with Carl and when you talk about your little girl Charlie. My mother doesn't have that, and it hurts my heart."

Nina's face changed in the blink of an eye. "You know what, you're right, Mini-Goddess. I lost my mother to drugs when I was a kid. I hate thinking she left this earth so fucking unhappy."

Quinn shot the vampire a look of pure sympathy. "I'm sorry, Nina."

Nina's look was far away. Khristos knew well the pain losing her mother had wrought in her life, but her grandmother, Lou, had helped ease that hurt since she was a teenager.

Nina nodded. "Me too. She had some serious problems. But I've got my Nana Lou, and she's pretty righteous."

Quinn sighed with a forlorn shrug. "The problem with my mother is, I don't know what to do about her unhappiness."

Nina strolled beside her, her long legs eating up the pavement. "It ain't up to you to do anything about it, kiddo. You can't be responsible for her happiness. She has to be."

Quinn appeared to give that some thought before she patted the vampire's arm. "Sage vampire is sage. But let's not talk about my mother anymore. There'll be plenty to talk about when we get back to my place. Tell me about that couple back there. How do you know so much about these people and why don't I know anything?"

Khristos dug out his phone from his pocket and held it up. "I get their information from the gods."

Her eyes grew wide and round when she clapped her hands. "Oh! Can I see?"

"Uh, no. You're not ready for the forums just yet."

"The gods have forums?"

"We're very twenty-first century, complete with wifi and everything."

Quinn let her head fall back on her shoulders when she laughed. "If you have apps, I'll just die."

"Don't start digging your grave just yet, but yep. With apps, too."

This time she laughed harder, hearty and rich with texture.

He really shouldn't like watching her laugh. He shouldn't like the sound of it in his ears. It shouldn't do that weird shift thing in his heart.

But it did.

Careful, Khristos. Be very careful.

"Quinn! So glad you're home!" Marty greeted her at the door, but it sounded more like, "Thank Jesus and all twelve you're back. Here. Take your mother." Her voice was tight and her eyes were bleary.

Ingrid sat between them, a consoling hand on each of their laps. She mouthed "help" to Quinn.

Aw, hell.

Wanda's face was weary when she looked up from her spot on the couch, a cold pack on her head. "Hi, honey. How was your day?"

Quinn rushed to the couch, ignoring the residual dull tremors still coursing through her body.

Her mother had struck. No one knew that look of total physical and mental exhaustion better than Quinn. "Don't worry about me. How are you two?" She motioned for Ingrid to make room on the couch then grabbed Wanda's hand and patted the space beside her for Marty to sit.

Wanda blew out a tired breath. "It would be a falsehood to say your mother is crazy hard to please."

"I'm *so* sorry. I knew she'd wear even you two down. She's difficult and critical and I shouldn't have let you offer to take her to the other room, let alone a day of shopping and the bird sanctuary."

Marty shook her head, tucking her mussed hair behind her ear and stretching her legs with a groan. "*How* did you do it, Quinn? That's what I wanna know. *Nothing* satisfies her. From where we chose to take her to lunch right down to the way the bird sanctuary tour was set up."

"She's not exactly cookies and warm milk, is she?" Quinn said, patting Marty's thigh.

"Oh no," Wanda murmured, closing her eyes and pressing the cold pack to her forehead. "She's shivs and testicle-hacking all the bloody way."

"That poor man who mistakenly bumped into her in line to see the penguins. Do you think he's scraped his ass off the floor of the sanctuary yet?"

Wanda giggled wearily. "Nope. But I bet he knows way more than he ever wanted to about male privilege."

"It's like she wrote it psalm and verse," Marty said on a moan.

Quinn sat up and moved to the edge of the couch. "I'm really, really sorry. I knew she'd spoil things because that's just my mom. It's why I live in Manhattan in a rundown apartment and she lives in Jersey. We need that bridge to keep me from committing homicide."

Wanda pulled the pack from her eyes. "You do know it's not you, don't you, Quinn? That you're absolutely not the reason she's so harsh and critical, right?"

Quinn shrugged. She'd tried for many years to convince herself it wasn't her, but everything had changed once her father left. "Most of the time, yes. Logically I know her ball-busting has nothing to do with me. In my heart? Not always so much."

Marty tilted her head and smiled, small lines of exhaustion wreathing her eyes. "Because you want her to find peace and it hurts to know she's in so much pain. I get that."

Guilt overwhelmed her. "You guys have done enough. I'd bet you want out of here pronto. So go home to your families. I'll be all right. And I'll handle my mother."

Wanda shook her head. "That's not how this works, sweetie. We stay for the long haul until we're comfortable that *you're* comfortable and all bad guys or the possibility of bad guys is eliminated. No man-hating mother can scare us off. It's what we do."

A commotion in the kitchen led to Archibald's terse tone. "I believe I've told you, madam, I have the roast well under control. It must sit for ten minutes before one slices it. To do otherwise is unseemly!"

"Isn't that just like a man to—"

"Mom!" Quinn was off the couch and around the corner to the kitchen where a harried Archibald stood, knife in hand.

"You're *finally* back," Helen said, readjusting her turtleneck.

Quinn held on to her patience—tight. "You say that as though I left you with Satan to the seventh level of hell. It's not like I knew you were dropping in for a visit, Mom. I had plans today."

"With your gay friend who couldn't charm a woman if he went to charm school."

Quinn felt that same old anxiety in the pit of her stomach her mother always stirred up. "Mom, *please* don't be so rude. Marty and Wanda showed you a lovely time, and you're in here harassing Archibald, who, by the way, is cooking you an amazing dinner."

"*Baby, you're a firework!*" Nina sang, gripping Helen's shoulders and almost lifting her off the floor as she guided her mother out of the kitchen. "C'mon, Mama Bear. It's time to yank that stick outta your keister and take a breather from your reign as Beatdown Queen. Even queens need a vacay."

Her mother prepared to protest, but Nina shook her finger in admonishment. "Nuh-uh-uh, Bruiser. This kitchen's too damn small, even for your mini butt. Now no more squawking. Get a move on, little doggie." Nina pointed to the living room and Helen actually clamped her mouth shut and listened, letting the vampire lead her out of the kitchen.

Quinn blew out a breath of relief before she glanced at Archibald and Darnell, the latter of whom wiped his face with one of her kitchen towels. "I'm sorry."

"Lawd ha' mercy. She's some kinda tornado wrapped in a hurricane, Miss Quinn," Darnell said, leaning his elbows on the countertop. "You okay?"

"She's done this all my life. I'm used to it."

Archibald smoothed his hair back into place, straightened his suit jacket, and shot her a gaze full of tea and sympathy. "My apologies, Mistress Quinn. I was sharp with your mother, but she'd been quite vocal for over an hour about my roast—"

"And we all know Arch here don't like nobody finaglin' with his food, right, Foodie?" Darnell cackled, his large frame shaking with laughter.

Quinn held up her hands and shook her head. "It's totally understandable. My mother could drive Jesus to drink. I'm sorry she's been hassling you when you've all been so kind to uproot your lives just to make me feel comfortable and help me get through this."

Darnell wrapped his beefy arm around her shoulder and squeezed. "It ain't no thang, Miss Quinn. That's what we're here for."

Archibald stared at her for a moment before his eyes became tender. "I simply cannot figure it."

She rubbed his arm in "Helen Was Here" sympathy. "Figure what, Arch?"

"How someone as lovely as you came from…well, from someone so cross."

Quinn beamed a smile at him and snatched a piece of the delicious bread Arch had placed in a basket. "That's the nicest thing anyone's ever said to me, Arch."

She popped the tasty morsel in her mouth and headed back out into the fire to find her mother sitting docilely at the table as Nina gave her the warning glare.

In all this, she'd forgotten about Carl. There were many things her mother might not question, being as wrapped up in herself and her anger as she was, but Carl—*Carl* Helen would take to task, and nothing, not even her mother's sharp tongue, would let Quinn allow that.

Khristos waggled a finger at her from across the room, summoning her.

Every time she looked at him, her heart skipped a beat, and that had to stop. She was still so fresh from her breakup with Igor, why was she reacting this way toward him? It had to be rebound related.

Yet, she found herself crossing the small space between them and taking his hand when he pulled her into the bathroom.

Closing the door behind him, he said, "Talk to me."

She backed up against the sink and leaned on it, attempting to create distance between them. There was hardly any space between them as it was, any closer and she'd pass out. "Wait, first, where's Carl? I'm so panicked my mother's going to find out about him and terrorize his sweet soul, he'll wish that crazy witch doctor had finished him off."

Khristos's lips twisted into a smile of complete understanding. "According to Darnell, he took him back to Nina's for the night—or at least until your mother goes home."

She took another deep sigh of relief. "Thank goodness."

"Now, that talk?"

"About?"

"About what happened today in art class."

"Um, I found the core of my discontent. Damn monkey bars."

He brushed her still tender cheek with his knuckles. "That's not what I mean, Quinn. What happened when you made that match? You were in agony—in real pain. I want to know what it felt like. What was going on?"

"Like someone was sticking a hot poker into my guts? Wait. Isn't a tough match supposed to feel like that? I was kind of going with the theory of no pain, no gain. I mean, those two were hell on wheels. If I didn't have this power, never in a million years would I have matched them."

Looking down at her, Khristos shook his head. "No, Quinn. It's *never* supposed to feel like that."

Oh, good. Her stomach plummeted as she gripped the edge of the sink. "So that means bad guys?"

"I don't quite understand how, but I'm swaying toward yes."

Now her breathing hitched. "So what do we do?"

"We find my mother and figure this out."

"You know, something's been bothering me for a while now. Why would your mother put her powers in an apple, of all things? Isn't that just a little crazy? I mean, for the love of God, she has the power to create life. It's not like you should leave something like that just lying around. Because I'm here to tell you, I'm keeping mine on the inside, not storing them in, say, a bunch of bananas."

Khristos laughed. It reverberated off the walls of her bathroom and landed square in her chest. "I guess in her defense, who'd think she'd stick the entirety of her powers in an apple? Because it *is* damn crazy."

"Right. Hide in plain sight. So now we need to find out who wants them and why they don't want me to have them. If that's what this is at all. I mean, maybe it was just some intestinal thing."

"Nope. Something's going on."

"Of course. Wishful thinking."

"Now, one more question."

Somehow, they'd managed to inch closer. Her body was just drawn to his like a magnet to a fridge, and there was nowhere else to go. "Shoot."

"Where's your father? Do you see him?"

Her smile was hindered by the fact that she didn't see him as often since he'd moved to California. "I do. He's remarried now to a really nice lady named Stella, and very happy. But he avoids my mother at all costs, and I avoid telling her I see him."

"It must be tough to hide how you feel about him. Tougher still not to share your moments with him out loud."

"Tough is an understatement. I can't even speak his name without her biting my head off. I still don't know why they divorced, but I remember the fights before they broke up. Epic. I know rationally they're better off apart, but it was hard on me at the time. What about you? Who is your father, anyway?"

His grin went facetious. "You really wanna know?"

"Duh. Especially if it's some awesome Greek god."

"If only my blood were that pure. My father was a poor peasant my mother fell in love with for about twenty-two seconds because a rival of hers had her eye on him. Then she dumped him. This was long before birth control was invented. He was a total mortal, but a great, honest, hardworking guy. Taught me to love my mom for who she was instead of offering her my love as ransom if she'd just change her wicked ways. But it was a long road getting there. Which was how I inherited babysitting the apple to begin with. From her anger when I wouldn't produce grandchildren with just anyone because she said I should."

Quinn's eyes flew wide open in surprise. "So you're half mortal?"

"Technically speaking, yep."

"So you sort of know my struggle with a strong, willful mother."

"Sort of," he responded. "My mother and I butted heads for many centuries over her poor behavior. She was a vengeful, exceptionally vain woman. Not in the violent, I'll-rip-your-limbs-off way, but in a spiteful, I'll-steal-your-man, have-your-luscious-hair-shaved-off-your-head-and-make-sure-it-never-grows-back kind of way. My father's the one who taught me patience and the value of kindness."

How bizarre to hear these insider stories after spending so much of her life reading about the gods. "You say your mother *was* vengeful and vain. She's not anymore?"

"Oh, she's still plenty vain, and we tease her incessantly about it by giving her gilded hand mirrors and wrinkle cream for Christmas. But she's mellowed over time. It's not that she wasn't a decent enough parent to me, because believe it or not, she was. Always around, always there when you needed her. But she's had some moments we've argued over. My father taught me to stand my ground if I believed I was right—and I did. Not always without detriment to my person," he said on a chuckle.

"So when she wanted you to marry and have children, she got angry with you and saddled you with the apple out of spite."

"She thought I was too much like her. Too busy playing the field, irresponsible, etcetera, and the apple was her lesson to me. And I let her *think* I was too busy playing the field."

Wait. What? "*Let* her think you were bed-hopping?"

"Yep. I worked hard at creating that reputation, too. A well-cultivated plan, if I do say so myself. I used plenty of my mother's tricks. I made up rumors, was seen in all the right places. I wasn't going to end up with the wrong person because of my mother's whim. I'd rather end up with the apple forever than be mated to the wrong person. I didn't do it out of spite. I did it out of a sense of integrity. What would my father's legacy mean if I wasn't true not just to myself, but the person I chose to spend the rest of my immortality with?"

Her mouth fell open.

He traced a finger over the outline of her lips, making her fight a shiver. "Your mouth is open."

"That's me and my astonishment. Give me a minute and it'll close on its own."

Khristos laughed, his minty breath fanning her face. "I sense you have a million questions, grasshopper."

Yeah, like who knew this man she'd totally believed had chosen the bed sport as his life's mission was so honorable? "Maybe more like a million and two—"

The sound of knuckles against the door made them both jump apart.

"Dinner, lovebirds! Knock off the spit-swap in there!" Nina called from behind the door.

Quinn cleared her throat and slipped under his arm, reaching for the door. "We'd better get out there before my mother finds out you're not gay and makes it her mission in life to tack your manhood to her wall—but we're not done here, Khristos with a K!"

She scooted out the door and around the corner to find her mother and everyone gathered at the table. Steaming bowls of food lined the center, just like the first night she'd come home after her initial bout with matchmaking.

Seeing all these people crammed into her apartment did exactly what it had the first night she'd witnessed it.

It made her smile. Filled her with warmth and friendship.

Until her mother just couldn't let well enough alone.

As Archibald prepared to slice the roast—a roast surrounded by fat red new potatoes, roasted carrots so orange they glistened under the glow of the candles; a roast that looked as though it had been pulled from the pages of a cooking magazine—he struggled with Quinn's one and only knife. A dull one that should have been sharpened long ago.

"So much for letting it *sit*," her mother said with a sneer of ugly glee.

Nina nudged Helen with a roll of her eyes. "Aw, c'mon, Mini-Mom. Didn't we just talk about this? Put your napkin in your lap, sit quietly, and behave."

Helen shrugged, tugging on the ends of her shortly bobbed hair. "I'm just making mention, men know nothing…"

Her mother's voice trailed off then, becoming a muted babble of sound. A sound that Quinn could no longer bear—and that's when something inside her snapped.

The break was almost physical, cracking in her ears when she popped up out of her chair and pointed at her mother. "*Get out!*"

There was a hushed silence that followed, painful and without even one gasp.

Helen looked up at her. "Excuse me, young lady?"

Quinn pushed her chair out and grabbed the back of her mother's, dragging it from the table. "I said get out! *Get out now.* Take your anger and your man-hate and your fury-filled rants about anything and everything you touch and quit shitting all over my life!"

Nina was the first to rise, putting a hand on Quinn's shoulder and squeezing so hard, she almost buckled. "Kiddo, chill. Think about this."

But Quinn brushed Nina's hand from her shoulder, her own shaking. "No! No more thinking, Nina! No more endless, ungrateful, angry, hateful words! These people are here to help me, Mom. Me, during one of the hardest things I've ever gone through. But you wouldn't know that because you didn't even ask me how I was. Not from the moment you put your foot over the threshold of my home. They put their families, their children, their lives on hold just to help *me*, and I will not have you taking unfair potshots at them because *you* hate your life and men and an endless assortment of things I can't even keep track of anymore. This is my home. Mine, and I don't want it filled with your vitriol! Now, get—out!" she roared, stomping toward the door and opening it with a harsh yank.

For the first time in Helen Morris's life, she didn't say anything. She gathered her purse and her coat, thin-lipped and a face full of fury, and leave she did.

To the stunned surprise of everyone in the room.

CHAPTER 11

Quinn gasped for breath as she hung on to the doorknob and slammed the door behind her mother's retreating form.

She closed her eyes, letting what she'd just done wash over her in wave after wave of sadness.

Khristos approached her first, his tall frame blocking everyone else out. He brushed the hair from her eyes.

But she shook her head, reaching for her own coat on the rack by the door, tears swelling in her eyes, her throat threatening to close up. "Don't. I just can't right now. I need…time. Just a little. *Please.*"

Nina dug Quinn's phone out of her purse and put it in her hand as Marty gently wrapped a scarf around her neck and Wanda tucked her gloves in the pocket of her jacket. "Call. Call if you need me—or us," Nina said. "We're never far behind."

She took one last look at Khristos before she ran up the stairs and broke into a light jog, ignoring her still sore ankle, ignoring the people she almost crashed into, ignoring everything but the need to flee her mother's oppressive hatred.

As her lungs began to burn, and her foot began to throb, she slowed down near one of her favorite parks where a swing set sat, abandoned in light of the freezing weather and hour of the day.

A sob finally escaped her lips when she sat on the swing—one of the deepest sorrows she'd ever experienced. Her mother was toxic, unable to climb out of her pit of anguish mired in hatred, but Quinn's heart was breaking for her.

Though the theme in their lives had almost always been a paranoia-filled rant of get-them-before-they-get-you, there had been good times. Few and far between, but still good.

But tonight…tonight when she was so happy about the matches she'd made, when she wanted to share that joy with someone—with anyone— she'd wished more than ever she could share it with her mother.

To hear her dig at the OOPS clan was the very last straw.

Leaning against the chain holding the swing, she let the years of frustration and fighting happen. Let them swell up inside, rising and falling with each memory that took her further and further away from her mother.

And she cried, tears dripping down her cheeks to splash on the hard dirt at her feet, her face raw from the salty wetness pelted by the cold wind, her heart one big ache.

She didn't care if crying made her weak. She had to let this relationship with her mother go, this soul-eating, agonizing tug-of-war go, or end up swallowed by the toxic waste, bobbing along until another hit came her way.

But she was damn well going to mourn it the way it deserved before she did.

Her sobs wrenched from her chest, a physical stab to her flesh with each gasp for air until hands, firm and strong, wrapped around her waist and pulled her from the swing.

Scooping her up, Khristos carried her to the park bench, tucking her to him and cradling her close as he sat down.

He set his chin on top of her head, now curled into his neck, and rocked her, a soothing lull of slow, rhythmic ease. His free hand cupped her face, letting her bury her chin in his shoulder.

She didn't know how long they sat that way or when her tears began to subside, but as the heartache of so many years full of anguish began to lessen, she realized something.

This was what she wanted in a man. A man who would silently hold her in the stormy sea of torment. A man who would provide safe harbor without condemnation or judgment.

"I kicked my mother out of my house," she finally said, her throat hoarse and raw.

"You sure did."

"I was awful."

He stroked her hair and continued to rock. "Nah. This has been coming for a long time. With the added pressure of being Aphrodite, you were bound to blow. I won't say I don't wish the two of you had found a better way to work this out, but it's a wakeup call for you both."

"Says the man whose mother tied him to an apple for eternity."

Khristos chuckled. "Says the man who willingly guards it in order to stick to his guns for eternity. What you did tonight was stick to your guns,

Quinn. Was it harsh and heated? Yep. But there has to come a time in your life when you stand up for what you want and let go of what's hurting you. You want to live a life full of love and happiness, and your mother only brings her worst to the table. It's hard to hold your head up above the water when someone's always dunking it back under. But you did."

She shuddered against him. Oh, she did all right. She really did. "I don't know what happened. I just lost it completely. Archibald had made such a beautiful meal and to have her pick it apart...one more hateful criticism and I think I would have lost my mind."

"And now you have to mend it."

She sat up and looked him in the eye. "Are you kidding me? My mother's never going to let that go—not ever. In her mind, I was disrespectful and rude and that won't go without some serious begging and scraping. I can't beg her to forgive me for telling her the truth, and I can't accept the way she behaves anymore. It hurts."

Khristos cupped her cheek, wiping the remaining tears from her face while she fought not to curl into the warmth of his palm. "Will you come somewhere with me? There's something I need to show you."

She slid off his lap more for her own self-preservation than her desire to go anywhere but straight to bed and bury herself under the covers. "Sure," she murmured.

Darnell popped out from behind an oak tree and smiled, his eyes sad. He held open his arms to her and she walked right into them without hesitation. "What are you doing here?"

"I'm on bad-guy watch and hug patrol," he said on a chuckle, giving her a tight, warm squeeze. "So you ready, Miss Quinn?"

She took a step back from his comforting embrace. "For?"

"Hold my hand," he said. "You, too, big guy."

In seconds, they were on a quiet sidewalk beneath a streetlamp.

Her eyes went wide. "Did we just...?" Had he just...No. She couldn't say it. It was too surreal.

Darnell grinned and snapped his fingers, the flash of his rings gleaming. "Poof. Just like that. I'll be across the street if ya need me, Boss." Hands in his pockets, the demon strolled off to a small square across the street with the wink of his eye.

Khristos pulled her to him and pointed. "Look over there, Quinn. Right inside that big picture window."

She peered in the direction of his finger and saw her mother.

Helen sat with Maude, one of her oldest friends, at a small table inside a charming café with red tablecloths and candles encased in enormous black lanterns. The glow made her face look softer, kinder, her eyes less like laser beams of death.

Maude was a nice woman she'd only met from time to time on her rare visits to Jersey. She'd been surprised by their friendship, due to Maude's easygoing nature. Maude was cookies and milk and her hair all done up in a soft, graying bun at the back of her head. Soft-spoken, gentle, easy to talk to. All the things her mother wasn't.

But seeing her mother looking across the table at Maude, with an expression she never though Helen capable of, dredged up residual hurt for Quinn.

She thought she was done after throwing her mother out of her apartment, but that helpless, angry thread she'd clung to when she'd screamed at her mother just wouldn't let her go.

Quinn wanted to rush in and demand she take back all the horrible words she'd flung at these people who were so giving, who'd stuck out this Aphrodite thing with her, because her mother was looking at Maude in a way she'd never looked at Quinn. And it hurt.

Khristos held her arm, pulling her close. "Please wait, Quinn. Don't do or say anything before you listen."

But this time, she shook her head and brushed him off. "You're always telling me to listen, but there's nothing to listen to. My mother said dreadful, awful things to people who've been very kind to me, and I just won't have it anymore. You were there. How can ask me to wait? Now, let me go!"

"No, Quinn. You'll stay right here," he ordered.

Just as she was about to protest again, he snapped his fingers and her mother's voice was in her ear, clear as a bell.

"Listen, Quinn. *Listen.*"

"Maude…there's something we need to talk about. Something *I* need to talk about."

Quinn rolled her eyes. *Good luck, Maude.* Her mother didn't talk to you. She talked *at* you as though you were the defense and she was the prosecution.

But Maude tilted her head in a question and nodded. "You can always talk to me, Helen. You know that." She reached her hand across the table and grabbed her mother's hand, giving her fingers a squeeze.

"I'm not a very nice person, Maude. I've been horrible to everyone around me for so many years. I've been critical and mean-spirited and ugly. Not just to other people, but to Quinn. The one person I love most in this world."

Quinn stood rooted to the spot. Her mother was admitting her faults? Out loud? In public? To Maude?

She peered up at Khristos in skepticism. "Is the world coming to an end? Should we gather up Carl and have him teach us about zombies so we're prepared?"

The rumble of laughter in Khristos's chest was deep, pinging off the buildings surrounding them. "No. But you do need to hush your pretty mouth."

Maude cocked her head, her brow furrowed in confusion. "You're being pretty hard on yourself, aren't you, Helen? You've never been cruel to me, and we've been friends for a hundred years."

Her mother's smile was full of irony. "That's because you wouldn't allow it, now would you? But I've run roughshod over Quinn and her life and it took a very pale, very smart woman to help me figure that out tonight."

Nina? Shut the front door.

"She reminded me today that, my unwarranted hatred toward the opposite sex aside, my daughter grew into an amazing young women who's kind and warm and believes in miracles—despite me. Maybe even to spite me."

Quinn gripped Khristos's hands, now securely around her waist. Who was this person? This soft soul, talking to someone else as though she actually cared about their opinion?

"Quinn's a great kid, Helen. I've always said so. A dreamer, no doubt, but dreams are what keep us alive, keep us reaching for something more."

Helen scoffed. "And I crushed all of her dreams. The woman she is today really has nothing to do with me. She did it all on her own—to survive me. While I was hating David for divorcing me, she was raising herself and living out the lives of the characters in her mountains of books."

"You really loved David. His betrayal didn't make any sense, honey."

Helen shook her head. "No. I never loved David, Maude. I wanted to. I tried to, and when I just couldn't, I took it out on him. Took it out on Quinn."

Maude's face was astonished, the wrinkles of concern on her forehead deepening. "But—"

"I know, I know. Appearances can be deceiving. When I got pregnant with Quinn, the only thing to do back then was get married or have my parents disown me. David was my first sexual experience and we were foolish. But he tried so hard to make it work. It just didn't. It could never have worked."

Quinn was floored, but she kept listening and clinging to Khristos.

"I came into the city while I thought Quinn would still be in Greece because I knew you'd be here visiting your sister this week, Maude, and I know how much you love this café. I wanted to tell you something here—in this place where we've shared so many happy memories."

Maude grinned and patted Helen's hand. "We've had some great times here, haven't we?"

"Some of the best in my life. *You're* one of the best things in my life, and I want you to just listen to my words. You can walk away when I'm done, and I'll understand, but will you please just hear me out?"

Quinn held her breath, sucking the cold night air into her lungs.

Maude held her breath, too. Quinn saw her slight chest rise as she nodded.

Her mother gulped, the hard sound of her swallow riddled with insecurity—something new and foreign to Quinn. "David was my first *male* sexual experience, Maude. Wouldn't you know I'd get pregnant, trying to please everyone but me? He was a good guy. Funny and smart, and it just sort of happened. And even though it was an accident, I'll never regret Quinn. But back then, well, you just didn't do what I'm about to do, and all these years, I've been angry about marrying someone I didn't want to marry. Would never have married in this day and age of awareness and rallies and Twitter."

Maude continued to sit quietly, her hand still in her mother's, the other on the stem of her wineglass.

Helen took a deep breath. "I married David because society said to marry him. Because my parents expected me to marry him. I thought by marrying him, I could hide who I was, stamp it out, but it only made me hate myself—hate everyone around me, and when he left, which was the right thing to do, he told me to be true to myself, no matter the cost. Instead, I lashed out until I didn't know I was lashing out anymore. Until it became second nature to bash anyone I could touch. Mostly anyone male."

A tear slid down Maude's and Quinn's cheeks simultaneously, but still, they both remained silent.

"My frustration at hiding who I am all these years boiled over this week as I tried to prepare myself for this conversation. I hurt Quinn and her friends and insulted them enough that she booted me right out of her house. And she was right to. I deserved it. I went too far over to the other side. But I want to come back. I so desperately want to come back. With you. *To* you, if you'll let me. I love you, Maude. I've loved you from the moment we talked about seeing the Black-cheeked lovebird in Zambia.

119

When we dreamed someday we'd take a trip somewhere exotic to observe rare birds."

Quinn and Maude gasped in unison.

That moment, that silent, palpable moment, would stay with Quinn forever as she mentally prayed Maude felt the same way about Helen. Prayed her mother had finally found peace, contentment—joy.

Maude slid from her chair, tears streaming down her face, and knelt in front of her mother. Letting her head rest on Helen's lap, she whispered, "I've waited for you for so long…"

Quinn's heart stopped beating then and she only heard the sound of *their* hearts. Of their love—a love her mother had been too ashamed to admit. A love she'd fought and tortured herself over. A love Maude had waited twenty years to experience.

Everything made sense in that moment. *Everything.*

She turned and looked up at Khristos with wonder. "Them," she whispered.

"Yes, Quinn. Them."

Closing her eyes, tears still falling from her face, Quinn mentally summoned Cupid, her pulse racing at this gift she'd been given—this ability to put one of the people she loved most in the world into the arms of someone who'd finally make her happy.

"Now!" Quinn murmured, shaking and hushed.

The arrow appeared out of nowhere, glowing more magnificently than it had in any of her matches so far, melting through the big picture window of the café, and landing perfectly on her mother. The shower of color sprayed over them, shooting upward and disappearing, leaving a residual glow.

Quinn shuddered a happy sigh and leaned back into Khristos wordlessly, enraptured, at peace,

A light snow began to fall, swirling around them in soft, wet flakes, and the wind howled, rushing against her wet cheeks as she stood and watched her mother and her new lover laugh, cry, sip wine and discover each other.

CHAPTER 12

Khristos pushed the door open to her apartment to find everyone sitting quietly around the table. They all jumped up, obviously prepared to offer their comfort to her, but Khristos, as intuitive as always, held up a hand to thwart them.

Quinn didn't hesitate when she sorted her way through the chairs and threw her arms around Nina's neck. "Thank you," was all she was capable of saying. "*Thank you.*"

Nina didn't speak, but she grabbed Quinn's hand and pressed it to her cheek and nodded.

In turn, Quinn gave everyone a hug, inhaling their scents of vanilla and musk, pinching Archibald's cheek, sharing a smile with Ingrid, thanking them silently before she made her way to the bedroom and closed the door.

She needed to absorb the information behind the doors her mother had unlocked tonight. To reflect on all the angry words her mother had once imparted and let this new light, this newest revelation, shine on them.

Pulling off her clothes, she didn't ever bother to put her pajamas on. Instead, she pulled Khristos's borrowed sweater into her arms and tucked it beneath her chin, inhaling the scent of him as she climbed under her covers and closed her eyes.

She smiled into the darkness just before she fell fast asleep.

Someone sat on the edge of her bed, and she stirred. Rolling over, she focused in on Khristos, his hair wet from a shower, his olive skin made deeper by the dark stubble littering his jaw. "A match needed?"

He shook his head and smiled down at her as she tried to sit up, placing his hand on her shoulder to encourage her to lie back down. "Nope. I was just checking on you to be sure you were all right, or if maybe you wanted something to eat? You missed dinner."

She knew he was doing this out of his sense of duty to the apple and his mother. She knew his kindness had a string attached. She just wished he didn't make her heart beat so fast or her knees feel so wobbly. Or worse, have that compelling way of making her feel as if she was important, as though he actually cared about her beyond her duties as Aphrodite.

But that was all in her head. She knew it. She'd do well to pay attention to it.

So she decided to avoid how she was feeling in favor of something she'd wondered about all the way home. "So, my dad…"

Khristos peered down at her, brushing her hair from her face. "What about him?"

"He knew. He always knew about my mom and he never said a word."

"I think he knew it wasn't his story to tell. Those words had to come from your mother. It was her secret to share, and no amount of reassurance from anyone would have helped until she was ready."

"I'm glad she was finally ready." The relief she felt over her mother's confession was full bodied.

"You were amazing tonight, Quinn. Exactly as Aphrodite should be."

His words of praise made her cheeks warm and her breathing hitch. "It was obvious my mom and Maude should be together. There wasn't much to do but let that arrow fly."

"Still, you're getting better, stronger, more sure. That's a good thing."

"Will it make a difference in leniency for you if I'm making the grade?" she asked.

"Don't think about me."

"I can't help it." She really couldn't help it. He was impossible to not think about.

"I just wanted to check on you, not put another issue on your plate. Go back to sleep."

But she grabbed his arm as he began to rise. "Wait. How did you know what was really going on with my mother?"

He sat back down, the scent of his freshly washed hair wafting in her nose. "I did a little digging. I couldn't put my finger on it, but something was off, ringing untrue for me. You were pretty wrecked and I hated seeing that. So I reached out on the forums—"

"And poof—like magic, right?" she whispered up at him. God, he was decent, and as men went, sensitive but gruff all at once, and so many adjectives she was rapidly losing count.

"Yeah," he whispered back with a grin. "Poof."

"Thank you, Khristos with a K. I feel like I'll never be able to say that enough."

On impulse, she wrapped her arms around him and hugged him hard, forgetting she was completely naked under the covers. When her nipples, rigid from the cool air, brushed his chest, Khristos groaned, and so did she. Long and low, their breaths mingled, their moans winding together.

Their mouths found each other on a surprised breath, their tongues tentatively touching before Khristos drove his deep.

Her hands clenched his thickly muscled shoulders in a moment of pure bliss. White flashes of light appeared behind her eyelids at the taste of his tongue.

His hands drove into her hair, wrapping the long length around his wrist, pulling her head back until his lips left hers and his mouth found the sensitive flesh at the base of her neck.

Khristos nipped it, running his tongue over her flesh to ease the sting then nipping again, making her arch against him.

Quinn pulled the hem of his T-shirt up and over his head, her mouth watering at the idea of touching his naked flesh. She flattened her palms and ran them over his pecs, relishing the tightening of his nipples, luxuriating in the heat of his skin as he rained kisses over her shoulders.

They fell backward on the bed, Khristos shoving the covers aside with his feet and pulling her flush to him. His cock was rigid beneath his jeans, rigid and pressing against the apex of her thighs.

He ran his hands over every inch of her, roaming the slope of her hip, the curve of her ass, setting her on fire with each pass he took. Skimming her ribs, he settled his hands beneath her breast, and she held her breath, forgetting about her impromptu boob job and instead arching into his palm.

Khristos grazed her nipple with his knuckle, making her writhe against him, press into his hard length until she thought her spine would break from the wave of heat settling in her belly.

Quinn fumbled with the zipper on his jeans, tearing it down and driving his pants over his hips until he was able to shrug them off.

And then they were both naked.

Just her and the descendant of a Greek god.

Khristos rolled her to her back, rising up above her on the palms of his hands, taking her mouth in a voracious kiss, licking at her lips, tasting her until she whimpered and wove her hands into his thick hair.

Tearing his mouth from hers, he kissed his way along her jaw, over her collarbone until he was at her breasts, lingering over her needy flesh.

Quinn sucked in a breath, fought not to drag him downward to her nipple, make him devour it until she screamed her pleasure.

But Khristos took his time, circling the flesh, nudging it with his nose, swiping at it with his hot tongue and blowing a breath of air across her rigid skin.

When he finally pulled her nipple into his mouth, she saw stars, all colors of the rainbow as her neck arched and her eyes clenched tight. Khristos ran his tongue over the sensitive bud, pulling at it, licking it, cupping her other breast while liquid heat pooled between her thighs.

Quinn's hands were as anxious to touch him as she was to be touched. Needy and desperate, she flattened her palm against his back, discovering the thick muscles and planes as she did.

As he left her breast and slid down along her rib cage, she gripped the sheets on either side of her, her hips jutting upward toward the heat of his mouth as he swooped down across her hipbone and spread her thighs.

Her heart stopped as Khristos hovered, his lips tormenting her with whispered kisses, his hands stroking her inner thighs, driving her mad with anticipation.

The first swipe of his tongue, just below her belly button, made her jump and hiss a sound of pleasure she had to fight to keep quiet. When he used two fingers to spread her wet flesh, Quinn thought she'd die.

Still, he waited, taking his time, using his thumb and rolling it over her clit, licking her belly, the crease where thigh met hip.

Her pulse pounded in her ears until he took his first stroke, his tongue sure and hot, dragging along her clit, drawing the hard bud into his mouth.

Quinn fought not to cry out, stuffing a knuckle in her mouth, reaching her other hand down to grip Khristos's silky hair. Pleasure, so deep, so intense her stomach coiled into a tight knot, settled over her, raced along her nerve-endings until she felt the white-hot need for release begin to wend its way upward.

Khristos slowed, pulled back, made her whimper her displeasure until he satisfied her craving once more by driving a finger into her. She was slick and wet when he thrust the digit as he licked her, and that was her undoing.

She writhed beneath his talented mouth, rose up, crashing against his lips until sweet relief found her. The aching swirl of desperation driving her to orgasm. Her neck arched, her back bowed, her legs widened as

Khristos slid a hand under her ass and held her flush to him, letting her ride out her climax.

Oh God. If she died right now, she'd be at peace with the passing. Nothing had ever felt like that before.

But Khristos wasn't done. He slid up along her body, his heated flesh finally pressed to hers, molding her to him, pulling her tight until her nipples scraped against his wide chest.

Her hands instantly slipped between his thighs, reaching for his rigid cock, grasping it in her hand, pumping it.

It was thick, long, blistering-hot and rock-hard. The dark of her room kept her from seeing all of him the way she wanted to, but her hands…her hands explored every delectable inch of him.

He groaned into her mouth as she stroked him, thwarted her from slipping away in order to wrap her mouth around the rigid flesh. "No," he whispered, husky and deep. "I need to be inside you *now*."

She shuddered beneath him, his words slicing through her ears like a knife through soft butter.

Without qualm, she lifted her hips, and wrapped her legs around his hips, inviting him to make love to her.

She knew this would only make the moment he left to go back to his life harder, but she didn't care right now.

Now, there was only their naked flesh touching, their sweat gluing their bodies together. Their hearts pounding in time with each other. Their mouths, hot and needy, open and willing.

Khristos positioned himself between her legs, slipping his arm under her waist, hauling her against him as she clung to his neck.

His first thrust was fluid, deep, making her clamp her mouth shut to keep from crying out. Khristos seared her, stretched her, groaned hot against her ear, rolling his hips to drive more deeply into her.

That rush of lava, that unmerciful, unrelenting pleasure, began to build again as their bodies crashed together. She clung to him, letting her hands slide over every inch of available flesh, savoring his skin under palms, loving the feel of her nipples scraping against the small patch of hair on his chest.

And when his thrusts increased, when the rhythm of their bodies synced so perfectly tears stung her eyes, she cried out, unable to hold back. Khristos's heavy weight, pushing her into the bed, his thick cock deeply embedded inside her, the amazing control he possessed as he waited for her to find relief first…

He pulled her tighter, taking her lips, driving his tongue into her mouth over and over, rocking into her with each slick stroke.

Quinn's toes curled as her legs tightened around his lean waist, holding on to his shoulders and letting the wave of hot orgasm sweep her away.

It pulsed from somewhere deep inside her, dragging her upward, raging between her legs with sharp pangs of longing. Digging her nails into Khristos's shoulders, she fought a scream of climax just as his body tensed beneath her, as his strong muscles flexed and tightened.

He kissed her deeper, groaning low and hot as he took one last thrust and came.

Their chests pressed against each other's as they gasped for air and she buried her face in his neck, inhaling the scent of them, fighting tears.

She shouldn't have let this happen. She was still in too much of a commotion about her life and her new job as Aphrodite to handle one more thing on her plate. To handle it in the proper state of mind.

But she couldn't regret making love to this amazing man, this man who had wise words and even wiser insights about who she was. He was decent and patient and nothing about this would ever make her regret her choice.

For tonight.

Tomorrow was a different story.

Tomorrow, he'd realize this was impulsive on both their parts. Realistically speaking, she knew sometimes in the heat of the moment things happened, and she wasn't going to allow herself to get carried away like she had in so many relationships before.

Of course, Khristos would feel the same way, and they'd carry on. Surely their time together was coming to an end anyway. And if someone was really trying to hurt her, the OOPS women would help. She knew they would.

But for tonight, she was going to lie next to this man made out of granite and enjoy the warmth of his delicious body against hers as he took her mouth in another kiss.

Just for tonight.

CHAPTER 13

"Khristos! Wake up!" she whispered urgently, forcing herself to look away from his sleeping form, as gorgeous as if he'd never experienced bed head.

He frowned, attempting to pull her to him, but she put her hand on his chest. "You have to get up and get dressed!"

He scrubbed his hands over his eyes. "What's going on?"

She pointed to her stomach. "I feel it. Like *really* feel it."

He sat up, the covers falling away from him and giving her the first glimpse of his chest in the full light of day. And of course it was perfect and tan and thick with cords of muscle.

Of course.

"A match?"

"Yes! Now hurry up! Get up and get dressed!" She didn't give him the chance to answer, or allow herself to linger with him for very long. This morning, she'd resolved to accept their moment for what it was, and rather than turn it into something it likely could never be, cherish the experience and keep right on moving.

He hadn't been a bachelor for centuries by chance—he was a bachelor by choice, waiting for the right person to come along. After hearing what his father taught him about love, she'd realized he wasn't someone who took the idea of finding a forever love lightly. That's what made him such a terrific, honorable man.

Khristos would want to woo the woman he fell in love with, get to know her, *really* know her. Not jump right into bed with her. They'd known each other less than a week. That wasn't who Khristos was. It wasn't who she was—or who she hoped to be now that her future had changed so drastically.

So no muss, no fuss, no regrets.

He slid from the bed, totally naked, but she turned her back to him as quickly as possible and grabbed a scarf from the drawer of her dresser. "Hurry—we need to move on this. I'm almost certain someone's waiting to be matched. Dress warmly, it's cold out today—looks like we might get more snow."

She pretended that she didn't hear his protests as she yanked the door open and ran for the living room. Anything was better than seeing him get out of that bed, full-throttle naked.

Nina handed her a cup of coffee, Buffy sitting on her shoulder. "You okay this morning?"

She looked down at her feet so Nina wouldn't see the red heat on her cheeks. "Of course I am. Slept great, ready to tackle another match. Sorry I woke you, but something's happening."

"Oh, you did *not* sleep," Nina razzed.

"How do you know?"

She tugged her ear. "Vampire hearing. But I appreciate you trying to keep it to yourselves."

"Could we not talk about this?"

"Aw, c'mon, Mini-Goddess. What's the fekkin' fun in that?"

Quinn gulped and took a deep breath. "*Please.*"

Nina lifted Quinn's chin with a cool hand. "Hey, kiddo. What the fuck?"

No. She couldn't do this right now. "Nothing. It's nothing. I'm just tired and this match is making me crazy and I don't want to muddy my emotional waters by talking about anything but this match that needs making."

Nina gave her a guarded look. "Okay."

Quinn's mouth fell open as she set her coffee down and quickly braided the length of her hair. "You're just going to let it go? No badgering, name calling, threats?"

Nina grinned. "Just like *Frozen.*"

Quinn giggled and rubbed the vampire's shoulder. "Aw, nice Nina is nice."

"Fuck you."

She giggled again, straightening as Khristos came out of the bedroom dressed in low-slung jeans, work boots and a fitted black pullover sweater. If not making more of their night together was the right thing to do, why did it feel as if it were ripping her in half when she looked at him? Tall, strong, good. So good.

But that feeling in the pit of her belly began to mushroom, trumping everything else—even how confused Khristos appeared, judging by the look on his face.

"We have to hurry!"

Grabbing her purse, she threw the strap over her head and ran for the door, following her gut, burning with a new urgency she hadn't experienced in her other matches.

Feet pounded behind her as Khristos and Nina caught up, flanking her on either side. Yet, she didn't have time to notice anything but the path before her. She followed this crazy pounding in her veins, slipping through the crowds of commuters, listening the way Khristos had taught her.

She almost didn't even look up until she landed exactly where she needed to be without even knowing the route she took.

Quinn stopped dead, the haze of the chase clearing enough to see where she'd landed.

The Spotted Pig.

Aka, Shawna "Cantaloupes" Sutter's place of employment.

No. This couldn't be right. Why, in all of the universe, would she have to make a match *here?* She dug her phone out and checked the time. *Shit.*

Igor always got his coffee here at exactly eight sharp on his way to work, and it was five after.

Khristos put a hand at her elbow. "Quinn?"

She peered through the glass window, etched artfully with the name of the coffee shop, and saw Igor playfully feed Shawna a piece of strudel. And the urge, deep and growing inside her, became more insistent.

But those sharp pangs had nothing to do with Igor or any type of longing for him. She didn't want to hack his testicles off with a butter knife. She didn't want to see him writhe in agony. She didn't feel that empty feeling of betrayal he'd left her with when he'd told her about Shawna.

Oddly, when it came to Shawna, she found herself admiring the skillful use of a scarf she'd made into a vest by folding it and tying the square edges into knots at her shoulders. It was a nice color on her, and accented her flame-red hair.

And she took great care managing the coffee shop. The orange and funky-green walls, dressed here and there with animated pictures of various musicians playing instruments, were artsy and fun. The pebbly surface of the sheet-metal countertops shone, and the multicolored mugs they used were hung perfectly from pegs on guitars and banjos that acted as racks all around the space.

But this had to be some cosmic joke.

"I take it that's Igor and Shawna?" Khristos asked, startling her from her thoughts.

"How'd you guess?"

"Those cans. How the hell does she stand up without tipping over?" Nina asked on a snort.

Khristos jammed his hands into the pocket of his down coat, obviously fighting a snicker. "The name of the coffee shop. You mentioned it."

"Right. The dreaded Parthenon confessional." She'd never live that down.

"So what do we do next, Aphrodite?" Khristos put his body between her and the coffee shop door.

And in the midst of all this, she still couldn't look at his handsome face. Her eyes sought the ground and her fuzzy boots. "I don't know. I *do* know I arrived here like some kind of homing pigeon, and my gut tells me to go inside. I don't like it, but there it is."

"Shall we?" he asked.

Yes! her mind screamed, even if her feet were reluctant.

Squaring her shoulders, she straightened and lifted her chin, marching past Khristos and Nina and walking directly into the coffee shop as if someone in the joint owed her money—boobs and all.

Which would have been fine if someone *did* owe her money. At least she'd appear as though she had a reason to be there other than a public, spiteful, jealous rage.

There were no tables where they could sit so her back would be to Igor and Shawna and she wouldn't have to watch them worry she'd bust out her hunting knife and take everyone out in the scorned-lover routine she was almost certain they were anticipating.

Igor's eyes bulged momentarily when he caught sight of her chest, stuffed into her red jacket like a sausage, but he looked away almost immediately.

So she plopped down at the table just two away from where they sat and folded her hands in front of her and waited for whatever was next.

"So, hot mocha lattes with a shot of espresso and some whipped cream in the shape of happy clouds?" Nina asked on a chuckle, sliding into the seat next to Quinn's.

"Or arsenic with a spot of rat poisoning so I can end my suffering. Because um, humiliating when the people who did you wrong clearly think you're here to end it all—or take them as hostages," Quinn joked.

But she didn't feel like she was suffering at all. Seeing Igor did nothing for her. It didn't evoke rage or grief or much of anything, and that was odd. There was a time when seeing Igor, his horn-rimmed glasses on the bridge of his nose, reminded her she had another half to make her whole—or so she'd thought.

Khristos pulled out the chair next to her and reached for her hand, but she snatched it away. She was determined to handle this with class and some dignity, and without the pretense that she'd brought this hot hunk in here to show Igor she was doing just fine.

It was like a Mexican standoff, a waiting duel of who'd look at whom first. Or which of the two would ask whom her plastic surgeon was first.

Igor and Shawna, in defensive mode, huddled together, their bodies covering each other protectively as they whispered. Shawna's red hair spilled down her lean back, her tight jeans revealing a pink thong at the waist.

How strange that she felt so indifferently about the fact that Igor had always said he didn't care for what he'd dubbed "trashy lingerie". Rather than be outraged, she chalked it up to yet another thing he'd done to pretend he was something he wasn't.

Khristos leaned into her, his eyes scanning her face. "What's going on in that head of yours?"

"In this game of awkward chess, I'm wondering who's going to make the first move."

The question was answered when Igor pushed off the table with his hands and approached them. His lean, tall frame moved across the floor with caution. His horn-rimmed glasses were nowhere on his boy-next-door face, and his blue eyes, eyes she'd always thought pretty enough to be a woman's, were wary.

Nina went into serial-killer defensive mode, her body language stiffening, her low growl menacing.

She patted Nina's hand to keep her in check. Igor might be a lying cheat, but he was as docile and non-confrontational as she was.

His smile was hesitant as he ran a hand through his sandy-blonde hair. "Quinn. Good to see you."

She straightened her tinted glasses, hiding her freakishly purple eyes. "You, too, Igor. How've you been?"

"Okay, I guess."

Quinn shook her head in amazement. He was minimizing his happiness to keep from rubbing salt in her wound. She saw it in his eyes, in the way he avoided Shawna's curious gaze.

"Can we talk?" she asked.

"Is it about the sheets? I'll give them to you, if you want. You paid for them—"

Quinn barked a laugh, cutting him off. The old, sad, misguided Quinn might have thrown the idea of those sheets right back in his face with a sharp retort about sloppy seconds and wisecracks about spending his time with a woman who thought picking the next *Bachelorette* was like taking an IQ test.

But the new Quinn, the new one who saw all the things wrong about them as a couple, all the cruel analogies she'd applied to Shawna out of anger, shook her head again.

Looking back now, she marveled at how she'd diligently ignored coming home to the lingering scent of Britney Spears perfume and Bubble Yum bubble gum in the air in favor of believing her Mr. Darcy would never cheat.

"I don't want the sheets, Igor. I'd just like to talk."

"Here? In front of your—"

"Friends," Nina provided with a snarl. "Scary, cheater-hating friends who'll—"

"*Nina*," Khristos warned, wrapping an arm around her shoulders.

"It's okay," Quinn said, though the word "friend" warmed her to her core. "Slow your roll there, Dark Overlord. I've got this."

Igor blanched when Nina snapped her teeth at him. "You upset her—one GD tear—and I'm comin' for you. Got it, *lover?*"

Quinn hopped up and placed her hand on Nina's shoulder, dropping a quick kiss on her cheek. "Have faith in me." Pointing to a corner booth, she asked Igor, "That work?"

Igor nodded, looking back at Shawna, who pulled a string of bubble gum from her mouth and wound it around her finger as she watched them.

Quinn slid into the booth and took a moment to reflect on how easy, at least for her, all this felt.

Igor took his place at the table directly across from her and began to defend himself. "Listen, Quinn. I know I did something really shitty to you—"

"That's not why I'm here, Igor. I'm not here to yell angry words at you, to humiliate you—or Shawna for that matter. Honest." She didn't even know why she was here. But then that urge she'd felt before came back tenfold, punching her in the stomach.

His eyes became guarded again. "So why *are* you here?"

Because the universe seems to think this scenario is LOL?

"Honestly? I don't know. It just sort of happened, but while I'm here, I just want to say something to you, if that's okay."

"Okay," he said, with hesitance riddling his tone.

"I hope you're happy," Quinn said with a smile, readying to slide out of the booth.

He grabbed her hand, to the tune of chair legs scraping the floor from across the room as Nina prepared to beat him down and Khristos warned her to ease up.

"Wait. Please, Quinn."

Quinn fought a chuckle and held up a hand to thwart Nina. "For?"

Igor swallowed hard, his Adam's apple bobbing in his nervousness. "I want to say something, too. I'm sorry I hurt you. Really sorry. It's been on my mind, keeping me up at night since we broke up. But I need you to know something. Shawna and I never slept together while you and I were together. I know that's what you thought, and I didn't do a very good job of defending myself. But she made it clear I had to leave you before any funny business happened, and she was right."

Quinn fought a gasp. Their last moments together had been fraught with angry words and her tears as she'd packed her things and stormed out the door. This revelation was a surprise. One she was glad of—it made Igor a better man than she'd originally thought.

"I've hurt a lot of people trying to figure out me, Quinn, but I'm sorriest I hurt you. This thing with Shawna...I know she's not what you'd expect, as smart and well-rounded as you are. But there's a quality to her, for lack of a better phrase, vocabulary skills I find endearing. I like that she needs me. She has a big heart. She's kind, nurturing. I can relax with her. I don't know...it just—"

"Happened. I get it, and it's okay. Sometimes the person you'd least expect ends up being the person you love the most. I'm actually okay. I know people say that out of spite when on the inside they want to gouge their ex's eyes out with a nail file, but for me, it's true. We were a mistake from the start, and I see that now."

His chuckle was as ironic as his smile. "I've been thinking a lot about that, too. About who I am for falling in love with someone else when you were so good to me. But I have this weird sort of self-discovery thing happening lately. I always felt like I was pretending with you. Pretending I was as well-read and knowledgeable. I don't have to pretend with Shawna. I don't have to pretend I'm something I'm just not. She's okay with the fact that we're pretty damn different. I don't have to outsmart her or outthink her. I'm not doing things I really don't enjoy just to keep from being lonely. And it's a relief. But how I ended up here? That's on me. I did those things to myself, and I regret every wasted moment."

Khristos's words came back to haunt her, but she wasn't angry about them anymore. She was grateful. Grateful to share this moment of closure with Igor.

"Funny you should mention self-discovery. I did those things, too, Igor. I turned you into someone you weren't in my head, and I let myself get carried way far away. I've done it before and it was wrong. So, I was wrong, too."

"Did this self-discovery also include breast implants?" Then he pressed his wrist over his mouth. "Sorry. That was insensitive and rude, but they're hard to miss. You really went all the way."

Yet, she wasn't at all insulted. Instead, she snickered. "Long story you'd never believe. They're not implants but some weird medical thing I picked up in Greece. It's almost too fluky to explain."

He paused a moment, the tic above his eye pulsing, the one that acted up when he was genuinely concerned. "So you really are okay, Quinn?"

"Yep. I've packed up my shivs and testicle-removers for good, where you're concerned."

Now Igor laughed, shaking his head. "I've dreaded this moment, you know. Thought about it. Visualized it."

"Bet it went a lot better than the movie you made up in your head, huh?"

"Yeah. That was filled with carnage and entrails," he joked.

"Then that's all that needs to be said. I'm glad you're happy, Igor. I'm glad Shawna's the one who helped you realize it was time to just be you." She slid out of the booth and Igor followed while Shawna hovered in the background, her face full of concern.

Facing him for what likely would be the last time, she smiled, wide, genuine, reaching up to cup his jaw as she did. "I hope from here on out you're always true to yourself, and most of all, that you and Shawna are happy." She stood on tiptoe, planting a kiss on his cheek before she turned to leave.

Hitching her jaw at the door in Khristos and Nina's direction, she plodded toward it until that damn feeling, the one pushing her to come to the Spotted Pig in the first place, grabbed her guts up in a fist and wrenched them.

Pushing her way out the door, she leaned against the side of the coffee shop as Khristos, always near, grabbed her around the waist. "Tell me what's happening, Quinn!" he demanded in her ear.

But she knew what was happening—it had just taken her by surprise with its velocity, with its truth.

"*Now!*" she whispered to her mental image of Cupid, looking up and into the coffee shop window just in time to see the arrow—gleaming and bright in the morning sun, whiz through the air and land on Igor and Shawna, hugging each other, under a shower of gold and silver.

Was that the scent of Bubble Yum and Brittany Spears perfume she smelled in the air?

Quinn smiled. Now, everything really was okay.

Which brought to mind one of her favorite Keats quotes: *Who shall say between a man and a woman, who is most delighted?*

"Good job back there, kiddo," Nina praised her upon their return to Quinn's apartment. "Personally? I woulda fucked him up so hard he woulda shit his teeth for a year. You're a better person than I am."

Quinn gave her a distracted smile, her mind on something else. "All in a day's work."

Marty and Wanda, both on their laptops, peeked over the tops of them and grinned. "We heard! Goooo, Goddess of Love!" Marty cheered, shaking her imaginary pom-poms as Wanda gave her a thumbs-up.

Archibald stuck his head out of the kitchen with Darnell just behind him. "How do you all feel about pizza night tonight? I have the most amazing recipe just garnered from the goddess of cooking herself, Ina Gartner. I can't contain my excitement!"

Carl, who'd returned while they were gone, thumped his hand on the table in agreement, shooting Quinn his lopsided smile when she gave him a quick hug. "Glad to see you, buddy. How about some *Goodnight Moon* tonight at bedtime?"

He leaned forward and grabbed his backpack from under the chair, pulling out a book she knew well—one near and dear to her romantic heart. "*Keats*, Carl?" She fanned herself and batted her eyes. "Be still my beating heart. Keats it is, my friend. You and me. It's a date."

Carl thumped her arm and grinned again.

What would she do when these people left her life? The notion made her sad, but there was a small part of her, the part who lived for love, that reminded Quinn her new job was forever.

It would be filled with plenty to do, and she'd keep busy matchmaking.

That was enough to fill up any romantic's cup, and she'd just have to be happy with that.

Khristos grabbed her by the arm and smiled. "Good news from the forums."

"Am I ever going to get a user ID and password for the forums? I feel a little left out of the loop," she joked.

He held up his phone. "Yep. I have them right here. Just texted them to you. Also, looks like I'm not having my liver pecked out anytime soon. No punishment for losing track of the apple. I escaped the guillotine."

"Yay for leniency!" she cheered, though she felt anything but cheerful. Khristos's possible punishment was one of her primary concerns before she tackled her next task. Relief flooded her veins. He would be safe. That was all that mattered.

"So, you did a great job today. You've really gotten the hang of this, Quinn."

Her heart pounded in her chest for what she was about to do next. But she was all about making the right choices in her life right now. Making sure she wasn't creating something out of absolutely nothing ever again. That hurt too much.

"Can we take a walk?"

"You bet. Lemme grab my coat."

Slipping out her apartment door, she waited for him at the top of the steps. Seeing his handsome face and thickly muscled body coming up the stairs made her throat tighten.

Quinn headed toward the small park he'd found her in the other night, aimlessly walking as the sun began to set and she attempted to gather up the courage to say what she had to say. To really live in reality for the first time.

She stopped at the park's entry and looked up at him in all his perfection. His smooth olive skin, his eyes, warm and brown with gold flecks. Those lips she'd savored like a fine wine last night.

"Wanna tell me what's up?"

No. No, she didn't. But she would. So she'd never get swept up in her daydreaming again. "I think I'm going to be okay now."

He grinned. "Of course you will. You matched your ex and his new girlfriend today. Nothing says okay like that."

Quinn shook her head, burying her chin in her scarf to keep the tears from falling. "No. I mean about being Aphrodite. I think I can handle it now. On...alone. On my own."

His gaze deepened, his eyes swirled with emotion. "Is this about last night?"

She put her cold fingers to his lips and gulped. "Don't say anything about last night. *Please*. It was amazing and wonderful, and despite the fact that I matched Igor today, I'm still a little raw. Maybe even a little unsure of my personal choice-making skills right now. But I'll never regret what happened between us, Khristos. Not ever. You've taught me so much about myself and love and given me insight into a million different things. I'm just not in the right head space…"

"I get it," he said—the very words she knew he'd speak.

Her pulse throbbed in her ears. If this was the right thing, if she was basing her new choices in smarter life journeys to avoid crashing and burning for the umpteenth time, why did it feel so differently than it had with any other breakup?

Why did it feel like her chest would explode and she'd never be the same if she didn't spend at least some part of her day with Khristos? She hardly knew him. Incredible sex wasn't the only kind of glue holding a relationship together.

Maybe this was what doing the right thing felt like—and it sucked.

Grabbing his hand on impulse, she looked up at him and forced a smile. "You were the best teacher ever. But you have a life I know you want to get back to—even if it isn't really filled with leggy blondes and big yachts. You're free now. You deserve the chance to live without the apple around your neck like some monkey on your back. I can handle this alone now, I think. We knew that was what would happen eventually, right?"

"That was the plan," he said quietly, his voice eerily tight.

"And I've already asked Nina and the rest of the girls if they'll stay with me in case these bad guys we haven't heard from since I was knocked on my ass show up. You said yourself; we don't have any super-strength or whatever to protect me. So if someone's still coming for me, why should you be in the line of fire?"

"Quinn—"

"No!" she almost shouted then pulled back and inhaled a steadying breath. "Don't say anything else. I can always get in touch with you if I find myself with a question. Just go enjoy your freedom, Khristos. Besides, before long, I'm sure we'll see each other around on the forums or maybe even at a virgin sacrifice," she teased.

Throwing her arms around his neck, she hugged him hard, savoring his scent, memorizing the way his hands felt at her waist.

She took a step away and smiled. "I'm gonna go get some of that amazing pizza Arch was talking about. We goddesses need our fuel. See you back at my place for one last dinner before you set your charge free on the world at large?"

He stared at her for a moment as snow began to fall, wreathing his body in shimmering white. "You bet," he murmured.

And then she turned and began to walk, trying to keep from running until she was out of his line of sight.

When tears stung the corners of her eyes, she fought them hard.

Because doing the right thing and making healthy life choices wasn't always easy or pain-free.

Right.

Right?

CHAPTER 14

As Quinn walked away, it hit him all at once. He wanted this woman—and she was letting him go so she wouldn't make another poor choice. She was playing things smart for her future. They didn't know each other on a deep, personal level yet. They'd spent a week wandering around New York City, matching people up, and then they'd made insanely incredible love.

Lovemaking he couldn't forget—her soft curves, her willingness, her sweet lips against his when she came. He'd only just begun to taste her, and she was out.

All in the span of the week, a week Quinn could have chosen to turn into one big fairytale. Which quite obviously, she was opting out of doing.

Yet, he felt as if he'd always known her. And the parts he didn't know, he wanted to know.

Did love happen that fast?

Of course it does, you dipshit. You've seen it hundreds and thousands of times in the course of your mother's reign as Aphrodite.

Just as it hit him and he made sense of his feelings after last night, just as he'd been about to confess he was falling in love with her—she'd dumped his ass like a she was making a deposit at a Jersey landfill.

He took his time walking back to her place, each step he took, feeling worse than he had the step before. His chest ached—tight with the words he'd wanted to say to Quinn.

When he approached Quinn's, peering around the railing to her steps and into the basement window like some lovesick fool, his chest hurt harder.

Fuck.

Marty was setting the table. Wanda was laughing about something with Carl. Archibald was waving his finger around with Darnell following his instructions. Ingrid sat in a corner, curled up with one of her medical books.

And Quinn was lying on the couch, a gel pack over her eyes.

Clearly, dumping him had been exhausting.

And that longing he'd once described to Quinn assaulted him once more.

He was going to throttle his mother's pretty neck when he got ahold of her for ever giving him the damn apple to guard in the first place.

His mother was…

His. Mother.

A memory slammed into his brain all at once. How could he have forgotten that screaming match with her over a decade ago?

Jesus. He could fix this insane longing for a woman who didn't want him in no time flat. All he had to do was find his mother, and if the forums weren't deceiving him, she was happily posting under the alias she thought no one knew about.

Except he knew about it, and it was time he and his mother had a long talk about apples and her lack of grandchildren and making him fall in love with a woman who very clearly had no interest in him.

Sending a quick text to Marty, Wanda and Nina, with a warming to keep a sharp eye on Quinn, he snapped his fingers. Because ending this shitty brand of suffering needed to happen now.

"Mother!" he bellowed, storming through her bleached-white, rose-filled cottage on Mt. Olympus. "You can't hide forever!"

His mother appeared from behind the column on the small patio overlooking the ocean, her hair piled on top of her head, her reading glasses perched at the end of her nose. Wind chimes tinkled and the ocean breeze wafted in on a perfumed breeze.

"Khristos! Oh, honey, it's so good to see you!"

He stopped short in front of her, pulling off his jacket and knit hat and letting them drop in a wet puddle to the floor. "First of all, don't you 'it's so good to see you, pookie' me like I haven't been trying to get in touch with you for almost a week," he growled.

She patted his cheek with a warm smile. "Don't get in such an uproar, it does ugly things to your skin, Khristos. And pick up those clothes. I just washed the floors and you're dripping all over them."

Patience. He pleaded with the gods for patience so he wouldn't throttle her pretty neck. "*Where* have you been?"

She shrugged her slim shoulders and said evasively, "Around. Resting, discovering a life that's all mine now to do as I please."

"How could you just abandon your duties like that?"

"They were no longer my duties, precious. You fixed that. Besides, you know how to take care of business. I taught you well. I trusted you'd teach that adorable Quinn everything she needed to know. And you did. Just look at her, making matches faster than *Match.com.*"

His gut stung. He didn't want to hear about matches or love. He just wanted this ache in his chest to damn well go away.

Khristos sucked in the sea air and clenched his jaw. "Okay. That aside, I need you to make it stop. Make it stop *now.*"

His mother's beautiful face, like creamy porcelain and peaches, looked astonished. "Make *what* stop, darling?"

"That overbearing, controlling, give-me-grandchildren-or-I'll-make-you-miserable love spell you put on the apple. You know, I almost forgot about it until today, when I was having my ass handed to me by my never-gonna-believe-in-fairytales-again Quinn. And then I remembered that argument we had, and it all made sense."

Her look of bewilderment almost had him. Almost. Damn, she was good. "A love spell on the apple? Argument? I didn't do anything to it but leave it in your care, Khristos."

"That's crap, and you damn well know it, Mom!" he thundered, glowering down at her, his jaw tight. "You've used that apple to keep me in check for centuries. You said so yourself."

She made a pouty face, crossing her arms over her chest. "Whoa, whoa, whoa. You just watch your tone there, son. How dare you come storming in here and yell accusations at me. Just who do you think you are?"

He tried to remember his father's words—to be patient with his mother. To love her for who she was, not who he wanted her to be. But goddamn it, this loving someone who didn't love you back was pretty shitty.

Knock it off, good man, next you'll be playing Air Supply and wandering around sniffing Quinn's frilly pillows. Fight for your man-card.

He had to fight not to seethe his next words. "You're joking, right? How can you stand there and tell me you had nothing to do with what's happening to me?"

"*What* is happening to you, honey?"

"Have you already forgotten what you said to me?"

Aphrodite yanked her glasses off and set her book on a nearby table littered with pictures of them, happy, laughing, playing badminton with Zeus and his brood. "What exactly did I say to you?"

"You told me if a woman ever got her hands on the apple—which the stats favored; I mean, how many men do you know who'd be kooky enough to confess their love woes to an apple in the Parthenon?—you said I'd fall helplessly in love with her. Yes, you did. Which to me meant, better hang on to that damn apple, Khristos, or possibly end up in love with a serial killer. It was your controlling way of demanding I get busy and make you some grandchildren."

Aphrodite appeared to pause in thought before she said, "Was your grandmother on that damn tour bus to the Parthenon again?"

"Bingo, Mom! She fed Quinn that crazy story about talking to the apple about her breakup with the man she wanted to marry to purge her soul of strife or whatever the story was. Quinn, being the mythology addict she is, and still pretty sore from the end of the relationship she thought would lead to marriage, *believed her.*"

"Does she still smell like a goat?"

"*Who?*" he all but shouted.

"Grams, of course."

"Rumor has it, yes."

Aphrodite grinned. "So she's still selling that story to the tourists? Gods, she's good. She cracks me up."

"Is that the point? No. The point is, Quinn is now Aphrodite, and I'm in love with her because you couldn't keep your nose out of my life! If I've said it once, I've said it a thousand times—let *me* find the love of my immortal life. But no, you just couldn't let it be."

"I'm still missing something here…"

He ran a hand over his jaw with an exasperated sigh. "How convenient you've forgotten that argument. I almost did, too. But then I remembered, it was like World War III. We didn't speak to each other for almost a decade. And I remember that threat—clearly. So make it go away. *Now!*"

Aphrodite laughed, a bubbling chuckle of casual abandon. "Oh, honey, no, no. no. I would never actually put a love spell on the apple. I said I *should* put a spell on the apple so you'd stop chasing women. Your memory's slipping, son. Try some ginko biloba. I hear it helps. I was just keeping you on your toes to teach you about consequences, give you responsibilities to tend. You know how I feel about my past, how remorseful I am for some of the horrible things I did in my misguided, orgy-filled youth."

Khristos cringed and held up a hand. "Stop right at orgy, please."

His mother shook her head as the room tinkled with more of her laughter. "I've told you at least a thousand times about all the trouble I've made, and not without good reason. I told you because I didn't want that for you, and the way things were shaping up, with you off chasing every toga from here to eternity, I had to do something, didn't I?"

He damn well didn't chase togas.

Wait—what?

There was no spell? He'd spent the better part of his adult life pretending to be something he wasn't to avoid getting caught in a web that didn't even exist?

Which meant—he really was falling in love with Quinn?

Oh, fuck.

"Do you mean to tell me that I'm not falling in love with her because of a love spell, but because…"

"Just because, honey." Aphrodite smiled at him, a smile beaming with love. "There's no spell, no shenanigans, nothing. That's your heart, telling you you've found the one. I'm so happy for you, Khristos! Oh, we'll have grandchildren in no time!" She whirled around, clapping her hands. "Mom!" she yelled. "Did you hear?"

His grandmother—or GG, as they called her—sauntered into the living room, a pink umbrella-ed cocktail in hand, her crazy Mohawk sagging from the humidity. "Yep," she said on a sigh. "I heard."

His mother threw her arms around his grandmother's neck. "Isn't this the most amazing news, Mother? Grandbabies!"

His grandmother pushed her false teeth from her mouth with her tongue before slapping Khristos on the back. "Hold onto your flimsy panties there, girlie. I got a confession to make."

His eyes narrowed in his grandmother's direction. He adored her, loved her as much as he loved his mother, but Grandma's first name wasn't Agape for nothing. Like her name, she was the scariest bitch.

Fear skittered up his spine. "GG, *what have you done?*"

She took a long sip of her drink through the straw, sucking on it noisily until she'd had her last drop. "You want it straight up, or do you want me to weave one of my stories like I do on the bus?"

He cracked his jaw. "Straight up, GG. Now. *Please.*"

She hiked up the front of her flowered orange-and-black bathing suit. "It was me who knocked the apple off the column. Now, don't go gettin' pissy. I did it to give you a break. You weren't ever gonna find the love of your life if you were too damned busy guarding the apple. Quinn's a nice kid. Never wrinkled her nose once on the bus. Even after I rolled in goat shit. Because you know how I am. I like to really become one with the peasant storyteller shtick. Anyway, she gets the whole dealio with love. She's good at it. She believes. Your mother's getting wrinkles around her eyes from trying to keep up. I had to do something, and she's such a control freak, she never would have quit. And that Iris is a twit. Who lets the

Goddess of Rainbows make choices the fate of the world relies on? We'd have a bunch of baby unicorns running around and no humans."

His mother bit her lower lip and winced. "Oh, Mother..."

GG rolled her eyes in disgust. "Don't 'oh, Mother' me. Look, it was time to take charge. So I whipped up a small seismic occurrence, and knocked the apple off the column when you weren't looking."

"And you chose Quinn because...?" Khristos asked.

His grandmother snorted. "After hearing your Quinn on the phone with her schmoe of an ex-boyfriend Igor, I knew she was right for the position because she's got moxie. Plenty of it. Told that Igor to shove his nose clippers into his anus-head."

His eyes almost rolled to the back of his head. "I can't believe *you* did this, GG."

She flapped her hand at him. "Yeah, yeah. I did this. If she hadn't taken a bite of the apple, I would have figured out another way to transfer the power to her. But she didn't go down without a fight, did she? She told you what was what. Loved it!"

But hold on. Maybe there was some measure of relief in this yet. "So you were the one who put a love spell on the apple?"

She wrinkled up her face and popped her lips. "Um, nope. No love spell. That's all on you."

He made his way to the couch and dropped down into it.

Shit.

His grandmother dropped down next to him and ran her knuckles over his head. "I'm sorry, kiddo. Sometimes you're the windshield, sometimes you're the bug."

His mother took a seat on the other side of him, blowing a long strand of hair out of her face. "Love stinks."

In the esteemed words of the J. Geils Band, *yeah, yeah.*

CHAPTER 15

"Hey. You okay in there?" Ingrid asked, peeking under the gel pack Quinn had over her eyes.

No. Right now, she was not okay. She patted the gel pack back in place. "I'm great. Just resting my eyes."

"I heard you matched anus-head with Cantaloupes. You're a better woman than I am. He's lucky I'm not Aphrodite or I'd have given him an arrow in his stupid ass."

"Wasn't it you who, just before we got on the plane to Greece, said I was frightening you when I went through my I'll-leave-Igor-drooling-in-his-own-spit-slash-Lorena-Bobbitt revenge phase and that I should knock off all thoughts of payback immediately? You said it wasn't healthy."

"Very fair. But looking back, you have to admit, you were super scary. I mean, I knew the Quinn who was rainbows and puppies and suddenly you were all three-sixty, looking to gank him."

"I was not going to gank him. I was just going to scare him—with a chainsaw. Remember, lots of great romances, in fact, some of the classics, end in tragedy."

Ingrid laughed. "You've come a long way since that day on the plane, baby. Especially if you matched Igor and Miss Cantaloupes."

Yeah. A long way. "Something you should know, by the way. Igor claims he didn't cheat on me. He said Shawna wouldn't allow it. Sure, they were emotionally involved, but nothing physical. He's more of a man than I thought."

"You believed him?"

"I did." She couldn't explain why, but she did.

"So where's our resident hottie Khristos?"

She shuddered a breath and scrunched her eyes shut to keep more tears from falling down her cheeks. "He went home."

"Where is home, anyway?"

"I don't know," she whispered. But she hoped it was somewhere nice with a stupid soul mate just waiting for him to show up and sweep her off her delicate feet.

Ingrid lifted the gel-pack again. "Let's talk about whatever's making you so glum, chum."

"I'm not glum. What makes you think I'm glum?"

"This," she said, pulling at the downward turn of Quinn's lower lip, "all thin, followed by the occasional tremble, is definitely glum." Cocking a pierced eyebrow, she gave Quinn's lip one last tug for good measure. "So let's talk about it."

"Let's not." *Please let's not.* She was still trying to do the right thing and the right thing was eating a hole in her heart.

"Why is Khristos gone then—which ironically happens to coincide with you trying to hide the fact that you've been crying? Don't bother to deny it. Your eyeballs look like someone plucked them out of your head and stuffed them back in. What's going on, Quinn?"

"Nothing's going on."

"It's because Khristos left, isn't it?"

"I told him to leave. It was time he got back to his life."

"And why did you tell him to leave, Quinn? Because I don't know if you were getting the signal, but he was pretty into you, and you were really feelin' him."

"Maybe you should be the Goddess of Love. Wanna bite my apple, little girl?" she joked to hide the dread in the pit of her stomach.

"I like human just fine, thank you. And you didn't answer the question. Why did you tell him to leave?"

"It was all just too soon, Ingrid. I'm fresh off an ugly breakup with Igor, and even though we mended fences today, I learned a lot about myself making these matches and why I make the choices I make where men are concerned. I don't want to make more wrong choices. Isn't that the smart thing to do? No rebound relationships unless they're wham-bams, was what you said. Just to help me get over the hump. Remember those words of wisdom?"

"He's no wham-bam, Quinn, and you damn well know it."

"I don't even know his last name, Ingrid. Does he even have a last name? How does he sign his Christmas cards? Khristos Aphrodite? Khristos hyphen Goddess of Love's Spawn?"

"That's a reason to chase him out of your life?"

She didn't respond. She couldn't.

But Ingrid wasn't letting go. "Still avoiding the question."

"Because he has a life, too."

"Nope. That's not why you did it, Quinn. If you're going to do all this reality, let's do it right. You did it because you're afraid you're getting too carried away with your romantic expectations again."

"How do you know?"

"My sleeping bag has ears. I was right out here on the floor last night. I know. You showed him your Cucamonga and he showed you his man-bits, and now you're freaked out."

God, she was smart. "So? What does that matter? It doesn't change the fact that I've never gotten a single relationship right."

"No. It says you've just picked the wrong men."

Quinn remained silent. Wasn't that the same thing?

"It also says you've gone too far the other side of reality. Come back before you miss something really great."

"Before it was too much romance, not enough caution. Now it's too much caution? Make up your mind," she said on a groan.

"No. Now it's just right, Quinn."

"How can you know it's just right? It's too soon to tell. We just met each other, Ingrid. Things like that don't happen overnight."

Ingrid grabbed her hand and held it to her cheek. "Sometimes, they do. In the past, if anyone defended love at first sight, it would have been you, sitting on the bleachers, megaphone in hand. But if you can't defend it right now, I will for you. Real love *can* happen in a glance or a touch or a week. You should know that after the matches you've made in the last few days. You've seen it. That's all I'm saying."

"Hey, Chatty Cathys, you two wanna go get ice cream?" Nina asked. "Marty and Wanda think it'd be fun to walk in the shitstorm out there and eat something cold when it's twelve degrees out."

"Need some quiet time?" Ingrid whispered in her ear.

"*Please*," she whispered back, utterly miserable.

"I'm in," Ingrid said, giving Quinn's shoulder a squeeze before rising.

Nina nudged her with a knee. "I'm gonna be right outside with Carl. Right on the sidewalk. Promised I'd help him build a snowman. Fuck if I don't regret buying him and Charlie *Frozen*. Anyway, you're not alone. All ya gotta do is give a yell if you need me. And for the record, you should flippin' listen to Ingrid and rethink this plan, Love Maker. It's fucking stupid." She reached down and chucked Quinn under the chin before gathering Carl and heading outside.

After everyone dropped a kiss on her forehead and shuffled out, silence fell over her apartment. She struggled to sit up, letting the gel-pack drop to the floor, her eyes sore from keeping the tears at bay.

Her line of sight fell on the sweater Khristos had left behind, his things in a neat pile by the side of the couch, and she ached.

Ached to see him, ached to talk to him. Ached.

Like someone had torn off a limb.

In all her failed relationships, she'd never felt quite like this when they'd ended. Though, technically, theirs had never even begun. He hadn't stopped her from walking away.

How would it have played out if he'd reminded her she'd gone *Pygmalion* on him and fallen for the teacher out of idol worship? What if he'd told her she still had her head in the clouds, dreaming up scenarios that didn't exist? What if he'd said exactly what she'd said to him? We had sex. Yay! Thanks for a good time. Good luck in all future endeavors.

Quinn let her head fall to her hands. Quite possibly, this was the smartest thing to do—just plow forward.

But what if it isn't? What if you didn't give him the chance to say anything because you were so busy dunking in the pool of reality, you forgot to come up for air?

"Alone at last," a sultry voice whispered into the dim light of her living room.

Quinn's head whipped upward. She scanned the room, her eyes darting around every corner.

"Do you have any idea how hard it is to take a bitch out when she's constantly surrounded by a posse like yours? Goddess, they're an annoying bunch. All that food and hugs and kisses and broccoli. I should torture you before I kill you, just because this has all been such a hassle. I think I actually broke a nail."

She fought a grating sigh. Okay, disembodied voices were on her checklist of things she'd like to take a pass on, going forward. They were unnerving and just a little unfair on the playing field of who had bigger powers.

"Who are you?"

"Who I am matters little. Who I'll be when you're dead is what matters."

Did the voice belong to Aphrodite? That moment when she'd shown up was still a little hazy. So she couldn't be sure. But it was worth a shot to ask. "Aphrodite?"

Laughter filled her small apartment. Maniacal and so earsplitting, her eardrums shook. "Uh, no. I *would* have been Aphrodite if you would've just died like you were supposed to. Alas, you're tougher than you first appeared."

Okay, not Aphrodite. Shit just got real. Bad guys were real, and in all her new realist state of mind, she was in trouble—for real.

"So it was you who knocked me down that night?" she asked into the room, hoping whomever the voice belonged to couldn't see her knees quaking.

A wistful sigh whistled in her ear. "Honestly, I'm better than that shot I took at you. I can't believe my aim was so off. But you really gave it a good effort when you hit the ground. Your tuck and roll was impressive."

Quinn nodded, looking around the room to find something to defend herself with. "Yeah. I took a gymnastics class for like a hot second when my mom thought I didn't get out enough. Funny what you retain, isn't it?"

"Oh, a laugh riot."

"And that match I made—afterward, when it felt like someone was sticking a hot poker in my colon?"

Another long, drawn-out sigh whizzed around the room, leaving an echo of disappointment. "I poisoned the apple just before you sunk your pretty white teeth into it. But it was the wrong poison. I forgot you're human. No residual effects. Just gas to show for my efforts. Bummer, right?"

Stall, Quinn. Stall. "You think my teeth are pretty?"

And then she remembered Nina was right outside.

Just as Quinn thought to call out to Nina was the moment an invisible hand grabbed her and threw her up against the far wall, pinning her there.

A woman, surreal, beautiful, perfect in almost every way, appeared in front of her, her wrist attached to the hand wrapped around Quinn's throat. "*Shut—up!*" the woman hissed in her face.

She was so caught off-guard, she somehow managed to marvel at this woman's beauty. From her long, graceful neck, to her almond-shaped sapphire eyes, to hair flowing to her waist in soft, full curls, she was amazing. It almost hurt to look at her.

And okay, it was scary to look at her in all this fury Quinn didn't understand the reasons behind.

But damn, she had some firm grip.

Quinn grabbed at the woman's hand, tearing at it, unable to breathe. Now probably wouldn't be the time to bemoan the fact that she hadn't been turned into a vampire or a werewolf with super-strength. But it had to be more useful than making matches.

As her feet lifted farther off the ground and her legs dangled, she tried to remember the fights she'd witnessed on the playground as a kid in school from a corner where she always hid from the chaos.

What did the person who lost always accuse the person who beat them of doing?

149

Fighting like a girl.

Why?

Because the winner had pulled her opponents hair.

As her eyes began to roll back in her head, Quinn forced herself to focus on one thing—yanking the shit out of this woman's amazing hair.

She couldn't even grunt her monumental effort when she reached upward with both hands and grabbed two lengths of this madwoman's hair as close to her scalp as possible and pulled for all she was worth.

The woman's mouth opened wide in a scream so chilling, Quinn was sure she'd shatter all the china Arch had brought in from Nina's mansion.

So she yanked harder. So hard, her fingers burned with the effort.

The woman dropped her, letting Quinn slam to the floor. She crashed into her end table, taking out the lamp, struggling for breath.

As she reflected on her small victory, she also noted the spinning wheel of fire, coming at her like one of those Chinese stars in an action movie. Coming at her and aimed right at her head.

So, yeah. Bad guys really did exist.

"What the hell's going on?" Khristos yelled over the wind whipping against Nina and Carl.

Nina had sent him a text that Quinn needed him, and even though it only took a second for him to snap his fingers and get back to Quinn's apartment, it felt like a century.

Nina clung to Carl, trying to keep him protected from the angry slash of wind, coiling, lashing at them, forcing them to almost double over.

"Dude, I don't know, but we need to get the fuck in there! Someone's got Quinn!"

His stomach twisted into a tight knot as he grabbed Nina and Carl, fighting against the wind to get back down the stairwell to Quinn's door and to a modicum of shelter.

A gust of icy air launched him against the brick, oddly scorching his back with agonizing, prickly heat. He fought to keep Nina's hand as he tried to inch his way to the handle in the tiny space, ignoring the searing pain of his back.

"We have to get in there!" Nina screamed, dragging Carl partially up the steps and pulling out some duct tape from her hoodie. She wrapped his hands to the railing in a blur of freakish motion. "Don't move, Carl! Stay here no matter what. If Wanda and Marty come, send them in. Okay?" she yelled above the roar of the wind.

Carl bobbed his head, but his sweet face held anguish.

"Whatever you do, Carl—hang on! Don't let go!" Nina ordered, fighting the howl of air to get to the door.

Her hand on the doorknob, she pushed Khristos out of the way. "Stay here!"

"The hell I'm letting you go in there alone!"

"Whatever the fuck's going on in there, you got shit to fight it with, dude. Let me assess this first. Stay the fuck here, and text Marty and Wanda again!" she ordered, twisting the doorknob he'd replaced and literally yanking the door off its hinges.

"Duck, Carl!" he bellowed as the door lifted and flew high in the air, the screech of metal scoring the wind.

Nina plowed in, her fangs bared, her hands in tight fists, and Khristos plowed in right behind her, ignoring every word of warning she'd spoken. Quinn was in danger, and the hell he was staying outside to await her fate.

Then everything went silent—so eerily silent, Nina stopped in her tracks.

"Quinn!" His heart crashed in his chest. *Please, let her answer.* His eyes scanned the small room, the floor littered in broken pieces of glass, laminate flooring torn and peeling upward. The table they'd spent so much time at this week upended and shredded.

He looked to Nina, who sniffed the air, her eyes blazing. She pressed a finger to her mouth as she took a long step over the flipped couch and peered around the corner to the kitchen.

Khristos went the other way to the bedroom, pressing himself against the wall in the short hall leading to it, fighting the urge to rush in rather than remain cautious.

"Kiddo?" Nina yelled into the silence.

"*Get out! Run!*" He heard the urgent whisper, experienced the utter anguish those words stirred in his gut. The words were an effort, a croak of a warning as the bedroom door creaked open.

Her room was no longer the size of a broom closet.

It was a coliseum—like back in the day, when his mother used to take him to the Panathenaic Games. Sprawling and wide, the walls made of concrete, the sheer size of it daunting.

And then he saw her—the woman he really was falling in love with—tacked to the wall of her former bedroom like a poster with a spike in each palm. Blood dripping from her hands, her neck purple with bruises, her feet just touching the ground, her eyes wide with fear.

CHAPTER 16

Quinn's eyes met Khristos's as the position of her arms, stretched to an abnormal width, tore her tendons and the nerve endings in her hands burned as though she were on fire, begging for relief.

"Go!" She mouthed the word, unable to explain, incapable of making her vocal chords cooperate.

But Khristos, this amazing, incredible, wonderful man, rushed at her rather than listen. Climbing over the bed blocking the entrance to this monstrosity, he knocked the pillows to the floor, spanning the short distance between them in seconds, his handsome face a mask of fury and concern, his eyes locked on hers.

He reached for her instantly, obviously afraid to touch the spikes nailing her to the wall. "*Who?*" he seethed, his rage clear as his hands fluttered over her, not knowing where to help first. "Who did this, Quinn?"

"Please, go. Please, Khristos," she murmured, knowing the woman was lurking somewhere in the massive space she'd created with a snap of her fingers.

She would never forget how the woman had turned her tiny bedroom into this vast venue Quinn had only seen in pictures. The room had transformed—walls lengthening, the ceiling rising to stratospheric heights, pillars erupting from the ground like seeds sprouting in fast-forward.

Chunks of rock had spewed and kicked up pebbles until everything clicked into place. All that remained of her bedroom were the furnishings, minute as dollhouse furniture against the new backdrop.

Nina flew up and over the bed, her eyes narrowed, her nostrils flaring as she saw what had happened to the bedroom and Quinn. "Holy fuck!" The vampire was across the coliseum in the blink of an eye, horror on her pale face.

"Go, Nina! Take Khristos. I'm…begging," she tried to whisper, her eyes pleading with them, her body shaking with violent tremors.

"Not gonna happen, Goddess-Lite!" she said, but her confusion about how to help, what to do next, was clearly written on her face.

A howl, a rush of furious rage, breathed through the coliseum, kicking up more wind tunnels of dust, and screeching through her ears.

The still unknown woman rose from the farthest corner like a serpent, bending, bowing, slithering upward and toward them. She morphed, changed, her head elongating, her body following suit, stretching until she was scaled, her tongue forked, slipping in and out of her transformed mouth.

A hiss omitted from her throat, sizzling and hot, swishing around the open space, growing louder, picking up speed. Her mouth opened wide again, just like it had before she'd broken all the glass in the apartment. She lashed her tongue at Quinn, a ribbon of crimson unfurled, flapping in a grotesque wave aimed directly at her head.

In those seconds, as she watched helplessly, her death imminent, she thought of only one thing—Khristos, who was as powerless as she was. He would feel the lash of that tongue if he didn't move.

"*Look out!*" Nina screamed, making a run to rush the woman, only to trip over a chunk of fallen pillar and hit the ground made of crumbled rock, leaving a cloud of dust in her wake.

But Khristos refused to move anyway. He placed himself between Quinn and the warp speed of the tongue.

To protect *her*.

And the last thought she had just before she used all her might to pull her knees to her chest, as sweat dripping down her face and the flesh of her hands tearing when she levered herself with them and kicked Khristos out of the way was, even in the throes of battle, he was a good guy. So, so good.

Khristos fell, his head hitting the post on her bed, crumpling to the ground as the tongue rippled toward her.

There was nowhere for Quinn to go, pinned to the wall, but Nina leaped up and forward and managed to wrap her arms around the neck of the python, yanking its head to the left with a scream of uncontained fury.

Then Marty was there, like a flash of motion and sound, with Wanda hot on her heels, tearing at this woman who'd become a slithering python of howling rage. They'd reached Nina just as the grotesque python attempted to strike again and the thunderous pound of hooves reverberated, shaking the structure.

In her sheer panic, as gold-bridled horses with flames shooting from their mouths appeared out of nowhere, set to trample right over Nina and the girls, Quinn wildly wondered how many more mythological creatures were due to make an appearance.

What was next, a chariot?

Which was exactly the moment she heard more hooves. *Naw. No way!*

More golden horses—attached to a chariot—melted through the walls, their galloping shaking the earth. The concrete starting to crumble while the python danced, twisting, turning, mesmerizing.

The hard surface at her back suddenly shifted and her right hand began to pull away from the wall with an agonizing rip of her flesh, making her bite her lip bloody to keep from screeching. And then her right hand was free—the spike still deeply embedded in her palm.

Quinn fought a scream of unimaginable, searing pain, fought the horror as Khristos lie at her feet with the walls falling all around them. If she didn't get to him, he'd be pummeled to death.

While madness raged around her, while every creature she'd ever read in her beloved books appeared before her eyes, she cooled on the inside. Found some strange focus she didn't know she possessed and, with a single-minded act, began to use her right hand to free her left, yanking, tugging, loosening, fighting the dizzying wave of nausea and fear tearing her hand from the wall produced.

The spike in her left hand loosened with a jolt, a white-hot rip of agony. Quinn used that to her advantage, clawing to pry her hand free.

Almost there, Quinn, almost there! It's gonna hurt, but pull!

With one last grunt of effort, her eyes scrunched tight, sweat pouring from her brows, horses and pythons and chariots whirling around, she ripped her left hand free with a long howl.

She hit the ground hard with her knees, unable to even brace her fall with her hands for fear she'd drive the spikes further back into her flesh. The velocity of the drop took the wind right out of her, but she was still capable of rolling.

She tucked her knees and turned toward the bed, where Khristos lay half under it, unconscious. Using her feet, she backed up against the crumbling wall for leverage and shoved him directly under the bed.

Nina's yowl of anguish had Quinn fighting to stand. As she rose, using the heels of her hands and the bed to do so, she saw the battle waging before her and felt a moment's helpless panic. So deep in her soul, so dark, she winced at the black talons scraping her insides.

How could she help? Her hands were torn to shreds, her knees so bruised she almost couldn't stand up, and she had nothing but gumption on her side.

And as if the whirling dervish of Greek mythology come to life wasn't enough—flying serpents took to the ceiling, their wings creating such a whoosh of wind it almost knocked her over.

One went directly for Marty's head, his webbed wings slashing the air, his tongue flicking debris out of his path.

Quinn grabbed the nearest thing she saw, her nightstand lamp, and hurled it upward, blood dripping from her open wounds and into her eyes. "Marty! Loooook out!"

Marty reacted by rolling her head then shaking out her arms and shifting into her werewolf form.

Oh God, oh God, oh God! Quinn had only heard from Ingrid about Marty's ability to shift, and after what had happened to Quinn, she had mostly believed.

But to see it, to see her bones melt and reshape themselves, to see hair sprout from her body like some sort of weird time lapse video, was amazing and frightening, rooting Quinn to the spot.

But the serpent kept flying straight for Marty. "Marty!" she screamed, hoarse and raw, her throat on fire.

Wanda knocked Marty out of the way, steamrolling her to the ground as Nina round-housed the python woman, landing a punch square on her head. Nina's fangs flashed, her arms landing punch after punch, the motion so rapid it left Quinn dizzy.

But from the corner of her eye, Quinn saw Carl at what was once the bedroom door, now a gaping hole, his gait slow, his eyes wide in his pale, greenish-tinted face.

Oh God! Carl was too slow, too awkward to move quickly enough to get out of harm's way. "Carl! Run, Carl! Ruuuunnnnn!" she screeched into the latest tornado-like wind.

But Carl kept moving forward, kept fighting the force of the air pushing him back. She fastened her eyes on him, forgetting the sharp stabs of pain in her knees, as she jumped up onto the bed, bouncing with her weight.

"Carl—get out!" she warned again, her head down to avoid being blown off the soft surface.

All at once, as though someone had sucked the air from the room, everything appeared to slow. Carl's determination was clear on his face, but his eyes were no longer fixed to hers. They were on something *behind* her.

She whirled around to see a cyclops running toward her, grizzled and thick-skinned, his eyeball rolling—his horn aimed directly at her chest.

Carl raised his hands high in the air, the effort clear from the grunt of pain his stiff joints must have caused, and he was holding something in them—something she had no time to identify as he head-butted her out of the way and brought his hands downward with a scratchy, uneven yell.

The cyclops screeched, arching his short neck, spewing his anger and going straight for poor Carl, charging him with so much fury it stole the very breath from her lungs.

But Carl just stood there, and as the mattress sank beneath her feet, she began to topple over, helpless to right herself.

Until, with a booming, "*Nooooooo!*" someone hard and heavy rammed into her, in turn hurling her into Carl.

They fell on the floor in a tangle of limbs and grunts of pain, her battered body thunking to the ground.

Khristos. It was Khristos! He reached for them both, his head bleeding, his body covering them, protecting them from falling debris.

"*Enooough!*"

Yet another voice, male and rumbling, ripped through the space, stopping everything on a dime. Concrete blocks hung in the air, particles of her shredded comforter and pillows floated motionless.

"*Eris! What have you done?*" the voice boomed, bouncing and thunderous.

What was it with these people and the disembodied-voice fixation? It was damn jarring.

"*Eris, explain yourself. Now!*"

Oh, shut up.

Eris? Like, *the* Eris, Eris? The Goddess of Strife and Discord?

Talk about living up to your myth.

Khristos rolled from her, grunting as he did, pulling himself to his feet and reaching for her, scooping her up in his arms to tuck her tight to his chest.

That was when she saw Carl.

"Carl!" she yelped, looking down at his broken body, sprawled and still. She tried to squirm from Khristos's arms, but Nina was on the ground in a flash, her hair covered in dust, her clothes torn.

She hauled Carl up, pushing his face from his hair, running her fingers over his head. Standing, she draped a limp Carl over her shoulder and headed straight for the cause of all this discord and strife.

"You fucking, fucking, motherfucking, stupid, dicklick, dumb, motherfucking bitch!" she hollered in the face of the woman who'd abandoned her serpent form and returned to still one of the most beautiful women Quinn had ever seen. "I'm going to make you bleed buckets, you crazy, out-of-control, motherfucking piece of mythological shit! And when I'm done, I'm going to do it *again*. You fucked with my zombie! You—*hurt—my—zombie—twatcicle!*"

Nina jammed her face closer to the woman, who now paled. "You know what that means? You have to die, and it's gonna hurt. Oh my God, it's gonna hurt like nothing's *ever* hurt your fucked-up, warped, pretty face before!"

Marty, in a scrap of what was left of Quinn's sheets, and Wanda, her face dewy with sweat, rushed to the vampire, pulling her back, but Nina, who'd fought so valiantly not to swear, was clearly on the cleanse plan.

"*Get the fuck off me!*" she growled at her friends. "I will kill this bitch! I'll rip her damn face off—eat my way through her delicate little intestines while she watches. Do you hear me, you batshit, boil-on-my-fucking-ass, chariot-driving olive-lover!"

"*Nina!*" that voice bellowed again, sharp and with a hard warning. Only this time, as though the very air in the coliseum had a rip in it, a man—an enormous man—slipped through the folds.

A beautiful, dark, enormous man dressed in a stark-white polo shirt and plaid golf pants.

Khristos's chest heaved in relief as he cradled her close. "Zeus. Jesus Christ, damn glad you showed up, man."

Zeus? Seriously? Zeus was in her apartment turned coliseum in lower Manhattan? Oh, this day was shiny-shiny.

Crossing his arms over his wide chest, he approached Eris with a frown that could only be described as deep disappointment. "So what do we have here?"

Eris lifted her head, her sapphire eyes flashing and wild, her creamy breasts rising and falling beneath the silky white gown she wore. "You know damn well what you have here, you scourge of the universe!"

Zeus's chuckle vibrated the entire room as he grinned. "Are you still angry with me, Eris? Did you do all this in my honor?"

Quinn's head ached, her hands throbbed, but not so much that she was going to miss this chance to find out why her apartment looked like a Sherman tank had driven through it. She squirmed in Khristos's arms, using her wrists to push off his broad shoulders and forcing him to let her slide to the floor.

He kept his hands protectively at her waist as she wobbled when her knees buckled. "Quinn." He muttered a warning in her ear. "Let Zeus handle this."

"The hell I will. You, you crazy—although I admit, utterly gorgeous—nutbag, just hold on. Just all of you hold right the hell on!"

Zeus caught sight of Quinn and winced, his tanned face pained. He lifted her hands with gentle fingers, examining the spikes embedded in them. "Gods!" he shouted. "Are you responsible for this, Eris?"

Quinn fought a whimper when he touched them, but that wasn't going to stop her. "You're damn right she is. This is my apartment, for the love of Pete! I'm not going to have anywhere to live. I'll never get my deposit back. Not to mention, I have spikes—*spikes*—in my hands! Cheese and rice, you people are insane! What the *hell* is going on?"

Zeus looked over her head to Khristos. "So this is the one?"

"She is indeed," Khristos answered with a hint of amusement in his tone.

"Aw, Quinn. Welcome to the fold!" He gathered her up in his bulging arms, making her cry out. "So sorry! Hang tight. I'll fix this right up." He took her fingertips and ran his lips over them, making the spikes and gaping holes in her palms disappear. With another snap of his fingers, her knees no longer felt as though someone were driving nails through the caps.

He cocked his head, looking down at her with sparkling green eyes. "Better?"

"So much," she uttered, then pulled her hands away, feeling guilty for admiring his beauty.

Cracking his knuckles, Zeus turned his attention back to Eris. "What is this about, Eris?"

Eris's eyes narrowed, her luscious lips thinning. "You know what this is about, you goddess-loving lothario!"

Zeus gave them all a sheepish look before he grabbed Eris by the throat, so fast her body jerked like a limp ragdoll from the upward swing. "What does this have to do with Quinn?" he hissed in her ear.

Eris's hands went to his thick wrist, struggling against it. "She has the power of Aphrodite now!" she cried. "If I could have gotten my hands on it, I would have made you—"

"Oh, I know!" Quinn jumped up and down, her arm in the air, everything making complete sense in a rush of understanding. "You wanted my power so you could make Zeus fall wildly in love with you and steal him from Hera! Am I right?"

"Yes!" she wailed a sob, her head falling back on her neck. "She doesn't deserve you! I do! Don't you remember all the things you told me that night on the Aegean, Zeus? Do you remember the sailboat and our lovemaking? You told me you loved me!" She let out a sob. "I've waited lifetimes for Khristos to become distracted enough to get my hands on that ludicrous apple. *Lifetimes!*"

Zeus clucked his tongue at her in admonishment. "Tsk-tsk, Eris. You know Hera's my one true love. I made that clear from the start. And now look what you've done. You've made a mess of everything."

She clawed at his wide hand, tears streaming down her face. "Let me go!"

Zeus made a sad face at her, puckering his lips. "I can't do that, Eris. We don't subscribe to the old ways any longer, and you know that quite well. You can't go around creating this kind of havoc anymore. Remember what I told you the last time you took it upon yourself to react out of spite when your candidate didn't win and you almost wiped out the White House with Talos? And what will Ares say when he sees you've stolen his horses—*again*? Unacceptable, Eris. You must be punished. Our new Aphrodite is to be celebrated, not nailed to a wall like some cheap art."

Carl stirred on Nina's shoulder then, slipping to the ground and landing on his feet, currently pointing outward to either side of his legs, his left hand completely torn off.

"You'd damn well better make her pay, Zeus, or I swear on all that's fucking holy, I'll hunt you *and* her down, and drop you both from the top of that damned mountain," Nina growled, cracking her neck by rolling her head side-to-side.

Zeus dropped a jovial kiss on her cheek, clearly not at all fazed by her threats. "As pleasant as ever, Nina! I assure you, punishment will be meted out appropriately. Let's do a Save The Date for another round of Vampires vs. Gods, yes? I've had some time to think up our line of defense."

Nina huffed at him, pulling Carl close to her and hissing up at Eris.

Khristos moved in closer to the dangling Eris and looked up at her, his face a mask of rage, an emotion that almost startled Quinn. "Let me make myself perfectly clear. If you ever, and I do mean ever, come near my woman again, I'll hunt you down, Eris. I'll hunt you down, I'll flay you alive. I'll kill you myself." And then he smiled, his expression light and easy as he held out his hand to Zeus. "Thank you for showing up. Sorry to bust up your golf game."

Zeus used his free hand to shake Khristos's, his smile warm. "Got here as soon as I could, but you know how hard it is to get a signal on the mountain. Sorry it took so long. I'll have Ares come collect the horses. The rest you can handle, yes?"

Khristos scrubbed a weary hand over his face, blood still drying on his forehead. "I can."

The god held Eris up for inspection, letting her dangle from his grip as her long hair streamed down her back. "Say goodbye to all the nice people, Eris. Quinn, it was great to finally meet you. See you around the forums, huh?" With a wink and a smile that would make women all over the planet melt, he and Eris disappeared.

Marty and Wanda shook their heads in unison, glanced at each other and squealed. "Was he not the most divine, Wanda?" she gushed.

Wanda grinned, half of her hair falling from the perfect chignon she favored, her red wool dress torn and covered in soot. "Not a lie! Did you see him just make everything stop? Like just done. Totally over. And the way he kissed Quinn's fingers to heal them? Sa-woon!"

Their giggles warmed Quinn's heart, and when their eyes landed on her, they held out their arms and she gave them each a tight hug. "Ingrid told me about you guys in action, and I thought I believed, but after seeing that, there's not a shred of doubt. Thank you. Thank you, thank you, thank you."

"Jesus," Marty breathed into Quinn's hair. "You pulled yourself off that wall, Quinn. To see you nailed there..." She stopped herself and audibly gulped.

Wanda pressed a kiss to Quinn's forehead, her breath shuddering in and out. "Thank God you're all right," she whispered before setting Quinn away from her. "Now let's get this mess cleaned up, ladies!"

Ingrid, Archibald and Darnell plowed into the coliseum—which was slowly returning to her tiny bedroom—their eyes wide. Ingrid stumbled over the littered floor and lunged for Quinn.

"Don't let me hear you ever call yourself a chicken again, Quinn Morris. And don't ever scare the shit out of me like that again. I'd never survive the rest of art history without you. I'm so glad you're all right."

Quinn took a deep breath and nodded. "You're right; you'd never survive without me in art history."

Ingrid giggled as Darnell wrapped his arms around both of them and hugged. "Daggone, Miss, Quinn. You tougher'n I'll ever be. I'm sorry I wasn't here for ya. I don't know what that crazy lady did, but she sealed the whole dang place after Marty and Wanda got through. Not even my magic could get me in here."

Thank God. Thank God Marty and Wanda had made it through.

Archibald stuck his head between them all and grazed Quinn's cheek with his knuckles. "I'm going to prepare the best chocolate cake you've ever eaten in honor of such a fierce warrior! But for now, we must make haste, family! Darnell, you get the shovel. Ingrid, locate a broom, would you?"

As they broke apart, each heading off to begin cleaning up, Quinn bent at the waist and breathed. The horror of those spikes in her hands hitting her once again.

But Nina patted her on the back, wrapping an arm around her neck and pulling her upward, dropping her chin to the top of Quinn's head. "Jesus fuck and a sidecar, Mini-Goddess. You're a GD badass, and you tried to save my boy Carl. Can't ever say thank you enough."

Quinn inhaled the scent of Nina, full of cinnamon and cloves, and rested her cheek on the vampire's shoulder, tears stinging her eyes. "Do you feel all gooey on the inside right now, Nina?" she teased, her voice gruff, her throat tight.

"Like a goddamn toasted marshmallow, Love Maker," she replied, hoarse and low.

Quinn squeezed her arm and pulled back, her eyes catching sight of Carl's missing hand. "Carl! Your hand, buddy!"

But Carl was busy picking through the rubble with Khristos, using his one hand to dig furiously through her shredded pillows and crumbled rock, grunting until he found whatever he was looking for.

He pulled something tattered from the remains of the mess and held it up, giving her his endearing lopsided grin.

She fell to her knees in front of him with a sob, right there in the middle of the mess, and hugged him hard.

It was a book. He'd tried to take out the cyclops with a copy of Jane Eyre.

"Carl," she whispered against his cold cheek. "Thank you. You were so brave."

He thumped Quinn on the back once more as Nina helped him up, giving Khristos's shoulder a squeeze. "Thanks for looking out for my Carl and Goddess-Lite, dude. You might not have any supernatural powers, but that was some damn tackle." She looked to Carl then, her eyes soft. "Now, c'mon, buddy, looks like we got some duct-taping to do." Leading Carl off, she left Quinn and Khristos alone.

Her chest throbbed, her heart pounded. As Eris had spiked her hands to the wall, one painful hammer to the metal at a time, Quinn had only one thought during those torturous moments.

She'd never see Khristos again. She'd never hear his voice, never laugh with him, never see his smile. Never get back the chance to say to him what she'd really been afraid of when she'd sent him away.

And it had been more unbearable than death.

Grabbing his hand, she looked up at him, cupping his jaw and running her thumb over the sharp, stubbled plane. "I'm sorry. I'm sorry I sent you away. *I'm sorry...*" she sobbed.

He pulled her hand to his mouth and pressed his lips to her palm. "I don't care if we end up being nothing alike, Quinn Morris. I don't care if you like to read poetry and I'd rather let a semi run me over twice. I don't care if you think this all happened too fast. I don't care if you still aren't convinced that anything deep can happen in so little time. I don't even care that you like those stupid pillows on your bed that are, by the way, of absolutely no use to anyone if you can't put your head on them. And I don't care if you don't want to hear me object to them. That's just who I am. But that's who you are, too, and I want to wholeheartedly object to the idea that because we only just met, we can't feel this connected. When I saw you nailed to that damn wall..." He paused, his eyes grim, his tone gruff.

His lips thinned and he clenched his jaw before he continued. "When I saw you, I knew none of it mattered. None of it. Know why it doesn't matter? Because I saw my life flash right there in front of my damn eyes. And I've had some lifetimes. It's a lotta life. I want to try this thing with you, Quinn, and in all my years, I've never said that to any other woman. I'm not the wrong damn life choice. I'm the right one. So just damn well say yes."

Her throat constricted and her eyes filled with tears before she stood on tiptoe and brought her lips just inches from his. "*Yes,*" she whispered before throwing her arms around his neck and kissing him for all she was worth.

He pulled her tight, molding her body to his, as she melted into him, sealing the deal.

And then everyone standing at the crumbled bedroom doorway holding their collective breaths, and those who had no breath to hold at all, cheered.

EPILOGUE

Six Months and Ten Days Later—Ten Utterly Implausible Paranormal Accidents And Counting, A Brand-Spanking New Aphrodite, One Relieved, Living-In-Boca-In-A-Cute-Condo Ex-Aphrodite, One GG/ Goat Herder Pleased As All Hell With Her Deceptive Yet Very Successful Tour Bus Stunt, Three New Amazing Friends Who Lunched And Shopped (some more reluctantly than others) With Their New Goddess Friend On A Bi-Weekly Basis And Possessed More Fangs And Fur Than A CW Show, One Still-Somehow-In-All-The-Chaos Human Study Buddy On Her Way To Being A Vet-Tech The Likes Of Which The World Has Never Seen, One Manservant Grandfather Who Remains The Best Gods vs. Vampires Chicken-Wing Maker Bar None, The Sweetest Teddy Bear Of A Demon Doubling As A Defensive Linebacker Ever, And A Vegetarian Zombie With A Joyfully Discovered, Surprising Love Of Classic Literature all gathered together on a beautiful, cloudless spring day to celebrate a surprise under the guise of a game-day feast…

Quinn hugged Marty and Wanda and gave Nina a quick punch on the shoulder—just to show she cared.

Nina flicked the end of Quinn's braid and smiled. "Ya look good, Aphrodite-Lite. It's a good day to kick your people's asses, right?"

Quinn threw her arms around Nina's neck and squeezed hard—to which Nina responded by untangling herself with a scowl. "You and the huggy-kissy shit. You act like we haven't seen each other in a hundred years. I just saw you last week, for shit's sake. Remember, when we fucking trudged through that stupid outdoor mall and made like girls?"

Quinn laughed. "I do. You bought me an ice cream. It was delicious, Marshmallow, remember?"

Nina scowled, fighting a grin. "That was just to shut you the fuck up, so I wouldn't have to hear you go on and on about Hot Dude. One more, 'OMG, he's so sensitive to my deepest girlie feelings' gush, and it was either yank your tongue out of your flippin' head or feed you. I chose feed, because if I don't, these two flappy-lipped whiners get upset with me."

Marty, wearing a football jersey and a cute pair of leggings, rolled her eyes and gave Quinn another tight hug. "We were so excited when Khristos called and invited us to game day! And you look so pretty, too. Just perfect for—"

"For an afternoon in Greece!" Wanda interjected, shooting Marty a look Quinn didn't quite understand. "Really, love that dress. It suits your figure."

Nina nodded, her grin wicked. "Yeah. That Barbie dress hides the fact that your cans deflated. Do you miss your boobs, McGee?"

She giggled, sticking her tongue out at Nina. "Not even a little."

Her cans had gone back to their rightful size, followed by her eyes and skin returning to normal, At first she'd been dismayed and she'd worried about Khristos's reaction when he saw her breasts in their original state.

But he'd reminded her, he didn't love her for her body parts. He just loved her.

Khristos's mother waved at Quinn from her lounge chair, set on the steps of the Parthenon. She'd begun to spend more and more time with the woman they lovingly referred to as ex-Aphrodite, when she wasn't off at her hot yoga classes or Garden Club meetings, learning helpful tips from her on matchmaking and hearing all the stories about Khristos's youth.

Quinn had a healthy respect for Khristos's mother, and truly enjoyed their binge watches of *Sons of Anarchy*—whom ex-Aphrodite declared she'd have done some damage to back in her youth.

Ingrid and Carl strolled toward her, Carl with his ever-present book in hand. He held it up for her to see. "Oh, Carl," she cooed, folding her hands together and placing them on her heart. "*Romeo and Juliet* so soon in the game? Are you sure you're ready for all that heartbreak?" She gave him a warm hug, careful not to squeeze him too hard and break off another body part.

He patted her back in return when she bracketed his face with her hands and smiled up at him. Carl was one of the greatest new joys in her life. Nina occasionally dropped both Carl and little Charlie at her apartment on she and Greg's date nights, and they all sat on the floor together reading.

Carl was constantly curious, and often made trips to the library with her to discover new books under the cover of a hoodie and some strategic planning on her part.

That Nina and Marty trusted her with their children was the ultimate compliment. It meant she really was a part of this crazy family, pieced together by accident.

Ingrid, dressed in leather, her eyes rimmed in charcoal, did a little dance. She clenched her hands together at her chest and swooned comically "Look at me, gettin' my Greece on. Now give me your hand, Quinn Morris. We're going to have one of those moments you've dreamt about since I've known you. The one you planned on so long ago, but instead got some big ol' boobies and a new job. Right here in the middle of the Parthenon."

Quinn's laughter echoed in the open space as she remembered all the dreams of her trip to Greece she'd shared with Ingrid before her breakup with Igor, giving her hand to her friend and squeezing it.

Rocking back and forth, Ingrid let out a dreamy sigh as she perused the shimmering white landscape, bumping shoulders with Quinn. "Isn't it romantic here in the Parthenon now that you're in love and happy, Quinn? Isn't it just like you've always dreamed? A perfect day for a pro—"

"Batch of Arch's chicken wings and artichoke dip," Khristos said from behind her, gripping Quinn's shoulders.

Ingrid's eyes flashed something odd at Khristos before they went warm. She lunged for him, giving him a hard hug. "You bet! It's the best day ever for some chicken wings and artichoke dip. In fact, I think I'm going to go stuff my face with some right now and see if I can find some hot god's abs to play like an xylophone." She blew them a kiss and ran off into the bright sun to join the others invited to this impromptu party Khristos had cooked up.

Marty, Nina, and Wanda followed suit, throwing themselves into their various roles of the day, and Quinn sighed, feeling content—included.

She turned to Khristos, slipping her arms up under his and letting her head rest on his chest, her favorite place in the world these days. "I wish my mother could have been here. Though it would really take some explaining, huh?"

His laughter rumbled against her ear, making her shiver with pleasure. "I gave Zeus strict orders there'd be no cows for him today."

Quinn grinned. Maude had surprised her mother with a trip to a bird sanctuary in Africa for their three-month anniversary and they'd waved the newly minted couple off just two days ago.

She and her mother talked often now. No less than twice a week, and they made a point of seeing each other, with Maude and Khristos included, at least once a month for family dinner night.

They'd been working hard to mend old wounds, talking things out and laughing more than Quinn could ever remember them doing her entire life.

Helen and Maude had moved in together, and Maude's influence on her mother, her calming, gentle effect, had done wonders for Helen's relationship with Quinn.

Plus, Maude made the most amazing sugar cookies this side of the universe. Most importantly, her mother was happy—blissfully so, and she was working toward accepting herself and letting go of all the anger she'd allowed to fester for so many years.

And it was a beautiful thing to watch her mother's relationship grow, flourish.

It was also pretty awesome to watch her romance with Khristos deepen.

Khristos had wooed Quinn, dated her one day at a time, showed her what falling in love with the right man was like, one who was true to himself, one who wouldn't let her turn him into something he was never going to pretend to be.

He sat with her while she read her beloved copy of Keats and he read posts on Facebook. She sat with him while he played video games and she planned the garden of English tea roses she hoped to one day grow.

He rolled his eyes while she shopped for more decorative pillows he saw as pointless if you couldn't lay on them, and she rolled her eyes back when he suggested they eat dinner on the bed.

He refused to eat frilly girl food like brie cheese on wafer-thin crackers, so she'd made him a cracker-and-cheese sandwich on a hoagie roll.

And they laughed—often—loudly—softly—together.

They talked. They were silent. They learned. They loved.

Khristos pointed to the space on the blanket he'd spread out. "Come sit with me, Quinn Morris, aka Aphrodite."

Quinn dropped down next to him and snuggled up against his chest, pulling her knees to her chin. "This is some game they have going on. Vampires are a cutthroat bunch, huh?"

He barked a laugh. "You have no idea. But it's damn good to see everyone together. So I'm okay with the virtual annihilation of my people."

She giggled, taking a bite of the strawberries he'd brought along for the Vampires vs. Gods Picnic—Round Two. "Nina's killin' 'em out there. I think she made Zeus cry for his mother."

"Nina is a warrior."

"A very pale one," she said on a chuckle. A pale one she'd come to care a great deal for. "You know, I've been wondering about something…"

"And that is?"

"What were you doing when GG knocked the apple out of the pillar?"

"I was in a minor fender-bender with a woman who hit a dog. She slammed on her brakes, I tapped her bumper. Total accident, but the dog—his name's Boo—was pretty smashed up. I was googling nearby emergency vets so we could get him help and I got distracted. He's fine now, by the way."

She leaned in and kissed him on a sigh, his good heart never failing to make her swoon. "Hey, did I tell you how beautiful all this is? I know you're not a huge fan of my girlie food, but you blended game-day food with it like a boss." Quinn waved her hand at the plates of cheese and fruit, the wine crisp and cold, the blanket he'd spread out on soft grass he'd created with a snap of his fingers.

"I don't believe you did."

"Well, then let me be the first to tell you, it's beautiful. Thank you for organizing this amazing celebration to annihilate our people."

Khristos laughed, his eyes warm. "Is it like you imagined?"

She pulled her hat from her head, one very similar to the one she'd worn to the Parthenon just a few months ago, and set it aside. "The annihilation of your people?"

He poured her a glass of her favorite wine and held it out to her. "Not so long ago, you were here, dreaming of your engagement to a man who was totally wrong for you. But is this what the setting looked like in that pretty head of yours?"

She leaned in and kissed him, letting her lips linger on his. Knowing he was hers was still as amazing now as it had been when he'd first told her he loved her. "It's a much better setting with you in it."

"Answer the question, Love Guru," he teased, skimming her lips with his tongue.

"You know, now that you mention it, it does."

He winked a gorgeous eye at her. "Perfect. So, I have something I'd like to read to you. You in?"

She mocked a pouty face. When Khristos read to her, it was usually a funny meme on Facebook or a snarky tweet from some guy who'd taken out an account on Twitter and called himself God.

"Is it going to be another tweet from God? Because telling everyone he hears their prayers and he thinks they're very funny is only funny after the first reading, Khristos with a K."

"Hey, he has one-point-nine million followers. He's damn funny."

She rolled her eyes at him and his reading material. No, it wasn't Keats or Shelley, but in the end, when they were together, it didn't matter as long as they were together. "Swear it's not from God and I'll give you the green light."

Khristos grinned. "I assure you, it is not."

"Then carry on." She rolled her hand with a chuckle.

He pulled out his phone and scrolled the screen, flipping it open and clearing his throat. "A poem, by Khristos with a K…"

"Dear Aphrodite,

"You are mighty

"Cute,

"And I'm pretty crazy

"About ute."

She spit her wine out when she laughed out loud. "*Ute?*"

"Shhh. It rhymes with cute."

"Oh, sorry. Please continue," she said on a grin.

He rolled his shoulders and looked back at his phone. "You also have nice hair.

"I like that it hangs down to there." He pointed to her breasts and wiggled his eyebrows. "I don't want to ever consider

"Not being able to read you God's tweets on Twitter,

"So it'd be pretty badass

"If you'd marry me

"Like really fast."

Quinn's shoulders began to shake with laughter. She fell back on the blanket, covering her mouth, trying to stamp out her squeals of hyena-like laughter until tears rolled down her face.

"Hey, now. I wrote you a gushy poem. You're not supposed to laugh."

That only made her laugh harder. So hard, Khristos peered down at her and mocked a frown. "If you don't knock it off right now, there'll be no shiny for you, Love Maker."

She grabbed him by the collar of his shirt and pulled him down to her, trying not to snarf. "I don't care about your shiny baubles. I love *you*. Not your riches. Right now, I care more about getting you into an emergency poetry-writing class so we can rectify that disaster of words immediately." And then she began to laugh all over again.

And it was perfect—and nothing like her dreamed-up proposal in her head, but still more incredible than anything she could have ever imagined.

Khristos rolled his tongue in his cheek and feigned insult. "Are we done making a mockery of my heartfelt profession of love?"

She snorted. "I'm done. No wait. Not quite." She barked another laugh, pressing her hand to her mouth once again to stifle it and clearing her throat. "Okay. Good to go." Quinn shot him a smile of encouragement and put on her serious face.

He pulled a ring from his shirt pocket and held it up, gleaming and amazing and in the shape of an apple. "So you wanna do this?"

She sighed in utter bliss, her eyes finding his, seeing the love she felt reflected right back at her. "No one in this world wants to be Mrs. Khristos with a K more than I do. I'm pretty crazy about you," she whispered.

Khristos rubbed his nose against hers then rolled her to her side, pulling her to his chest. "Right back at'cha, Aphrodite."

The gathered crowd all stopped and cheered. Marty and Wanda cried. Nina and Ingrid high-fived. Archibald and Darnell dabbed at their eyes with the tablecloth for the game-day feast, and Khristos flipped open his laptop to reveal her mother and Maude in the middle of a park, their beloved birds surrounding them, clinking two glasses of champagne in celebration.

How could her mother have known Khristos would propose today…?

And then she realized, as tears of joy gathered in the corner of her eyes. "Today wasn't about a rematch at all, was it?"

He winked. Her man. Her forever. Her soul mate. "Today was about how much I love you, and how I want to spend the rest of my eternity with you."

In this moment, this precious, perfect moment, Quinn couldn't help but remember yet another of her favorite quotes from John Keats: *The imagination may be compared to Adam's dream—he awoke and found it truth.*

She was wide awake now, and it was better than anything she'd ever dreamed.

Cupid and the now-relaxed, refreshed, and totally retired Aphrodite poked their heads around a pillar in the Parthenon.

She winked at her old partner in crime as he readied his arrow. "Whatever you do, avoid Nina's mate Greg. Gods help us all if we were to mistakenly match him with someone else. I like my innards in a nice, neat coil on the inside, thank you very much."

Cupid nodded, lifting the brim of his Yankees cap to clear his line of vision. "I hear she'll eat your face off."

Ex-Aphrodite shivered, running her hands over her arms despite the heat. "Never doubted it for a second."

He looked to where Quinn and Khristos sat, curled into one another, Quinn's chest pressed against her son's. "You think they really need our help? Seems like they got it pretty well covered."

"I'm not taking any chances with this, C. I'm sealing this deal for eternity. I've waited centuries. That's long enough."

Cupid pulled the bow tight, his arm up, his elbow high. "You ready?"

"Like a god on bring-your-own-virgin-to-slaughter night."

"We don't do that anymore," he chastised on a snicker.

She sighed wistfully in remembrance. "But do you remember it, C?"

His sigh mimicked hers. "Yeahhh. Like it was yesterday. Glory days, Boss. Er, ex-Boss? What the hell do I call you now?"

She took her position behind him with a wink and a wicked smile. "Grandma. Just call me Grandma."

At ex-Aphrodite's nudge, Cupid sent the arrow high; white and blue in color in Quinn's honor, it shot straight through the air in a perfect arc, glowing and brilliant against the deep blue of the Grecian sky.

The arrow melted through Quinn's chest and disappeared into Khristos's, leaving in its wake an upward spray of sparkling hues.

And Ex-Aphrodite and Cupid fist-bumped as they happily sighed—in unison—for the last match they'd ever make together as a team.

The one match dearest to their hearts.

The match they'd waited lifetimes to make.

The End

(But do come back for more in the upcoming *Accidentally Ever After*, won't you? Nina would miss you if you didn't!)

AUTHOR'S NOTE

I do hope you enjoyed Accidentally Aphrodite! I'd so appreciate it if you'd help others enjoy this book, too.

Recommend it. Please help other readers find this book by recommending it.

Review it. Please tell other readers why you liked this book by reviewing it at online retailers or your blog. Reader reviews help my books continue to be valued by distributors/resellers. I adore each and every reader who takes the time to write one!

ABOUT DAKOTA CASSIDY

Dakota Cassidy is a *USA Today* bestselling author with over thirty books. She writes laugh-out-loud romantic comedy, grab-some-ice erotic romance, hot and sexy alpha males, paranormal shifters, contemporary kick-ass women, and more.

Invited by Bravo TV, Dakota was the Bravoholic for a week, wherein she snarked the hell out of all the Bravo shows. She received a starred review from Publisher Weekly for *Talk Dirty to Me*, won an RT Reviewers Choice Award for *Kiss and Hell*, along with many review site recommended reads and reviewer top pick awards.

Dakota lives in the gorgeous state of Oregon with her real life hero and her dogs, and she loves hearing from readers!

Connect with Dakota online:

Twitter

Facebook

Join Dakota Cassidy's Newsletter The Tiara Diaries!

Other Titles by Dakota Cassidy

Accidentally Paranormal Series
The Accidental Werewolf
Accidentally Dead
The Accidental Human
Accidentally Demonic
Accidentally Catty
Accidentally Dead, Again
The Accidental Genie
The Accidental Werewolf 2: Something About Harry
The Accidental Dragon
Accidentally Aphrodite
Interview With an Accidental-- a free introductory guide to the girls of the Accidentals!

Wolf Mates Series
An American Werewolf In Hoboken
What's New, Pussycat?
Gotta Have Faith

A Paris, Texas Romance Series
Witched At Birth
What Not to Were
Witch Is the New Black

Non-Series
Whose Bride Is She Anyway?
Polanski Brothers: Home of Eternal Rest

The Hell Series
Kiss and Hell
My Way to Hell

The Plum Orchard/Call Girls Series
Talk This Way
Talk Dirty to Me
Something to Talk About
Talking After Midnight

The Ex-Trophy Wife Series
You Dropped a Blonde On Me
Burning Down the Spouse
Waltz This Way

Urban Fantasy from Dakota Cassidy writing as Nina Blackman
Fangs of Anarchy Series
Forbidden Alpha
Outlaw Alpha